ECHOES
of a
MURDER

A DI MATTHEW STANNARD NOVEL

C.K.
Harewood

ISBN (Hardback): 978-1-912968-51-0

ISBN (Paperback): 978-1-912968-50-3

ISBN (eBOOK): 978-1-912968-49-7

ECHOES OF A MURDER

C. K. HAREWOOD

Chapter One

22nd March 1930

When Pauline Bowen leaned her body against the guardrail and lifted her face to the stars, she had no idea she had less than half an hour to live.

As she stood there, Pauline was considering her future in terms of years, not minutes. Empty years. Lonely years. Years she had thought would be the same as her past, crammed with dinner and bridge parties, bizarrely named cocktails, even more bizarre dances, and luncheons with the other wives. She would applaud her husband as he played polo and cricket and she would perform in the amateur dramatic productions at the club.

Pauline considered herself an excellent performer. For the past twenty years, she had played the part of Mrs Geoffrey Bowen to perfection. She'd given her husband two healthy children and packed them off to boarding school so they wouldn't be in the way, hung off his arm at his work and social functions, pretending not to be bored, and listened attentively to his complaints and soothed them away. And she'd kept herself in as good condition as was possible for a thirty-seven-year-old mother of two, so he needn't be ashamed of being married to a frump.

But none of that had made any difference in the end, for Geoffrey had told her one morning during breakfast that he was leaving her for another woman. He'd prefaced this announcement by telling her not to make a scene in front of the servants, to be calm, and she had done as he wanted, but only because she couldn't quite believe what she'd heard. 'It's unfortunate, but there it is,' Geoffrey had said. 'I can't live with you anymore, so I'm leaving.' Just as if he was telling his barber how he wanted his hair cut. He'd spread marmalade on his toast and drunk his coffee, then thanked her for taking it so well before leaving for the office. Pauline had sat at the table while it was cleared, staring at the embroidered pattern in the cloth, trying to work out what she had done wrong.

After the first shock had passed, after her disbelief had turned to anger, Pauline's primary emotion had been shame. Remembering the broken-off glances and the whispers that had followed her around for months, she realised Geoffrey's affair had not been a secret among their friends. She could picture the men's conversations over their port and cigars. 'I say, Geoffrey, how's it going with that young filly of yours? Wearing you out, is she?' And Geoffrey would have smiled that smug, guilty schoolboy grin of his, raised his eyebrows in 'a gentleman never tells' kind of way, then told them everything. And the chaps would have wordlessly agreed to keep it among themselves, then gone home and told their wives. Pauline's ignorance of the affair would be bandied back and forth in the hairdressers, in the Ladies' room, talked about over the heads of manicurists and pedicurists and before the servants, but never in front of Pauline. When Pauline was around, amused glances would be exchanged behind her back, her friends revelling in their secret knowledge while pretending to feel so sorry for poor dear Pauline.

Pauline found that humiliation the hardest to bear, everyone knowing and thinking her a fool. It was why she hadn't been able to stay, why she was returning to her family. Back to her parents, who had no idea she was coming. She hadn't dared write to them, knowing what they would say. Her mother would have written back, telling her to stop being so silly with all this talk of leaving. She would have to let Geoffrey have his mistress – that's what men did and Pauline would have to put up with it – but she must put her foot down and tell him there was no possibility of his leaving. Appearances must be kept up. That was all that mattered.

But Pauline didn't have it in her to keep up the lie that her marriage was fine, and so she hadn't written to her parents to warn them of her intentions, but simply left. But if Geoffrey thought she was going to slip away and let him and his tart have everything she'd spent her lifetime building, then he could think again. Geoffrey would pay through the nose for his betrayal, so much so that his mistress would wonder if he had been worth all the trouble.

Pauline was resolved on one other point. She would not let Geoffrey ruin the rest of her life as he'd ruined all that they'd had together. She would seek pleasure in life; if Geoffrey could have his fun, then so could she, and to hell with reputation. After so long worrying about what other people thought of her, Pauline was determined not to care anymore. She would be the woman she wanted to be rather than the woman society expected her to be.

And tonight, the woman Pauline wanted to be was a woman who was desired. Her mind had already conjured a lover for her, and so, the breeze lifting the curls from her forehead was not the cool wind from the north but the breath of a stranger. The goosebumps pimpling her arms had not risen because she was feeling chilly but were the effect of his touch.

She shivered. Her imagination was powerful, but even so, she couldn't fool herself for long. There was no lover beside her and Pauline heaved a deep sigh.

It was as she turned her head away from the wide, dark expanse of night that she saw him standing in the shadows. She'd noticed him before at dinner, handsome in his way but with an air of awkwardness, looking away whenever she caught his eye, and that had discouraged her from considering him as a lover. Woefully out of practice in flirting, Pauline needed a man to make the first move.

Or did she? The old Pauline would have thought so, would have shied away from being so forward, but the new Pauline was a much bolder woman. Why should she not do the chasing?

Making sure there was no one around to witness her first attempt at seduction, Pauline hooked her hands behind her on the rail and showed him her body. He took a long look, appreciative, she thought, and her confidence grew.

'Why are you hiding there?' she said in a voice she hoped sounded like a purr. Pauline crooked her finger at him. 'Come here.'

He came towards her, a little shyly, like a child unsure whether to take the treat offered to him.

'What's your name?'

He told her in a whisper.

'That's nice.' She slid her hand down his shirt, knowing this was no time to be coy.

He stroked her cheek. The gentle gesture surprised and dismayed her. It seemed to promise affection and that was something she didn't want. Pauline angled her face away with a 'don't do that' smile. His fingers brushed her throat and moved down to stroke the collarbone peeking out from the edge of her green silk dress. She expected, wanted, his hand to move lower, but it came back up to curl around her neck, and she grew impatient. Silencing a tut, Pauline slid her hands around his waist.

She had expected to feel his arousal, but his body didn't respond. Instead, his other hand curved around her neck and both thumbs rubbed either side of her windpipe. Pauline gave in, closing her eyes and tilting her head back. She'd waited this long for a little passion in her life; she could wait a few minutes longer.

But then his fingers tightened. His thumbs squeezed.

Pauline couldn't breathe. Her eyes snapped open in alarm and she tried to pull out of his grasp, but he held on tight. She tried to push him away, but he stood firm. She would have kicked at him if she could, but her legs were giving way beneath her and everything was turning dark.

The last point of light Pauline Bowen saw was the gleam in her would-be lover's eyes.

Chapter Two

11th April 1930

Detective Inspector Matthew Stannard held his breath as the foreman of the jury stood.

He hated this moment, when all his hard work, all the hours he had put in, the sleepless nights he had endured, came down to one or two words. It didn't matter that the evidence he had gathered was irrefutable. It didn't matter that Matthew knew he'd done well in the witness box, giving his testimony clearly and concisely, and standing up to cross-examination with a conviction the defence barrister hadn't been able to break. There was no question of a mistake having been made. Eric Hailes and Donald Spencer were as guilty as any two men could be, but as Matthew had learnt over the years, you never could tell with juries.

'On the count of murder, how do you find the accused?' the clerk of the court asked.

The foreman raised his chin, cast a quick glance over his audience, and declared, 'Guilty!'

The court erupted with a loud cheer and energetic applause, and Matthew breathed again. The foreman resumed his seat and the judge called for order. By the time silence fell, a black square of felt was sitting upon his wig and he addressed the prisoners in the dock.

'Eric Hailes. Donald Spencer. You have both been found guilty of murder. It is the sentence of this court that you will be taken to a lawful prison, there to await execution. Do you have anything to say in stay of execution?'

Matthew looked up towards the dock. Eric Hailes was sobbing and seemed incapable of speech. Donald Spencer screwed up his arrogant face and spat into the well of the court, a gobbet of spittle landing on the sleeve of his barrister.

Unfazed by this show of vulgarity, the judge ordered the prisoners to be taken down to the cells to await transportation to prison. He rose, exiting through a doorway behind his chair and the court became all bustle and noise as belongings were gathered and conversations begun.

It's over, Matthew thought as he pulled on his raincoat. *I can relax now.*

The last few months had been hectic. The excitement over his promotion and new posting to Craynebrook; being thrown in at the deep end with a murder on his very first day; the investigation that ensued, rippling out to uncover criminal activity that no one in the sedate suburb could have imagined; and the trial that followed so swiftly, as if everyone wanted to put the whole sorry mess behind them as quickly and quietly as possible. With all that, there had been no chance to take it easy.

Matthew made his way outside. The trial had attracted a great deal of attention and the pavements were filled with people. He elbowed his way through those crowding around the doors only to have a young woman block his way.

'Sign the petition, sir?' she asked and thrust a clipboard into his hand.

Matthew read the paper clamped beneath the metal clip.

At the top of the page, in large, bold type, were the words '*Save Nancy Price!*' He flicked through the pages beneath, counting nine pages filled with signatures. 'You want her sentence commuted?'

'To life imprisonment,' the woman nodded. 'Nancy Price doesn't deserve to hang.'

'She did kill three men and try to kill two more,' Matthew pointed out.

'We're not claiming Miss Price was right to take the law into her own hands,' she said with weary patience, as though she'd heard this argument many times before. 'We agree she should be punished, but after what was done to her...' She broke off, Matthew suspecting delicacy preventing her from detailing the horrors Nancy Price had suffered at the hands of The Five, the dissolute members of the Empire Club. 'Those beasts have been found guilty, you know? Spencer and Hailes?'

'I know,' Matthew said, taking the fountain pen from her hand. He signed his name and handed the clipboard and pen back.

'I'll sign too,' a voice behind him called out and Matthew turned to see Dickie Waite holding his hand out for the clipboard. Equipped with his own pen, the reporter scribbled his signature beneath Matthew's. 'There you go.' He smiled at the young woman as he handed the clipboard back to her. She thanked them both and hurried off.

'Do you think it will do any good?' Dickie asked, watching her approach another man who waved her irritably away.

'It might,' Matthew said. 'Especially now Hailes and Spencer have been convicted.'

'I hope it does. Those buggers deserved everything they got from Nancy Price. Craynebrook's a cleaner place because of her.'

Matthew raised an amused eyebrow. 'Is that tomorrow's headline?'

'Front page of *The Chronicle*,' Dickie smirked. 'And if you're very lucky, I might put your name in the copy.'

Matthew shook his head. 'Leave me out of it. I don't need any more publicity.'

'Tough. My editor will insist you're mentioned.' Dickie took out his handkerchief and blew his bulbous nose. 'Are you heading back to Craynebrook or home?'

'Craynebrook. Superintendent Mullinger wants to be kept updated. You?'

Dickie waved his reporter's notebook. 'Back to the office and write up the trial verdict for the morning edition. We can go back together.'

Matthew nodded and they set off for the train station.

'It's going to feel a little dull in Craynebrook after all this excitement,' Dickie sighed.

'I don't mind dull,' Matthew said. 'It'll be nice to just have routine police work to deal with for a while.'

'Don't give me that. You enjoyed it all as much as I did. Oh, not the murders and the rapes and all that. But the investigation, working it all out, putting all the pieces together. That's what it's all about, isn't it? That's what you're going to miss. If solving crimes didn't interest you, you would have stayed in uniform. Go on, Matthew, confess it. Finding murderers is what you're good at. There's no harm in admitting you enjoy it, too.'

'All right, I enjoy it. Satisfied?' Matthew said. 'Now, do me a favour, Dickie, and stop talking about murders. I've had enough these past few months to last me a lifetime.'

Georgina Moore walked slowly through the rooms of Driscoll's Care Home in search of her son. She found him in the garden, sitting on one of the wooden benches, smoking a cigarette. He was wearing a thin, shapeless cardigan over his blue-striped shirt and house slippers, and it worried her to see him sitting there without a coat or outdoor shoes.

'Hello, Oliver,' she said quietly, so as not to startle him.

'Hello, Mother,' Oliver Moore replied, making room for her on the bench.

She sat, propping her walking stick against the arm and setting her handbag on her lap. 'How are you today, dear?'

'All right.' He held up the half-smoked cigarette. 'Don't mind if I carry on smoking, do you?'

'Of course not,' she lied. Georgina had never liked the smell of smoke. 'But Oliver, dear, aren't you cold out here?'

He didn't answer, and Georgina sighed to herself. She hated it when Oliver was in this kind of mood. It made conversation so difficult. It wasn't as if they could just sit there, not saying a word to one another. If they did that, she might as well not come. And she needed to talk to him today. What she had to say couldn't wait until Oliver was in a more communicative mood. But how to tell him? She looked back towards the house, hoping to see Dr Avery and be able to ask for his help. But the doctor was nowhere to be seen. She would have to struggle on alone.

'You're very quiet, Oliver. Is something wrong?'

'Nothing's wrong, Mother. I just don't feel like talking, that's all.'

'As long as that's all it is.' *Just tell him*, she chided herself, and took a deep breath. 'Oliver,' she said, turning on the bench to look at him, 'I have some news about Dominic.'

There was a long pause before Oliver said, 'What about him?'

'He's coming home. Just for a holiday. A few weeks. He wants to see you. I haven't promised him anything, just in case, …but it would be nice to see him, wouldn't it?'

'It would be,' Oliver said. 'It's been such a long time since I saw him.'

'Yes, such a long time. Six years.' Georgina laughed nervously. 'I've been wondering if I'll recognise him.'

'Will he recognise me? I expect I've changed quite a bit.'

'So, you will see him?'

'Yes, I will see him.'

'And you'll be all right? I don't need to worry?'

His brow creased. 'Why would you need to worry?'

'I don't,' she insisted, a little too shrilly, and clutched her handbag tighter. Nibbling her bottom lip, Georgina watched a squirrel run around the trunk of a tree. 'So, what have you been doing all week, Oliver?'

'The same as usual. Reading, playing cards.'

'But you have been out? You mustn't neglect your walks. Dr Avery said exercise is good for you.'

'I'm not neglecting my walks.' Oliver smiled and pointed at a man wearing a brown overall standing before an easel. 'And I sometimes walk with Peter to the public house.'

Georgina looked over at Peter Treherne. 'I didn't know Peter painted. It's a pleasant hobby. Perhaps you should take it up?'

'I don't want to take up painting, Mother.' Oliver flicked the ash from his cigarette.

Some fell on his trouser leg and Georgina tutted and brushed the ash away. 'Do be careful, Oliver.'

Oliver swatted at her hand. 'Don't fuss over me, Mother. I can't stand women fussing.'

'I'm sorry, dear. I didn't mean to fuss.' Georgina sighed and checked her wristwatch surreptitiously.

'Don't feel you have to stay,' Oliver said. 'Not if you don't want to.'

'It's not that,' she snapped. 'It only seems you'd rather be on your own.'

'I'm not in the best of moods today, Mother,' Oliver admitted, and Georgina knew he meant it as an apology. 'It's probably best if you go.'

'Well, if that's what you want.' She hoped she didn't sound as relieved as she felt. She grabbed her stick and rose, looking down at him and wishing she knew what was going through his mind. 'I'll say goodbye, then. Until next Friday, Oliver. And remember, I'll have Dominic with me.'

'Yes, Mother,' Oliver nodded. 'I'll remember.'

Chapter Three

Matthew heard singing as he opened the door to his flat. 'Pat?' he called as he hung up his hat and coat.

The singing broke off, and his sister poked her head into the hallway. 'You're home early,' she said. 'It's only half-past five. What happened? You get the sack?'

'Very funny. You didn't say you were coming over.' He leaned against the kitchen door frame and watched his sister as she put the dishes he had left out to dry away in the cupboard.

Pat slammed the cupboard door. 'I had to get out of the house.'

Matthew folded his arms and sighed. 'What's Mum done now?'

'Oh, the usual, but she's ratcheted it up a few notches the past few days, having a right go at Georgie. Nothing the poor sod does is right. If he brings home sausages for tea, Mum wants chops. He makes her a cup of tea. She wants coffee. He picks up her magazines from the newsagents. She says he's come back with the wrong ones. And you know Georgie. He just says sorry and walks away. I wish he'd stand up to her, just once. I tell him not to take it from her, but does he listen?

Says it wouldn't be right to answer Mum back. And I say I answer Mum back all the time, but I can't get through to him.' She folded up a tea towel and put it down on the counter. 'I wish you'd have a word with him, Mattie. He listens to you.'

'Can't Fred talk to him?' Matthew asked hopefully.

Pat gave him a despairing look. 'You know Fred doesn't like to get involved when it's about Mum.'

'I know he's scared of her.'

'He's not scared. He just can't win with her. You know what she's like. Oh no,' she said, throwing up her hands in mock despair, 'what am I saying? She's not like it with you, is she?'

'It's only because I'm not there for her to get annoyed with.'

'Balls! You can't do no wrong in Mum's eyes and you know it. That's why if you talked to Georgie, or even talked to Mum and told her to leave him alone, she'd listen. I know she would, if you told her.'

'I'll have a word,' Matthew promised.

'On Sunday? You are coming, aren't you? If you're working again—'

'I'm coming.' He cut her off sharply, not willing to listen to another lecture on how hard he worked. 'I'm always there for Easter Sunday, you know that.'

Pat grunted. 'I know it's the only day we can count on you.' She looked around the kitchen to make sure her job was done. 'Now, I've put some biscuits and tea in your cupboard. I've taken your socks to mend and I've done your dusting.'

'You don't have to do all that.'

'I know I don't.' She looked him up and down critically. 'You eaten?'

Matthew shook his head.

'I'll do you something before I go, then.' She banged a

frying pan down on the gas ring and knocked a nob of butter into it. 'Busy?'

'I have been.' Matthew turned on the tap and filled the kettle. 'I've been at the trial every day for the past few weeks. But it's over now.'

'And?'

'Guilty. Both to hang.'

'Good. Your guv'nor pleased?'

'Not so you'd notice.' He ignored Pat's raised eyebrow. She knew of the antipathy between him and Superintendent Mullinger and Matthew wasn't in the mood to go over it again. 'You remember Dickie Waite?'

'Yeah. That friend of yours what came to the pub. Reporter, ain't he?'

'That's right. He was at the trial too and met me after-wards. Do you know what he said? That's it going to be dull in Craynebrook now and I'm going to miss all the excitement because I won't have anything interesting to investigate.' He waited, but Pat said nothing. 'Well? Don't you think that's a bit of an odd thing to say?'

'No,' she said, turning a rasher of bacon over in the pan. 'Put your eyes back in your head, Mattie. He's right.'

'What do you mean, he's right? You think I want people to be murdered just so I have something to do?'

'Hark at you,' she chuckled. 'All put out.'

'I think I have a right to be put out. You make me sound like a monster.'

'Oh, go and sit down,' Pat said, smiling. 'I'll bring your tea in.'

Matthew grabbed a knife and fork from the drawer and sat down at the rickety drop-leaf table beneath the window in his sitting room. Glancing around, seeing how Pat had tidied for him, he noticed the picture of his father on the mantel-piece was slightly askew. He reached over and set it straight.

Pat entered and put a plate of bacon and eggs and a mug of tea in front of him. 'Eat up,' she ordered, pulling out the other chair and sitting. Leaning her chin on her hand, she studied the photograph of their father. 'You don't get it from Dad,' she mused. 'The working things out in an investigation, I mean. I don't remember him ever talking about wanting to be a detective, do you?'

Matthew shook his head. 'Dad was happy to stay in Uniform.'

Pat made a face. 'I wouldn't call him happy. It was a job, that's all. It paid the bills. But as soon as you said you was joining the police, we all knew you'd be a detective one day, Mattie.' She looked back at the picture. 'Handsome, weren't he? Not as handsome as you, mind, but nice-looking.' She suddenly straightened. 'Well, I've never noticed that before.'

'What?' Matthew asked, following her gaze.

She reached over and grabbed the photograph frame. 'Looking at him, it's like looking at Georgie.' She turned the frame around to show him. 'Don't you think so?'

Matthew shrugged. 'I suppose.'

'He's the spitting image of him.' She put the frame back on the mantelpiece and frowned. 'You don't think that's why Mum's got it in for Georgie, do you? Because she reminds him of Dad?'

'Why would that make her have a go at him?'

Pat gave Matthew a 'don't be stupid' look. 'They were never happy, Mattie. Remember what happened the last time he came home on leave? From the minute Dad stepped through the door, they was arguing. They'd been at it for hours by the time you came home.'

Matthew did remember. It was 1917, and he'd gone to work that day so happy because he knew when he returned, his father would be home. But as Matthew turned the corner into his road, he'd heard the shouting and saw the neighbours standing outside their front doors, muttering to each other and shaking their heads in disapproval.

He'd rushed into the house to find his mother screeching at his father, her face blotchy with anger, and his father standing by the window in his army uniform, fists clenched at his sides, jaw set hard. Matthew had seen his father angry many times before, but he'd never seen him rigid with fury. Worried what his father might do with his white-knuckled fists, Matthew had gone to his mother, grabbed her hands and begged her to stop. She'd struggled at first, her rage too intense to be so quickly cooled, but he'd made her look at him, and as always, the sight of her eldest son calmed her. His mother stopped struggling and threw her arms around Matthew's neck, holding on tight. He held her until her little heaving body stilled, then released her to turn to his father.

But his mother had one last thing to say to James. 'Thank God I've got Mattie,' she'd cried. 'I don't know why you even bothered to come back. We don't need you. We don't want you here.'

And his father had left without a word, grabbing his kit bag and storming out of the house. Matthew started after him, but his mother grabbed his arm and pulled him back to her. 'Let him go, Mattie. He's not worth it.'

Matthew had tugged his arm free and run after his father. He was in time to see his father climbing into a van at the end of the road and called out to him. But he either didn't hear or didn't care and the van drove off. It was the last time he ever saw his father.

Matthew hadn't spoken to his mother for days after that, hating her for what she'd said and hating himself for hating her. And when she'd come to him in tears, begging to be forgiven, he'd given in and accepted her embrace.

His father had been killed not long after; his mother received the War Office telegram on Easter Sunday. She had cried at the news, so fervently that Matthew almost believed she genuinely grieved for his father, but her tears hadn't lasted long. It was Pat who kept up the family tradition of remembering their father by going to church every Easter Sunday – the only time they ever did – and cooking a roast dinner with all the trimmings, no expense spared.

Pat rose and tucked her chair under the table. 'I better be off. Make sure you eat all that. You're looking too thin.' She planted a quick peck on Matthew's temple. 'Ten o'clock at the church on Sunday, Mattie. Don't be late.'

Chapter Four

Edna Gadd shifted her bulk from one foot to the other and wiggled her toes in her boots. Her feet were so cold, she could barely feel them, and she stamped to gee up her poor circulation.

'Oh, come on,' she muttered, glaring at the prison gates, willing them to open. She checked her watch and saw the minute hand jerk towards the number twelve. Eight o'clock. Any moment now.

Right on cue, the small door in the prison gates opened and two men stepped out, one after the other. The first was a dark-haired man wearing a flat cap and a knee-length over-coat. Despite the shabbiness of his clothing, his looks were quite striking with his long, straight nose and full lips, and Edna studied him with interest for a moment before shifting her attention to her son, who came out blinking at the sunlight, his white-blond hair flopping over his forehead.

Poor circulation and numb feet were forgotten in an instant. Edna's face broadened into a smile. 'WILF!' she shouted and waved at him.

Wilf raised his hand and called back, 'Hello, Ma.'

Crossing the narrow street, she threw her plump arms

around his waist, tears flowing down her ruddy cheeks. 'Oh, Wilf.'

'All right, all right, don't go on.' Wilf pulled away, embarrassed at such an emotional display in front of the other man. 'You only saw me last week.'

'I know,' Edna said, wiping her cheeks, 'but I'm just so glad you're out.' She jerked her head at the other man. 'Who's that?'

'He's nobody,' Wilf said.

The other man grabbed Edna's hand and wrung it. 'Frank Crowther,' he introduced himself. 'You must be Mrs Gadd. I've heard a lot about you.'

'Have you?' Edna looked at Wilf enquiringly.

Wilf shook his head to tell her not to pay any attention. 'See you, Frank,' he said, and turned Edna away.

'Yeah, see you, Wilf,' Crowther called after them as they walked towards the main road. 'I'll be in touch.'

'He a friend of yours?' Edna asked.

'Sort of,' Wilf said and took a deep breath. 'Even the air smells fresher out here.'

'Fresh?' she scoffed. 'With all these petrol fumes?'

'I love it. Reminds me of home.' The smile fell from Wilf's face. 'Or it would do if we were going back to Addison Road.'

'Now, Wilf, don't start all that again. We had to move from Addison Road. I told you why.'

'I know what you told me,' he said sulkily. 'Don't mean I have to like it.'

'You ain't even seen the new place. It's nicer.'

'I liked Addison Road. All me mates were there.'

'What mates? We didn't have any left after what you did.'

'Don't go on about that. I've done me time. It's over with.'

'Just don't do anything like it again, that's all. You get settled and you get a proper job.'

'I ain't getting a job, Ma,' Wilf said, as they joined the end of a bus stop queue. 'I don't need one.'

'What do you mean, you don't need one?'

'We got money coming in regular, ain't we? And we'll have more when I've done a bit.'

'Oh no.' Edna grabbed his arm. 'You're not going back to that. You'll go inside again.'

'Keep your voice down, Ma,' Wilf growled, glancing at the other people in the queue who had turned their heads at Edna's words. 'I'll be careful. That last time was a one-off. It won't happen again.'

'I can't go through all that again, Wilf,' Edna groaned. 'That poor woman—'

'Enough, Ma. I don't want to hear about her. I just want to get home and put me feet up.'

'All right. I'll let it drop for now,' Edna agreed. 'But promise me, Wilf, that you won't do nothing until we've talked about it.'

Wilf rolled his eyes and nodded. 'Promise.'

'Well, what d'ya think?' Stanley Tompkins asked as he watched Frank Crowther bounce on the bed. 'I know it's not much, but at least you've got a roof over your head.'

Crowther patted the lumpy mattress appreciatively. 'It's like a bleeding palace compared to where I've come from.'

'Good. It's three bob a week.'

'That's a bit steep, ain't it, Stan? I thought we was pals.'

'We are, but that's the price for the room and the use of the kitchen. I can rent this out three times over, you know? There's plenty what wants it.'

Crowther got up from the bed and looked out of the

window. 'Nice view,' he said, raising an eyebrow at the graveyard below.

'Don't look out the window if you don't like it,' Tompkins shrugged. 'Do you want it or not?'

'Yeah, all right. Three bob.'

'Up front.'

Crowther's face hardened. 'You're 'aving a laugh, ain't ya? I've just come out of prison. I ain't got that on me.'

'How you going to pay me, then? You got work lined up?'

'Might have.' Crowther opened his suitcase and took out a folded shirt. 'A fella I was inside with got out this morning, too. He might have something I can get in on.'

'Anything in it for me?' Tompkins asked hopefully.

Crowther grinned as he put his few clothes in the rickety chest of drawers, but didn't give Tompkins an answer. He shut his suitcase and slid it under the bed. 'Where's the nearest boozer? I could murder a pint.'

'At the end of the road. I'll come with you.'

'Nah, you're all right,' Crowther said, waving the suggestion away. 'I don't want company. You'll cramp my style.'

Tompkins shifted uncomfortably. 'You're not going back to your old tricks, are you, Frank? Didn't being put away for it teach you a lesson about that?'

Crowther shrugged. 'It's not something I can learn not to do, Stan. I read about it while I was inside. It's what doctors call a compulsion. I can't help it.'

Tompkins looked unconvinced. 'Well, don't do it round here, right? I don't want no bother.'

'You won't get none.' Crowther clapped him on the shoulder. 'See you later,' he called as he thundered down the stairs, leaving Tompkins to wonder how his friend could afford to drink at the pub when he claimed to be potless.

Andrew Monckton sidled into the corridor, took out the hip flask from his inside pocket, checked to make sure no one was around to see, and tipped half the contents down his throat. He gasped as the whisky burned and screwed the cap back on the flask, stowing it in his pocket.

God, but he needed that drink. How he had got through the luncheon with only a glass of vinegary red wine he didn't know. Why had he agreed to do this? he asked himself as he ran the flat of his hand over his thick, dark-brown hair that already had the odd strand of grey. Graydon Heath wasn't even in his ward. Yet here he was, attempting to breathe life into the Liberal Party, standing in for the candidate who claimed to be too unwell to attend, but whom Monckton suspected was shamming.

He knew he'd made a poor show over lunch. He'd been sat next to a particularly tiresome man who'd wanted to know about his war service. Irritated, Monckton had told the man the truth, that he had not wanted England to go to war and that he had hoped for a diplomatic resolution to the problems engulfing Europe rather than a military one. The man had recoiled at this, his mouth puckering in readiness to deliver a rebuke about his lack of patriotism until Monckton had declared that, despite his personal feelings, he had served and done his duty. Mollified, and perhaps a little embarrassed, the man had dug into his plum duff and turned to his opposite neighbour to engage in a more satisfactory conversation.

And now Monckton was supposed to deliver a rousing speech to this bunch, men and women who ought to know by now that the Liberal Party was finished. Monckton had reached this conclusion months before, though he kept it to himself, not telling anyone he was thinking of joining one of the other political parties. He hadn't yet decided whether he would join the Conservatives or Labour. In his most cynical moments, he would make his choice depending upon which party offered him the most. When he was feeling more ideal-istic, it would be whichever party best fitted his personality.

'Andrew!'

Monckton jumped. His party agent, Charlie Ezard, had poked his head around the corner and was glaring at him.

'What are you doing out here? They're all waiting for you.'

Monckton's eyes widened in mock astonishment. 'Really? All twelve of them?'

Ezard sighed impatiently. 'What do you want from me, Andrew? They're a willing audience. That's not bad for a Wednesday afternoon.'

'I'll be preaching to the converted, Charlie. It's a waste of time.'

'Fine. I'll tell them you can't be bothered, shall I? That'll go down well.'

'Oh, stop nagging,' Monckton growled. 'Just give me a minute and I'll be in.'

'Thank you very much.' Ezard looked him up and down. 'And have a mint or something, will you? I can smell the whisky from here.'

Monckton waited until Ezard had gone, then took out the flask and swigged another mouthful. He'd give the damn speech, then dash off to The Green Man just around the corner and drink until he ran out of money.

Where the hell am I supposed to get a mint from? he wondered as he fixed a smile on his face and returned to the hall.

Chapter Five

Maggie Longford threw her cigarette stub away and crushed it beneath her shoe. She imagined the stub was her husband's face, and Maggie smiled to herself as the paper casing broke and the wisps of tobacco spilled out.

It was seven months since Paul had walked out on her and their two children leaving her with the rent arrears. Her bitterness towards him had only grown in that time and with good reason. It was because of his desertion that she'd been forced into working the streets. When all her savings had been used up and she'd sold or pawned all she had of any value, she'd realised she had only one saleable object left – her body. Renting it out had been an obvious and necessary step to take if she wanted to keep herself and her children from starving or being thrown out of their house by an unsympathetic landlord.

But Maggie had not found selling herself easy. Her first night had been spent standing on a street corner, being jock-eyed and harangued by the seasoned prostitutes who resented her encroaching on their patch. These were women of whom Maggie had had no previous experience, and their aggression, not to mention their colourful language, had appalled her. So, she had taken herself off to a quieter part of Graydon Heath, where passing punters were less frequent but still adequate for her means.

And as the weeks passed, she became accustomed to her new job. The patter of solicitation now tripped easily from her tongue. The business was admittedly unpleasant but ultimately bearable because there was money at the end of it. Her fortunes had improved, if only by a little, while her opinion of men had never been lower.

Maggie scraped the bottom of her shoe against the kerb and decided it was time to go home. She had had a good night; four punters and not a nutter amongst them. Enough money in her pocket to keep herself and the kids for a week, if she was careful. As she made her way home, her heels clipped on the paving stones, the only sound on the quiet residential street.

And then, her heels weren't the only sound. Another set of footsteps had joined hers and was even keeping time. She halted and turned. A man came to an abrupt halt about twelve feet behind her. He was wearing an overcoat that reached to his knees and a flat cap that cast the top half of his face into shadow. A scarf covered the bottom.

'Cold, are we?' she asked.

He nodded.

Maggie studied him for a moment. A nutter, she wondered, or just shy? Her fingers toyed with the money in her pocket. She'd made enough for one night, it was true, but a little more would come in handy. She smiled her professional smile. 'Want to be warmed up, love?'

He nodded again.

Maggie looked around and spied an opening between two semi-detached houses. It was far from ideal, but it would do. She'd just have to warn him to be quiet.

'Come on, then,' she said and set off for the alleyway, hearing his boot heels on the pavement behind her, telling her he was following. Turning into the opening, she went in about six feet, backed up against the brick wall and hitched up her skirt.

'It'll be two bob,' she said as he drew near. He hadn't drawn the scarf away from his face and all she could see were his dark eyes. 'And you need to keep quiet.' She pointed at the small, open window above. 'Don't want to disturb the neighbours, do we?'

He reached for her, cupping her face with his hands, and for a horrified moment, Maggie thought he was going to remove his scarf and kiss her, until his hands slid down to her collarbones, the thumbs stroking the bony protrusions. Then his hands came back up and fingers curled around her neck as his thumbs caressed the front of her throat.

'Oh, get on with it, love,' she chided. 'I haven't got all night.'

His eyes hardened, and for the briefest of moments, she thought she'd blown it. He might leave her before paying, or worse, hit her for her cheek.

'I just meant—' she began, but was unable to say more because his thumbs were pressing either side of her windpipe and she couldn't make a sound. Terror flooded through her. She'd been treated roughly by punters before, but not like this. This madman wanted to kill her! She could see it in his eyes.

Maggie pounded at his arms, but he was strong, and her blows barely seemed to touch him. Her legs were giving way and she felt herself sliding down the brick wall.

Light suddenly shone out overhead. Someone in the room above had switched on a light and Maggie, despite the blood throbbing in her ears, heard the sound of a door closing noisily.

He looked up at the window, then released her, shoving her away so roughly she slammed into the ground, hitting her head. By the time she was able to open her eyes, black spots dancing before them, he was gone, and she was, mercifully, alone.

Chapter Six

Georgina cast her eye over the bookstall, wondering whether to buy one of the many paperback novels on sale. The titles were tempting but, affordable as they were, buying one would be an extravagance she could ill afford, and she turned away from the bookstall, her mind dwelling unpleasantly on money.

In her younger days, Georgina had always considered herself well off, someone who would never have to worry about money. But that had been before everything went wrong and income suddenly became a problem. Her husband's army pension didn't stretch as far as it used to, her shares dividends were paying out less and less while Oliver's care home fees kept going up and up. Her friends had suggested ways she could economise, such as moving to a smaller house, which held some appeal; making do without a maid, which held none. While she agreed a housemaid wasn't exactly a necessity – she imagined there were plenty of women who managed without one – getting rid of Lucy would signal to everyone she was struggling and that was a humiliation she could not bear. If only Oliver didn't need to be in the care home...

Georgina shook the thought away. There was no point thinking of 'If onlies'. If only her husband hadn't died; if only there hadn't been a war; if only Oliver's wife had been a better woman. She could go on and on, and this was no day to be thinking of the past. Dominic was coming home and she must keep her mind on the present.

She smiled as she turned towards the platform's exit gates, as if she could see Dominic already. When she'd put him on the boat to India in 1924, Georgina had never imagined it would be years before she saw him again. Back then, she had thought he would be away for perhaps six months, just time enough for all the madness at home to die down. But his letters to her in those first six months were full of how much he was enjoying India, of how well he was doing in his job with the Imperial Civil Service and that he'd made many new friends. She hadn't pressed him to return home. After all, what would he be coming home to? The family house had been sold, his mother was buried and his father was in a care home. Of course, it would have been nice for her to have Dominic around, but she wouldn't allow herself to be selfish, knowing he wouldn't want to be with her all the time. Dominic was young. He would want to be with his friends, walking out with girls and having fun, and that was how it should be.

A whistle blew, and Georgina heard the chug of a train arriving. She paced outside the gates, every few seconds looking beyond them, hoping she would know Dominic when she saw him. What if they passed one another believing themselves strangers? Dominic might think she hadn't bothered to come, that she didn't want to see him, and oh, how awful that would be.

And then, suddenly, there he was, a suitcase in each hand, hat set at an angle that was so like Oliver. As he drew nearer, Georgina wondered how she could ever have worried she wouldn't know him. Dominic was the image of his father at the same age; the same dark hair, the same dark eyes. There was, perhaps, just a touch of his mother around his mouth, but she pushed that thought away.

Their eyes met and Georgina's smile faltered a little. The face, being so like Oliver's, was familiar, and yet, somehow, it was the face of someone she didn't know.

'Grandma?' Dominic asked tentatively.

'Yes,' she said, her eyes filling with tears at the use of the word so long absent from her ears. 'Oh, Dominic, come here.' Georgina held out her arms and Dominic set down his suitcases and stepped into her embrace. She held him tight. 'It's so good to have you home.'

'It's good to be home,' he said, pulling away.

'You look well,' she said, holding him at arm's length. 'How was your journey?'

'Fine.'

'Oh! Good,' Georgina said, a little dismayed by the monosyllabic response, something else he seemed to share with his father. She pointed at his suitcases. 'Pick those up and we'll get a cab.'

He grabbed the suitcases and they made their way to the exit.

'How's Father?' Dominic asked as they stepped out onto the pavement.

'Oh, he's well,' she said brightly. 'I've told him you were coming home and he's so looking forward to seeing you.'

'When will I see him?'

'On Friday.'

'Why not today?'

'You've only just arrived, Dominic. Surely, you're tired after all your travelling?'

'No,' Dominic insisted. 'I'm not tired at all.'

Georgina had to admit he didn't look in the slightest

weary. Oh, what it was to be young and full of energy! A three-week sea voyage from India and several hours on the train would have exhausted her and sent her to bed for the rest of the day, but here was Dominic, fresh as the proverbial daisy. She shook her head. 'I'm sorry, but we can't see him today. Friday's my day for visiting your father.'

A cab pulled up at the kerb and Dominic lifted his suit-cases into the space beside the driver. 'You make it sound like he's in prison.'

'Not at all,' Georgina protested, gesturing him to get into the cab. 'It's a care home. Your father's there for his health and he has his routines. It would upset those if we went to see him today. Besides, he might not even be in.'

'He is free to leave, then?'

Georgina sighed as she settled into the seat and the cab pulled out into the traffic. 'Of course he's free to leave. Your father goes out whenever he wants. He's really very happy there, Dom. You must believe me.'

Dominic nodded. 'If you say so, Grandma.' He took a small black box out of his pocket and held it out to her. 'This is for you.'

Smiling, she opened the box. Inside was a gold brooch in the shape of a serpent with green paste gems for eyes. It was a little gaudy and not at all to her taste but she kissed his cheek and said, 'Oh, it's lovely, Dominic. Did you get it in India?'

He smiled and pinned it to her lapel. 'Something like that.'

Dickie glanced up from his typewriter as Bill Edwards shuffled into *The Chronicle*'s office. He noted the flushed complexion and the belly straining the buttons of the shirt as the editor hung up his coat and hat.

'Good lunch was it?' Dickie glanced at the clock on the wall. 'All three hours of it.'

Edwards scowled. 'What are you? My missus?' He dragged a chair over to Dickie's desk and sat down with a loud exhalation. 'I had lunch with the mayor. You know how he likes to talk.'

Dickie didn't know, having never been invited to dine with the dignitary. 'What did he have to say for himself?'

Edwards belched. 'Bloody heartburn,' he muttered, giving his chest a thump. 'What did he have to say for himself? Well, to summarise his three-hour rant into one sentence, he's worried about Craynebrook. He's got this idea that the Empire Club murders and everything that came out of the investigation has given Craynebrook a bad name.'

'I don't blame him,' Dickie said, thumbing tobacco into the bowl of his pipe. 'You've only got to read all the letters we've been getting to know that what went on at the Empire Club shocked a lot of people.'

'I know,' Edwards nodded. 'He's been getting letters, too. Anyway, the long and the short of it is, he wants to improve Craynebrook's image.'

'And how's he going to do that?'

'With our help. Now, hear me out before you knock this back. It might not be as daft as it sounds. The mayor thinks a series of articles about Craynebrook's war heroes will remind people of how decent the area is. Interviews with some of the men who made it back. Women who volunteered to help the war effort. Proud parents who lost their sons in the fighting, that sort of thing. Well, what do you think?'

Dickie puffed on his pipe. 'It's a good idea. Most of the people who live in Craynebrook are honest, law-abiding people. Articles about heroes and heroines might just remind people that The Five were the exception rather than the rule.'

Edwards's eyes widened in astonishment. 'I thought I'd have to arm-wrestle you into agreeing.'

'I surprise myself sometimes,' Dickie shrugged. 'I suppose you want the first article for this week's edition?'

'The sooner the better. So, I can tell the mayor it's all in hand, can I?'

'You can,' Dickie nodded. 'And you can tell him what the first article will be about, if you like.'

'And what's that?'

Dickie rolled a sheet of blank paper into his typewriter. 'Craynebrook's war memorial. What else?'

Chapter Seven

Edna took the stairs one step at a time. Whoever was banging on the front door would just have to wait for her to get down-stairs. She wasn't going to rush and do herself an injury. Who could it be, anyway? she wondered. No one knocked on her door except for the man who read the gas meter and the milk-man. She reached the door and opened it with a laboured sigh.

'Mrs Gadd,' Frank Crowther hallooed her cheerfully. 'How nice to see you again.'

Edna scowled. 'What you doing here?'

'I came to see Wilf. He in?'

'He's in the lavvie.'

'That's all right. I can wait.' Crowther stepped inside before Edna could argue. 'I wouldn't say no to a cuppa if you've got the kettle on.' He brushed past her down the passage.

Edna followed him into the kitchen, putting the kettle on while he made himself at home.

'You must be pleased to have Wilf back,' he said, watching her as she shuffled around the kitchen.

'Too right I am,' Edna said, peering into mugs to check they were clean. 'What about you? You got family?'

'Nah,' Crowther said. 'It's just me on my ownsome.'

'Where you staying?'

'Over in Graydon Heath. I got a room with a pal of mine. It ain't much, but it's better than prison.'

'What were you inside for?'

Crowther shook a finger at her. 'Now, you're not supposed to ask that, Mrs G.'

'Oh, ain't I? Pardon me, I'm sure.'

'He was in for flashing.'

Both Edna and Crowther turned towards the back door. Wilf was standing in the doorway, hooking his braces over his shoulder.

'Flashing?' Edna looked at Crowther in disgust.

'And more,' Wilf said, taking a biscuit from the tin. He bit into it and crumbs tumbled down his front. 'Frank don't like women much, Ma.'

Crowther glanced uneasily from Wilf to Edna and back again. 'Now, now, Wilf, enough of that. You'll give your lovely mum the wrong idea about me.'

Wilf sniffed. 'What you doing here, Frank?'

'Said I'd pop by, didn't I?'

'I know you did, but I weren't expecting you so soon.'

'Well, it ain't as if I've got anything else to do. Besides, I didn't want to miss out on anything.' He gave Wilf a meaningful look.

Edna frowned. 'What's he on about, Wilf? And how'd he know where to find us?'

'Wilf gave me your address, Mrs G,' Crowther said. 'He thought we might work together when we got out.'

'You want to work with him?' Edna pointed savagely at Crowther.

'It's all right, Ma. Calm down,' Wilf said, patting the air. 'It was just an idea.'

'Well, you can forget it. We don't work with no one.'

'I ain't no one,' Crowther protested. 'I know all about Wilf's business affairs.'

Edna glared at Wilf. 'What have you told him?'

'He's told me all about that Monckton fella,' Crowther went on. 'That's a nice little number you got going there.'

'There's nothing in that for you, Frank,' Wilf said, avoiding Edna's eyes.

'If you say so. But what about the other?'

Wilf shrugged. 'Maybe.'

'That'll do, then.' Crowther rose. 'I won't stop for that cuppa after all, Mrs G. Best I get off.'

'I'll see you out,' Wilf said, and pushed Crowther into the passage as the kettle whistled.

Edna filled the teapot with boiling water and banged the kettle back on the gas ring as Wilf returned. 'Are you out of your bleeding mind?' she demanded.

'Frank's all right,' Wilf said.

'A flasher?'

'We can trust him.'

'What did you go blabbing to him for? Telling someone like that all our business?'

'It just came out, Ma. Stop having a go at me.'

Edna shook her head as she poured out the tea. 'I don't like him, Wilf.'

'You don't have to have anything to do with him. If he comes round again and I'm not here, don't let him in. You hear?'

'I won't,' Edna declared. 'If he waves his whatsit at me, I'll chop it off.'

Wilf laughed and stirred two spoonfuls of sugar into his

mug as Edna sat down. His expression became serious. 'Listen, Ma, as Frank brought the subject up...' He tossed the teaspoon into the sugar bowl. 'I've been thinking about Monckton.'

'What about him?'

'I reckon he's had it easy for too long. He ain't been giving us enough.'

'Twenty quid a month's not to be sneezed at, Wilf.'

'Fifty would be better.'

Edna's mouth fell open. 'You're mad. He won't pay fifty quid a month.'

'He will if he's knows what's good for him.'

'Oh, Wilf,' Edna groaned. 'It's too much. He's paid the twenty every month like a lamb. You push him up to fifty and he's going to...' she gestured helplessly.

'Going to what?' Wilf challenged. 'I tell you, Ma, he ain't going to do nothing but pay up.'

'He could go to the police.'

Wilf shook his head. 'He's in too deep. And besides, what could he tell 'em? He don't know me from Adam. You've picked up the money every month regular for nearly six years and nobody's got a sniff of what we've been doing.'

'But we're doing all right on the twenty,' she whined.

Wilf banged his fist on the table. 'I don't want to just do all right. I want to be set up for life. I want you to be able to take it easy, have some young girl doing all the cleaning and shopping for you, so you ain't wearing yourself out all the bleeding time.'

'People like us don't live like that.'

'We're going to live like that, Ma,' Wilf insisted and banged the lid on the biscuit tin. 'And I don't want to hear no more about it.'

Georgina put a hand on Dominic's knee to stop it jiggling. 'There's no need to be nervous, Dom.'

'I'm not nervous,' he said unconvincingly, his eyes darting around the day room with its half-dozen armchairs and low tables. Some of the tables were littered with dog-eared magazines and newspapers while others had packs of cards laid out, some in unfinished games of solitaire. Two of the armchairs were occupied and Dominic was watching the men in them with a mixture of curiosity and alarm.

Although she was doing her best to hide it, Georgina was as nervous as her grandson about this first meeting between father and son. Dominic had plagued her with questions about Oliver all during dinner the previous evening. Was he really happy at the care home? Was care home a euphemism for something more sinister? Was his father actually incarcerated in a lunatic asylum?

She'd done her best to allay his fears, explaining the care home was exactly that, somewhere Oliver was cared for, and that it was the best place for a man afflicted with a chronic nervous condition such as his father had. She'd had to admit that some of the men were more troubled than his father, that they sometimes experienced what the doctors called episodes when, to a layman's eyes, they did indeed appear a little mad. But, she'd hastened to add, Oliver wasn't like that. She didn't say Oliver too had had his episodes in the past. There was no need, she reasoned, for he hadn't had one of those for a long while and she didn't want to frighten Dominic with talk of something that might never happen again.

Georgina winced as one of the armchair occupants suddenly cried out. Casting a worried glance at Dominic, who was clutching the arms of his chair, Georgina looked appeal-ingly at the white-coated attendant who kept watch in the day room. He understood her silent appeal and went over to the man, bending low to murmur calming words in his ear. Whatever he said seemed to work; the man fell silent.

She glanced at Dominic. His face was stony, his eyes fixed on the floor. 'Dom?' Georgina whispered.

'If I'd known it was like this...' He shook his head, shrugging off the hand she placed on his.

The day-room door opened and Oliver walked in. He came towards them silently, his slippers making no sound on the carpeted floor, and smiled awkwardly as Dominic jumped up.

'You've grown,' Oliver said, looking his son over. 'Hasn't he, Mother?'

'Yes,' Georgina said, keeping her eyes on Dominic. 'He's quite the young man.'

'Well,' Oliver said when Dominic didn't speak, 'shall we sit down?' He gestured at the chairs.

They sat. Oliver rubbed his palms on his knees, a gesture Georgina knew was a sign of his discomfort. He didn't know what to say to his son, that much was clear. And Dominic? He was just staring at his father as if he couldn't quite believe it was him.

'Dominic's enjoyed India. Haven't you, Dom?' She gestured for Dominic to say something.

'Yes,' he said. 'It was fun.'

'I thought about going out there when I was young, didn't I, Mother?' Oliver said. 'But I didn't think I could endure the heat.'

Dominic nodded. 'It does get very hot.'

Another silence, and Georgina felt her skin prickling. *Find something for them to talk about*, she told herself, and racked her brain for a subject.

'Dominic's met up with an old friend,' she said. 'Do you remember Daniel Green, Oliver? He lives over the road to me?'

Oliver shook his head.

'Oh,' Georgina said, disappointed. 'Well, he and Dom used to play together. But isn't it nice for Dom to have someone to go out with while he's home? Where did you say you were both going tonight, Dom?'

Dominic didn't seem to hear her. He leant forward and put his hand on Oliver's knee. 'Are you all right in here, Father?'

Oliver blinked, a little taken aback by the question. 'Yes. Why wouldn't I be?'

'Because you're in here with...' Dominic jerked his head at the man who had called out earlier, 'madmen.'

Oliver chuckled and raised his eyebrows at Georgina. 'Is that what you've told him, Mother?'

'Certainly not,' Georgina cried. 'Dom, I've told you—'

But Dominic wasn't paying her any attention. 'Because if you're not all right in here, then I should get you out.'

'Dominic! No!' Georgina jerked out of her chair.

Dominic and Oliver looked up at her in surprise.

'I'm sorry,' she gasped. 'I didn't mean—' She sat back down and clasped her handbag tightly to her chest, trying to ignore their astonished, confused stares.

The man in the armchair began moaning, a continuous, high keening that Georgina had heard him make before and knew was the prelude to an episode. *Not today*, she mentally begged. *Oh, please, not today.*

Dominic stared at the man and Georgina saw horror in his expression. The keening grew louder and more insistent, and Dominic bolted from the room.

The attendant came over to Georgina. 'It might be better if you go,' he said, looking worriedly at Oliver, whose hands were gripping his knees so tightly the knuckles had turned white.

Was it because of his fellow resident or because of how

Dominic had reacted? Georgina wondered as she got to her feet. 'Will he be all right?'

'Don't worry,' the attendant said with a sympathetic smile. 'We'll see to him. You better go after your grandson. I think he was a bit upset.'

'Yes, he was,' Georgina nodded unhappily. 'I'm going now, Oliver,' she said loudly to get his attention, but Oliver didn't give any sign he heard. She hurried out in search of her grandson and found Dominic at the care home gates.

'I'm sorry,' he blurted as she put a hand on his arm. 'I just couldn't stand it in there.'

'I know,' she stroked his arm soothingly. 'That poor man. If you haven't seen that sort of thing before, it can be quite alarming.'

'And my father's in there with men like him! Why do you make him stay? He's not mad, is he?'

'No, of course he's not mad.'

'Then why is he here?' Dominic yelled.

Georgina took a deep breath. 'Dom, please don't shout at me. I know you're upset, but I won't have you speaking to me like that.'

'I'm sorry. I didn't mean to shout.' Dominic grabbed his hair and tugged. 'Ugh. It's just I can't help feeling that if I'd been here, if I'd never been sent to India, Father wouldn't have ended up in this awful place. We would have been together, just him and me. I would have looked after him. That's how it should have been.'

Dominic turned and walked away. Georgina let him go, not knowing what to say or how to comfort him. There was a low stone wall over the road from the gates, and she crossed to it and sat down. She would wait for Dominic to come to her.

Chapter Eight

Agnes Trent took her customer to the haberdasher's doorway.

The porch was deep; it could have been designed for obscuring an indecent act. It was the best spot for servicing punters, and this was her patch, her stretch of high street. The other women knew not to come near, for Agnes's claim to territory was notorious and few were brave enough to challenge her.

She'd been at this game a long time and there was little that could surprise her. Agnes had had them all; the shy ones, the arrogant ones, the rough ones, the inadequates. But she couldn't quite work out which type this punter fell into. Shy, maybe. That would explain the scarf over the lower half of his face and the cap pulled low. Quiet, definitely, for he hadn't said a word. Inadequate was her next guess. He wanted to pretend this was a romance, that they were sweethearts enjoying a stolen moment of intimacy. That explained the gentleness of his hands on her throat, the stroking, his thumbs slightly catching on her sagging skin. Funny, she thought, what men liked to do. Most got straight down to business and she preferred it that way. This unnecessary foreplay bored her and she felt for his trouser buttons, keen not to drag their transaction out. He wasn't paying her enough for that. But as her fingers probed, he jerked his hips away and she tutted in irritation.

'What's the problem, dearie?' she asked before his fingers tightened around her neck.

Agnes tried to breathe and found she couldn't. She clamped her hands around his wrists and tried to push him away, but couldn't dislodge him. *Scream*, she told herself, but she couldn't make a sound. His grip was so tight. It felt as if her head was going to explode.

She could feel her legs buckling. Blackness was coming upon her when a whistle sounded a little way off. She heard him gasp and his fingers slackened, just a little, but it was enough for Agnes. She seized her chance and croaked out 'Help!'

The whistle sounded again.

He threw her aside and ran. Agnes fell, her knees slamming into the cold, wet tiles of the doorway. She cried out in pain and tears flooded her eyes, surprising her. She hadn't cried in years. Heavy footsteps came running and, for a terrible moment, Agnes thought he was coming back to finish her off.

She looked up and, for the first time in her life, was thankful to see the outline of a policeman against the moonlight.

Wilf climbed over the wall and dropped down lightly on the other side. He swore as his small lock-picking set fell out of his pocket and he scrabbled around in the dirt to find it.

A light came on in the window in the house next door and he froze. A minute later, it flicked off, and he breathed again. *You're out of practice, Wilf, old son*, he told himself as his gloved fingers closed around the leather pouch and he replaced it firmly in his pocket.

Wilf tiptoed to the back door of the house and tried the handle, just in case luck was on his side. The knob turned, and he grinned as he opened the door slowly, waiting for the squeal of hinges. The squeal was quiet, barely louder than a mouse's squeak, and he stepped into the kitchen. He listened, ears pricked for the slightest sound, but he heard nothing and moved further in.

He tried the pantry door first. Usually, there were only foodstuffs in a pantry, but sometimes the owners put their silverware there and experience had taught him the pantry was always worth a look. Not this time, though. Wilf helped himself to a biscuit from a tin, then moved into the hall. He went through the dining room, opening the sideboard and finding a canteen of cutlery that went straight into his sack. A silver platter, cake knife and sauce boat followed before he moved to the sitting room. Here, he found two silver candlesticks, a cabinet of silver trinkets and a cigarette box. He searched a small study, found a money box of five-pound notes in one of the bureau's drawers, and stuffed the notes into his pocket.

He returned to the hall and put his foot on the bottom stair, waiting to hear a creak. It didn't make a sound, and he made his way up, grateful for the thick carpet underfoot, and entered the first bedroom he came to. This one didn't appear to be used often, for there were none of the usual signs of regular occupation and nothing worth taking. He moved on to the next room; this was a child's, and he walked straight out. He pushed open the third door, and in the dim light coming through the curtains, checked the bed. There was no one in it.

All the tension drained from his body, and Wilf laughed out loud. All his tiptoeing around and there was no one home.

He moved to the bay window where a dressing table

stood. A silver-backed hairbrush and hand mirror went into the sack. The jewellery box was opened, and he whistled as he picked out a silver locket necklace, three pairs of earrings and a gold bracelet. A wooden box on the other end of the dressing table revealed cuff links. They all went into the sack.

Wilf stepped away, but not before he caught sight of himself in the dressing-table mirror. His lips tightened, and drawing in a deep breath, he picked up a small crystal vase from the dressing table and threw it at the mirror. He enjoyed the noise the breaking glass made, enjoyed too the cracks that resulted, but his pleasure was short-lived. He hurried from the room, annoyed at succumbing to his emotions again, down the stairs and out through the back door, closing it behind him. He always closed doors when he left; there was no point drawing attention to the fact the house had been entered. His sack clanked a little as he made his way down the street, keeping out of the pools of light shed from the street lamps.

It was a good haul for his first time out, and bloody hell, but he'd enjoyed it!

Chapter Nine

Matthew checked his wristwatch, wiping off the drops of rain that speckled the glass. It was coming up to a quarter to ten, and he was supposed to be at the church in Bethnal Green by ten o'clock. Pat's warning not to be late rang in his ears, but she could forget about him being late. At this rate, he would miss the church service entirely, and he groaned inwardly at the recriminations he would have to bear from his sister.

'What are you going to do about this?' a man yelled from amongst the crowd that had gathered.

Matthew gave him a polite smile and looked up at the war memorial that only the day before had been gleaming white stone. Now, it was covered in red paint, the names of the dead carved into the stone hidden beneath the viscous liquid.

'Anything?' Matthew asked PC Rudd as he came over.

The constable shook his head. 'Nothing, sir. Whoever did it took the paint tin with them. No paintbrush, either, but then, it doesn't look like they used a brush. They just chucked the paint over it.'

'They certainly did.'

'Why would someone do this?' Rudd asked, gesturing at the despoiled memorial. 'I mean, I'd understand if they had chucked the paint over a shop window because they were short-changed or something. But vandalising a war memorial. It's nasty.'

'I suppose it makes sense to whoever did it.' Matthew squinted at the base of the memorial and pointed. 'What's that?'

Rudd bent down by the stone plinth. 'Looks like a piece of paper, sir. The paint has stuck it to the stone.'

'Can you peel it off?'

Rudd used a thumb and forefinger to grab hold of a small section of the paper that was sticking out. He gave it the smallest of tugs, and slowly, the paper came away.

'Don't rush,' Matthew ordered. 'I don't want it torn if you can help it.'

Rudd continued to pull. 'The paint's still a little tacky down here, so it should come away all right.' He straightened and held out the scrap of paper for Matthew to see. 'Looks like a newspaper, sir.'

Matthew tilted his head to read the name. 'It's *The Chronicle*. Can you make out the date?'

Rudd wiped his finger over the paint. Some of it came away, enough to see the text beneath more clearly. 'The eighteenth.'

'Friday's edition,' Matthew said. 'Get it dried out and log it as evidence.'

Rudd made a face. 'You don't think it has anything to do with the vandalism, do you, sir? It was probably just blown there by the wind.'

'Maybe, but let's not discount it as evidence until we're sure. Dry it out, please.'

'Straight away, sir.' Rudd walked off with the sodden newspaper, holding it away from his body to avoid getting paint on his uniform.

'Any idea who did it, inspector?'

Matthew turned to the young man with a camera hanging from his neck and a notebook and pencil at the ready. 'Reporter?' he asked.

'Teddy Welch, *The Chronicle*,' the young man smiled and held out his hand.

Matthew shook it. 'Mr Waite not working today?'

'Not today, no. I'm standing in for him. But I do know what I'm doing.'

'I'm sure you do, Mr Welch,' Matthew smiled at the young man's insistence. 'But to answer your question – no, I don't know who did this.'

'Do you know why whoever did it would want to vandalise a war memorial? On Easter Sunday, of all days?'

'I've really no idea. When I catch him, I'll ask him.'

'Can I put that in my article, inspector?'

'If you think it's worth printing,' Matthew said, angling his hat to shed the rain that had pooled in the brim. 'Now, if you'll excuse me, Mr Welch, there's somewhere I'm supposed to be.'

Georgina watched Oliver as Lucy set the platter with the roasted leg of lamb on the table. He seemed perfectly normal and she allowed herself to relax a little.

She'd telephoned the care home that morning and spoken with Dr Avery, wanting to make sure her son was in the right frame of mind to visit her for Easter Sunday. Dr Avery had assured her that though Oliver had been a little unsettled after Dominic's visit, he had been well enough the past two days and that he should be fine to visit her for lunch, though he thought it best the visit not last more than three or four hours as longer might tire him.

Maybe she should have been more worried about Dominic, Georgina thought as she shifted her gaze to her grandson. He'd been a little on the quiet side since his visit to his father, and he hadn't said a word about it or about Oliver since. That worried her more than his constant questions had done.

'Hungry, Oliver?' she asked as Lucy left the room, closing the door behind her.

'Very. It looks delicious.'

'It does, doesn't it? Would you like to carve?'

Oliver took up the carving knife and began slicing the lamb. 'What's Easter like in India, Dominic?' he asked, putting a slice on a plate and handing it to Georgina.

'Much the same as here, I'd say. Everyone goes to the club and has lunch, just like this.' Dominic took the plate Oliver passed to him.

'But surely, the food isn't the same?' Georgina said. 'You don't have lamb and mint sauce out there for Easter, do you?'

'Of course we do,' he said, spooning buttered Jersey potatoes out of the bowl. 'Easter wouldn't be Easter if they served curry and rice.'

Oliver sat down and unfolded his napkin, laying it over his lap. 'That was another thing I didn't think I would take to. Curry.'

'It is an acquired taste,' Georgina agreed, pushing the mint sauce towards Oliver, relieved her son and grandson were at least able to make conversation. 'Lucy made a curry once, and it was so hot, I was drinking water all evening. Did you ever eat the local food, Dom?'

'Sometimes, when me and the chaps went into the town.'

Oliver spooned mint sauce onto his plate. 'What chaps were they? Anyone we'd know?'

'I don't think so. Just chaps I worked with.'

'But who were they? What were their names, Dom?' Georgina insisted. 'We might know their people.'

'What does it matter if you do?' Dominic said testily. 'I

50

hate the way everyone knows everyone else here. That's what I liked about India. I could go into the town and no one would know who I was.'

Georgina's head was beginning to hurt. 'I expect you're eager to get back to India,' she said, cutting into her lamb. 'As you like it so much.'

There must have been an edge to her words, for Dominic didn't answer and when she looked up to find out why, she found her grandson staring at her.

'Do you want to be rid of me, Grandma?' Dominic asked quietly.

'Of course not,' she cried. 'I'm so happy to finally have you home.'

'I don't want to be a nuisance to you.'

'But you're not. Oliver, please, tell him he's not.'

Oliver pushed peas around his plate. 'You're not a nuisance to Mother, Dom. I am, but you're not.'

'Oh, for heaven's sake,' Georgina cried and felt tears pricking at her eyes. 'Stop it, both of you. I won't have you talking like this.'

The table fell silent, the only sound the scraping of cutlery on china. Georgina blinked back her tears and tried to eat, but her appetite had gone and she gave up, setting her knife and fork on the plate. Both Oliver and Dominic, however, didn't seem to notice or mind the silence and tucked into their lamb and potatoes eagerly, even helping themselves to more.

Georgina glanced at the clock on the mantelpiece. *Only a few more hours*, she thought, *and then Oliver will return to the care home and Dominic will go out for the evening with his friend, and I can have my house all to myself again for a few hours. How lovely that will be.*

Sebastian Monckton put his knife and fork together on his plate and wiped his mouth with his napkin, folding and setting it down by the plate, just as his nanny had taught him. He looked first at his father, filling his wineglass from the decanter at one end of the table, and then at his stepmother at the other.

'May I be excused, Mother?' he asked quietly.

Felicity examined his plate before answering. 'Yes, you may. But don't make any noise.'

The boy slid from his chair and hurried from the dining room.

'Why did you have to tell him to be quiet?' Monckton asked irritably.

Felicity lit a cigarette. 'Because I need to rest this afternoon before our guests arrive. I can't do that if he's hurtling around the house, yelling at the top of his voice.'

'He doesn't hurtle. And anyway, he's a boy. He's supposed to make a noise.'

'Not in my house.'

'It's *my* house. It's the one thing I can call my own.' He tried to ignore the mocking rise of her eyebrow by snapping a grape off its stem from the bowl in front of him. 'So, who's coming this evening?'

'Mark and Annabelle. Alex and Jane. Freddie and Grace.'

'Oh, for Christ's sake.'

'They're our friends, Andrew.'

'They're *your* friends. And a more tiresome lot I can't imagine. I'm not staying here for them.'

'Oh yes, you are. If you think you're skulking off, you're very much mistaken. How would it look if you weren't here when they arrived?'

'I don't expect they'd care a jot. They don't like me any more than I like them.'

Felicity tapped her cigarette out into the ashtray. 'You will be here when they arrive, Andrew, and you will stay for dinner. After that, you can do as you please.' Her lips curved in a sly smile. 'It's probably for the best you go out. We'll be playing bridge then. You can't play, so you'd only be in the way.'

'Not can't. Don't,' he corrected. 'And I'll be more than happy to leave you and your cronies to it.' Felicity bristled at the use of his word 'cronies' and that gave him pleasure.

Her eyes narrowed. 'Before you go out,' she said, 'please make sure Sebastian is ready to leave early in the morning. I won't have him keeping the driver waiting.'

'Leave?' Monckton cried. 'What do you mean, leave? The boy's only just got here.'

She sighed dramatically. 'Must you become hysterical, Andrew? It's not at all attractive. I've arranged for Sebastian to stay with a friend for the half-term.'

'What the hell for?'

'I have a busy week and I don't want him under my feet. Anyway, he'd be bored here all day. He's pleased to be going.'

Monckton banged both fists on the table. 'You had no right to arrange it without talking to me first. You knew I was looking forward to him coming home. I want him here with me. I hardly see him as it is.'

'Oh, honestly!' She crushed her cigarette in the ashtray. 'You sound like a woman. Not like a man at all. But then,' she looked at him contemptuously, 'you're not much of a man, are you?'

His rage erupted instantly. Monckton grabbed the decanter and hurled it across the room. Felicity shrieked as it passed by her, only an inch from her ear, and crashed against the wall. Footsteps hurried down the hall and the dining-room door burst open.

'I heard a crash, madam,' the maid said, her eyes widening as she saw the dripping wall and broken glass.

'I'm afraid Mr Monckton's temper has got the better of him again,' Felicity said, composure regained. 'He's made rather a mess. Clear it up, please.'

'Yes, madam.' The maid hurried away to fetch a dustpan and brush.

Felicity rose with a weary sigh. 'I trust you won't make such a fool of yourself again, Andrew. In front of the servants is bad enough, but in front of my friends would be too too embarrassing.' She strolled out of the dining room, closing the door quietly behind her.

A moment later, the maid came back in. 'I'm to clean up, sir,' she said nervously.

'Then get on with it.' Monckton reached across the table and snatched up Felicity's half-empty wineglass. He drained it and set it down, listening to the sweep and crush of broken glass as the maid swept the debris into the pan. 'And when you've done that, you can bring me another bottle.'

Pat banged the lid on a saucepan of cabbage. 'You promised you wouldn't be late.'

'I didn't promise,' Matthew said, 'and I didn't do it deliberately. I got called out.'

'Today of all days?'

'Well, I would ask the criminal fraternity not to commit crimes on my days off, but I'm not sure they'd oblige.'

'Oh, that's very funny. You should go on the stage. So, what was the emergency this morning?'

'Someone threw red paint over the Craynebrook war memorial.'

'Why'd they do that?'

'I don't know.'

'Was it kids?'

Matthew groaned. 'I don't know that either, Pat.'

'I was only asking, you touchy sod.' She bent and opened the oven door, basted the leg of lamb, and slammed the door shut, making Matthew wince.

'I didn't want to miss the church service, you know?' he said. 'It's important to me, too.'

Pat turned to him, her face softening. 'I know. I'm sorry. It's just that Mum started when you didn't turn up at the church and said we shouldn't be bothering to remember Dad after all this time.'

'Is that why you've been crying?'

'I haven't,' she protested.

'I'm a detective, Pat. I can tell when someone's been crying.'

'You're going to start me off again.' Pat's chin dimpled and she shook her head. 'Do you want to stop? Am I making it worse by insisting on all this?' She gestured at the pots and pans.

'No,' Matthew said emphatically. 'Just because Mum couldn't care less about Dad doesn't mean we should too, and I'll tell Mum so. Don't let her upset you.'

'Easy for you to say,' she sniffed.

Matthew stifled a sigh. 'Is Georgie all right?'

'He's helping Fred downstairs.'

'That's not what I asked.'

Pat threw a tea towel at him. 'Yes, inspector, he's fine. He wasn't close to Dad, so it don't bother him. All that bothers him is he thought you weren't coming today. So, now you're here, he's happy. Mum's happy. Everyone's happy. Satisfied, Mr Policeman?'

'I'm satisfied,' Matthew nodded, trying not to smile. 'Do you still want me to have a word with Mum about Georgie?'

'Oh, I'd forgotten about that.' The saucepan with the

cabbage was boiling over, and Pat turned the gas down. 'No, leave her alone. She hasn't been so bad with him this last week. She'll only sulk about it when you've gone.'

'I won't say anything, then. And how's this for an idea? Next year's Easter Sunday, you and me go to a restaurant for lunch? If the others don't care about all this, we leave them behind and we go somewhere nice and remember Dad as we want to. What do you say?'

Pat's eyes moistened again. 'Really?'

'Really.'

'Oh, Mattie,' she said, the tears flowing freely now. 'That would be so lovely.'

Chapter Ten

Frank Crowther buried himself in the bushes.

His heart was beating fast, his blood was rushing in his ears, and the palms of his hands were damp with sweat. He felt as if he'd explode with excitement.

He'd been making his way back to his room, eating chips he'd bought from the stall outside the pub, the only thought in his head that of wondering when Wilf would be in touch with news of a job. But as soon as he heard the clack of a woman's heels on the pavement, he crammed the last of his chips into his mouth, tossed away the vinegar-stained newspaper and waited.

She was getting nearer. It was too dark and her face too much in shadow for him to tell how old she was or whether she was pretty. Not that it mattered. He didn't need her to be attractive. He just needed her to be afraid.

Aching with impatience, he unbuttoned his flies and delved inside. Oh, he remembered this, the delicious, desperate anticipation. It had been too long. He was going to enjoy himself.

She was only a few feet away when he sprang, bursting out of the bushes and onto the pavement before her. She halted, giving a cry of surprise and alarm. When he didn't move or speak, he saw her relax, just a little, and that was the moment Crowther had been waiting for. He drew out his penis and saw her eyes drop down to his crotch, widening in horror as he worked himself.

This was the best bit for him, that delicious moment when his victim froze, unable to take her eyes off his jerking hand. Sometimes, he could really make it last, slow his hand down and revel in the panic and terror on the woman's face. Most times, though, he knew he could only enjoy their terror for a few seconds if he was to get away safely. He closed his eyes as his pleasure mounted.

It was a mistake.

She cried out. It wasn't a scream exactly, more like a strangled cat, and Crowther's eyes snapped open, his hand tightening on his swollen member. For a fraction of a second, it was his turn to freeze, but then self-preservation took over his brain and he fled, his now flaccid penis bobbing against his open fly. He didn't stop running until his lungs threatened to burst and he had to bend over double to catch his breath. Curses and obscenities spilled from his mouth against the bitch who had cut short his fun.

Breathing normally again, he straightened and looked around to make sure he hadn't been followed. There was no one. Crowther grinned and buttoned up his flies. He'd do better next time.

Chapter Eleven

William Hayden paid off the cab driver and picked up the suitcases, sighing as he watched his wife stride up the garden path to the front door.

The Easter weekend was supposed to have been a much-needed rest, a few days away at his parents' house in the country with nothing to do but be waited on and fussed over. And it would have been just that if only Katherine hadn't been determined to find fault with everything his parents said or did. If they said he was looking a little thin, Katherine had to take it as a criticism she wasn't looking after him properly. If they asked him about his work, Katherine complained they never asked her what she got up to, as if she couldn't possibly do anything of interest. William had spent the entire weekend trying to prevent an argument between her and his mother, something Katherine decided was a betrayal of his wedding vows. And so, the journey home had been filled with angry words from Katherine for not supporting her, punctuated by long moments of silence. It had all made him wish they'd never gone away.

William had reached the front door when Katherine screamed his name. His hope of sneaking away for a lunchtime drink at the pub was forgotten in an instant as he rushed into the hall. 'What is it?'

Katherine appeared in the sitting-room doorway. Her mouth was open, her eyes wide and teary. 'Look,' she said, waving him in.

He went, wary of what he was walking into. At first, he saw nothing to explain why his wife was so upset. The room appeared to be as they had left it. Then his eyes fell on the display cabinet on the far side of the room and he realised it was empty. All the silverware he had painstakingly collected over the years was gone.

'Someone's been in here, Will,' Katherine whimpered, and William dropped the suitcases and took her in his arms. 'They've taken all our things.'

He kissed her temple and murmured soothing words, feeling her hot tears on his neck. His eyes roamed around the room, realising now that the candlesticks from the mantel-piece were also missing, their candles strewn on the floor, and the cigarette box was gone from the coffee table.

'I'm calling the police,' he said, peeling her away from him and sitting her down on the sofa. 'Don't touch anything.'

William returned to the hall and snatched up the tele-phone receiver. As he demanded to be connected to Crayne-brook Police Station, he shook his head. What an all-round bloody mistake it had been to go away for the weekend.

Edna groaned as she pulled up her bloomers and smoothed her skirt over her ample hips and thighs. She'd sat on the lavatory for more than a quarter of an hour, she reckoned, pushing and grunting, and she was still bound up. Every morning was the same and she was fed up with it. The stuff the quack gave her didn't do her any good, even though he charged an arm and a leg for his bottle of jollop. She'd have to go back to the castor oil, she supposed.

Reaching up to pull the chain, Edna's gaze turned to the shelf near the cistern, noticing a bag on it that hadn't been there the day before. She grabbed the handle and pulled. There was a sound of metal and the bag dropped heavily from the shelf, nearly hitting her in the face.

'Bloody thing,' she cursed, grabbing the other handle and setting the bag on the toilet seat. She drew back the zip and peered inside. Pressing her lips together in irritation, she unlocked the lavatory door and stamped into the house.

Climbing the stairs to the first floor, Edna threw open the bedroom door and dumped the bag on the bed. 'Wake up,' she ordered and sank onto the rickety chair beside the bed.

There was movement beneath the blankets and the holdall wobbled as Wilf turned onto his back. 'What is it?'

'You've been at it again, haven't you?'

Wilf prised his eyes open and looked down at the holdall lying on his legs. 'What did you bring that up here for?'

'We were going to talk about this, Wilf. You promised me you wouldn't go out on a job before we'd talked.'

'Oh, leave off, will ya, Ma? I ain't even awake yet.'

'Do you want to go back inside? Is that what you want?'

'Where's me tea?'

'Sod your tea. I want to know what the blooming hell you think you're doing.'

Wilf sat up and glared at his mother. 'I like it, all right? The same as you like your books. I ain't telling you to stop reading, am I?'

'Reading books won't put me in prison,' Edna retorted. 'And don't you ever think about me? All that time I spent worrying about you while you was inside. I get you back and you're at it again.'

'I'm doing it for you,' Wilf protested. 'This,' he kicked at the holdall, 'and Monckton. I told you why.'

Edna shook her head, knowing it was useless to argue with him. 'Where did you go for this lot?'

'Craynebrook.'

'You didn't?' she gasped. 'Not back there?'

'It's good pickings, Ma. You look at what I got and you'll see I'm right.'

Edna peered into the holdall. 'Yeah, the stuff looks good. But going back to Craynebrook... That's risky, Wilf. What with Monckton living there and what happened.'

'You're worrying over nothing.' Wilf fell back onto his pillow and yawned, showing his yellowed tombstone teeth.

She prodded the holdall. 'How we going to get rid of all this, then?'

'Same as always. Nobby Webber.'

'Wilf,' Edna said in exasperation, 'I told you the other night. Nobby's dead.'

'He's what?'

'Been gone six months or more.'

'Blimey. Poor old Nobby.'

'Don't go getting sentimental about him. He was a rotter and you know it. So, tell me. How are we going to get rid of the stuff now?'

'Shut up, will ya? I'm thinking,' Wilf snapped. 'If we were still at Addison Road, it'd be easy, wouldn't it? I'd know someone we could go to if we were still there.'

'Don't keep going on about Addison Road, Wilf. I've had it up to here.' Edna gestured to the top of her head.

'Yeah, all right.' He shrugged. 'I'll have to use Frank.'

'Oh no. We're not using him.'

'Why not?'

'Why not?' she echoed incredulously. 'A filthy bugger like him?'

'Frank ain't that bad, Ma. And it ain't any of our business what he does for kicks. The fact is Frank Crowther knows plenty of people round this way and we don't. He could be useful.'

'He'll have us over a barrel, Wilf. He already knows about Monckton. You bring him in on your housebreaking and he'll know everything.'

'It don't matter if he does. Frank ain't a snitch. So, there you go. I'll take the stuff to him in a day or two.' Wilf fell back onto the pillow and yawned. 'I don't know what's the matter with you lately, Ma. You never used to worry so much. Carry on like this and you'll make yourself ill. Now, go and get me tea.'

DC Gary Pinder unwrapped a boiled sweet and aimed the wrapper at a wastebin about four feet distant. The wrapper landed in the bin and Pinder threw up his arms and cheered, 'Goal!'

God, he was bored. Why did he never get anything interesting to work on? Even Barnes had more exciting cases and he was the most junior detective in CID. Rolling the sweet around in his mouth, Pinder dragged over the case file he'd been working on for the past five weeks, knowing Matthew would be on his back if he didn't make some progress soon.

He heard footsteps in the corridor and looked expectantly towards the door. A moment later, Detective Sergeant Justin Denham walked in.

'All right, Just? Where have you been?' Pinder asked.

'Bedford Street,' Denham said, taking off his coat and hanging it over the back of his chair. 'A couple go away for the weekend and come back to find they've been burgled.' He shook his head. 'You should have seen the wife. She was really upset.'

'Yeah, well, if all her furs and jewellery's gone, what is she going to wear to the hunt ball?'

'It wasn't that,' Denham said, his lip curling at Pinder's scorn. 'I think it was knowing that someone had gone through the house that really got to her. You know, looking into all their private things. Have you ever been burgled?'

'Nah. Not that they'd find anything worth taking at my place. Not on my salary.'

'You're always moaning about your salary. Give it a rest, will you?'

Pinder unwrapped another sweet. 'What was taken?'

'Silverware, mostly,' Denham said, shaking his head at the paper bag of sweets Pinder offered. 'Candlesticks, a canteen of cutlery, cigarette box, jewellery, a bit of cash.'

'Any idea who done it?'

'I've been thinking. There's Denny Carter, but he broke his ankle jumping out of a window and hasn't moved for weeks. Pete Harriman, maybe, though silverware's not really his thing. It could be Alan Young, though.'

'Why him?'

'The dressing-table mirror was smashed for no good reason and Young likes to cause damage.'

'I thought he usually pees on the carpet and furniture.'

'He does, but I still reckon he's worth a tug.' Denham moved to the filing cabinets to retrieve Alan Young's file. 'Where is everyone?'

'Barnes is over at the primary school. Some petty cash has gone missing and the headmaster wants all the pupils lined up and interrogated. Bissett went out with his bag of tricks about an hour ago. I suppose that was for you?'

'Yeah, he's dusting the house. Probably a waste of time, but you never know. We might get lucky.'

'Which leaves Lund up with the Super and Stannard out

on enquiries for vandalism of the war memorial.' Pinder chuckled. 'He didn't look happy.'

'Probably because he knows he won't get anywhere with it,' Denham said, opening the file on his desk and taking a note of Young's last known address. 'Anyone could have done that.'

'If you ask me, he's got the hump because it's not exciting enough.'

Denham frowned at him. 'What do you mean?'

'Well,' Pinder spread his hands as if it was obvious, 'he won't get his name in the 'paper for a bit of red paint, will he?'

'The DI's not interested in getting his name in the 'paper,' Denham said irritably, pulling his coat back on.

'So you say,' Pinder said, 'but I'm not the only one who thinks it.'

Monckton knew he had acted badly.

He wished it had been one of those times when he couldn't remember what he'd done, when the drink had blotted out all his words and deeds and he didn't have any notion he should feel guilty.

Monckton should have known there would be a row after dinner; after all, a quarrel before bed had become routine for him and Felicity for months now. But he had used language he'd never used to Felicity before and said foul things about her not being a proper wife. He'd wanted to hurt her, to offend her, and he'd certainly managed that. Felicity flounced out of the sitting room and up the stairs, forcing him to follow her to their bedroom door. She turned to him in the doorway, her hands on either side of the frame, barring his entry. Raising that contemptuous eyebrow of hers, she told Monckton he was a miserable, tiresome drunk and pointed him to the opposite bedroom. 'You're not sleeping in here. I don't want a lout in my bed.'

'Fine by me,' he shouted through the door she slammed in his face. 'It's no fun sleeping with a frigid bitch like you.'

And so, into the spare bedroom he had gone, banging the door shut, hoping the noise would annoy her. His head swimming, he dropped onto the bed fully clothed and fell asleep almost at once. When he woke up, it was to an acrid taste in his mouth and the realisation that not only had he thrown up on the carpet during the night, but that he'd wet himself, too.

Shame flooded through him. True, it wasn't the first time he'd found himself in this state, but it was the first time it had happened at home. Knowing their maid would have to clear up his mess, and knowing Felicity would hear of how he had disgraced himself, made him groan out loud.

Monckton ran a bath and climbed into the hot, soapy water, placing his feet with exaggerated care, for his head was still swimmy and he feared slipping. How humiliating would that be? If he broke an arm or a leg and had to call Felicity for help? *This can't go on*, he told himself as he lay back in the water and closed his eyes. *I have to stop drinking.*

Presentable after his bath, and a shave that had resulted in only a few painful cuts, Monckton headed downstairs to find Felicity. She wasn't in the dining room having breakfast and it was only the clock chiming ten o'clock that made him realise how late he'd slept. He found his wife in the morning room, and stood like a naughty schoolboy brought before his headmaster, head bowed, hands clasped before him, ready to apologise for his behaviour. Before he could utter a word, however, Felicity spoke.

'If you're about to say you're sorry, don't bother. I don't want to hear it. You'll mean it now, but it won't stop you from acting like a beast again the next time you drink too much. All your things will be moved to the spare bedroom. You'll sleep in there from now on.'

'Felicity—'

'Be quiet, Andrew. There's nothing you can say that will make me change my mind.'

The telephone rang and Felicity went out to answer it. Monckton followed her into the hall and watched as she picked up the receiver. She turned her back on him as she said, 'Hello, Mummy,' and he walked past her into his study.

Closing the door, Monckton leaned his head against the wood. If Felicity had been angry, if she'd shouted at him, he could have coped with that, but he couldn't bear her indifference. It was proof, if he needed it, that Felicity simply didn't care about him anymore.

With a sigh, he pushed away from the door and slumped down in his desk chair. His post was on the blotter before him, put there by the maid as she did every morning. He slid the first letter off the pile and ripped open the envelope. It was a letter from Charlie Ezard asking if he'd make another speech, this time in Islington. Monckton made a face and tossed the letter aside. Ezard could forget that; he wasn't doing any more favours for the party. He picked up the next. This one was a brown envelope, a reminder from the butcher's that payment was overdue and that it would be greatly appreciated if the account could be settled within the next few days. This one joined Ezard's letter.

Monckton frowned as he slid the third letter from the pile. This pale blue envelope looked cheap and old, as if it had been in a drawer for a long time. The writing on it was unfamiliar, the address written in untidy capitals. He ripped it open with curiosity. As he unfolded the single sheet of paper, his mouth turned dry. On the page were the words: THE PRICE HAS GONE UP. FIFTY QUID FROM NOW ON.

His hand shook as he pulled open the bottom drawer of

his desk and took out the hip flask. Setting the letter down on the blotter, he stared at the bold words as he unscrewed the cap and lifted the flask to his lips. Today had just turned into a bad day to give up drinking.

Georgina put her ear to the bedroom door and tutted in irritation as she heard snoring. She'd expected Dominic down for breakfast over an hour ago – she'd waited for him, telling Lucy not to cook the eggs and bacon just yet – but now it was gone ten o'clock and her grandson was still lying in bed. She had had her breakfast alone.

She turned the handle and pushed the door open. The bottom of the door caught on a pair of trousers thrown on the floor, and Georgina had to give it a shove to open it wide enough for her to enter. Stepping inside, she peered around the door and looked down at the bed. Dominic was lying on his side, his back to her. The rest of the clothes he had been wearing the day before were also littering the floor, and a strong odour of salt and vinegar hung in the air. Coming, Georgina realised angrily, from the screwed-up newspaper lying near the waste bin.

'Dominic?' Georgina said, her voice loud in the quiet room.

The snoring ceased and Dominic stirred. His hair was sticking up and his eyes opened blearily as he looked over his shoulder at her. 'What?' he mumbled.

'It's past ten o'clock. Don't you want any breakfast?'

Dominic turned onto his back and stretched. 'I'm too comfy to get up. I'll have it up here.'

'You'll come down for it, young man,' Georgina declared. 'I'm not making Lucy bring a tray up here.'

'That's what she's paid for, Grandma.'

'Well, I don't like it. I don't approve of young men lazing in bed. It's not good for you.'

'For God's sake.' Dominic thumped the mattress angrily. 'I did it all the time in India. Why are you making such a fuss?'

'Oh, all right,' Georgina said, stung by the accusation. 'I'll have Lucy bring up a tray. But only this once, Dom. I won't have you making a habit of it. Why are you so tired, anyway?'

'I don't know. I just am.'

'You're staying out too late,' she said, picking up his clothes and folding them over her arm. Her nose wrinkled as she caught the smell of beer. 'Were you and Daniel drinking?'

'I'm not five years old anymore, Grandma. You can't stop me drinking.'

'I don't want to stop you. I just want you to—' She broke off as there came an odd, muffled noise. 'What was that?'

'Nothing,' Dominic said, sitting up and bunching the blanket around his thighs.

'Dom, what was it?' she demanded.

With a sigh, Dominic peeled back the top of the blanket. A small, furry head poked out and round, wide eyes blinked at Georgina.

'Where did you get that?' she cried.

Dominic lifted the black and white kitten out of the bedclothes. 'I found it last night, shivering in a box.'

'Why did you bring it home?'

'I couldn't leave it, Grandma. It was crying and all alone.'

'You know I don't like cats, Dom. They make a mess in the house. You'll have to get rid of it.'

Dominic hugged the tiny creature to his chest. 'No. It's staying with me.'

'I won't have a cat in the house.'

'It's not doing any harm.'

'I don't care. This is my house and I say it can't stay.'

'If you make it go, then I'll go too.'

'Dom!'

'I will. I'll go. You should be pleased. You don't want me here, anyway.'

'How can you say that?'

Dominic turned his face away and didn't answer.

'Oh, very well.' Georgina tossed his trousers across the end of the bed. 'The cat can stay. And don't say I don't want you here. It's very hurtful.'

'Sorry,' Dominic muttered, and then smiled and kissed the little furry head. 'Now, can I have my breakfast?'

Chapter Twelve

Joanne Cooper pulled her fox stole tighter about her shoulders as a draught passed across her. Why had she taken an aisle seat near the door? she wondered as the black and white images flickered across the big screen. She should have paid the extra and taken a seat upstairs, but then penny-pinching Maureen would have complained. 'It doesn't matter where you sit,' Maureen would have said. 'It's what going on up there on the big screen that matters.'

That was all very well and good, but what about what was going on all around them? Here, in the cheap seats, were the young couples, their arms around each other, heads together in the dark, doing God knew what with their hands. She'd never done anything like that. Heavens, she hadn't even had a proper kiss until her wedding night, and what a disappoint-ment that had been!

Joanne looked at the couple sitting in the next row with envy. They hadn't come up for air for about ten minutes; her ears had picked up the slurping sounds of wet kisses and the odd moan of pleasure from the girl. How she would have liked to be in her place, feeling the young man's roving hands, squeezing and stroking, to feel his heat, to taste him.

She tutted, annoyed with herself for the thought. It was ridiculous to feel so, she told herself. She wasn't a young girl, but a sensible woman with two children and a husband at home. Her cheeks burned at the idea of Laurence's disgust if he knew what she was thinking. Why, he'd been shocked when she asked him to leave the light on when he made love to her.

Joanne glanced at Maureen beside her, wondering if she had noticed the couple in front, but there was no chance of that. Her friend's eyes were glued to the silver screen, watching as Ronald Colman wooed Lili Damita. Maureen never had fantasies like she did, Joanne felt sure. Maureen's imaginings were strictly reserved for the actors she adored, fantasies that had no hope of ever coming true and probably would have horrified her friend if they did.

Joanne drew a deep sigh, her eyes wandering over the rows of seats to her right, across the aisle where a man sat by the wall. He looked odd, sitting there alone, hunched in his coat, the collar up, a cap on his head. Only a narrow triangle of cheek was visible.

He must have sensed her watching, because his head turned slightly in her direction. A mouth came into view, a full, sensuous mouth that begged to be kissed.

Her breath caught in her throat. Where had that thought come from?

Behave yourself, Joanne told herself sharply, and dragged her eyes away, fixing them on the film. She was feeling hot and flushed, and knew it wasn't the hot flushes she'd been getting of late, but the flush of stifled desire.

It wasn't fair, she suddenly decided. Laurence was wrong. Why was desire only supposed to be for the young? Desire was wasted on them. They rushed through their fondling and fumbling, never stopping to enjoy it. That was something to be said about age. You learnt to appreciate taking things slowly, not to go headlong at a thing and then wonder what all the fuss was about.

A rebellious urge crept into her mind; the desire to rebel against her husband and acknowledge that she wanted passion in her life. And why shouldn't she? Every film she and Maureen saw together proved women her age were being passionately seduced by men they'd only just met. Why should she be any different?

Joanne turned her head once more towards the man by the wall. His face was still angled in her direction and her heart beat faster. Was he looking at her? Did he want her as she wanted him? She imagined getting up without a word to Maureen and sitting down beside him, taking his hand and putting it on her knee, letting go so he could move it where he wanted. She shivered at the thought of his fingers curving around her thigh, disappearing beneath her skirt.

'I'm just going to powder my nose,' Maureen whispered in her ear, and stumbled past Joanne into the aisle, knocking her heel against her leg.

Her fantasy brutally cut short, Joanne rubbed her shin to ease the pain and pulled her skirt straight. She heard the squeal of hinges as the seat behind her was pulled down and glanced towards the wall again. Her heart sank. Her fantasy lover had gone.

Joanne rested her head on the back of her seat, her eyes closing as the figures danced on the screen, and was drifting off when fingers brushed her neck. Her eyes snapped open, widening as the fingers continued to stroke. She didn't move, didn't jerk away or turn in her seat and demand to know what the man thought he was doing. Because she was sure it was a man and she thought she knew who. She didn't want to do anything, say anything that would make him stop. Oh, this was a dream, wasn't it? A delicious, wonderful, exciting dream?

Joanne heard footsteps in the aisle beside her and the fingers snatched themselves away. She almost groaned in frustration as Maureen tapped her on the shoulder to move her legs so she could get back to her seat.

She put her head back like before and waited to feel his fingers on her skin. But the minutes passed and she realised they were gone for good. As the screen faded to black and the lights came up, she glanced behind and saw the seat was empty.

'That was a lovely film, wasn't it?' Maureen said as she rose, waiting for Joanne to do the same.

'Yes,' Joanne said mechanically, letting the seat flip back up and moving into the aisle. Her fantasy was well and truly over, and she felt like crying.

Chapter Thirteen

'For heaven's sake, Jo, will you tell me what's wrong?'

Maureen sank down on the end of the bed and stared at her friend slumped against the headboard.

'I can't,' Joanne whimpered, tightening the collar of her bed jacket around her throat. 'I can't tell anyone.'

'You can tell me anything, you know that,' Maureen wheedled, tapping Joanne's foot beneath the eiderdown. 'And you want to talk to me, I can see it. You're desperate to get whatever it is off your chest.'

Joanne let out a shuddering breath. For all her annoying ways, Maureen was right. She did want to tell her. But would she understand? Joanne felt tears pricking at her eyes and she decided she had to speak. She just had to, or she would break down later in front of Laurence or the children, and then what excuse could she make for her behaviour? Laurence would tell her it was her nerves again and that she should go to the doctor for a tonic. As if a tonic could make her forget last night!

'Promise you won't tell anyone else,' Joanne said.

'I promise,' Maureen said, drawing her finger over her chest in the shape of a cross. 'Tell me. You'll feel better.'

'It was last night at the cinema. There was this man.'

'What man? I didn't see a man.'

'He was there all the time we were watching the film. He was over by the wall at first, then he moved to the seat behind me when you went to the Ladies.'

Maureen leant forward. 'Did he say something to you?'

Joanne shook her head. 'He stroked my neck.'

'He stroked—' Maureen broke off, frowning. 'Why did he do that?'

'I don't know. He just did.'

'And you let him? You didn't stop him?'

'I was so shocked,' Joanne lied. 'And anyway, he stopped when you came back. I didn't like to make a fuss.'

'You should have told me then what he'd done,' Maureen declared. 'I would have told him what for and called the manager. But is that what all this,' she gestured at Joanne in the bed, 'is about?'

'No,' Joanne cried, annoyed her friend was implying she was upset over something so trivial. 'After the film, after we said goodnight, he followed me.' She broke off. She could stop there, make out that was all. Being followed by a stranger was enough to unnerve a woman. Maureen couldn't scoff at that, could she?

'And then what happened?' Maureen asked impatiently.

'He caught up with me at the bus shelter.' The words tumbled out before Joanne could stop them. 'He pushed me up against the wall. He didn't say anything, just put his hands on my neck.'

'What was he like? How old was he?'

'I don't know. It was so dark and he had a cap on. It was pulled down low and he had a scarf over his mouth. I couldn't see his face properly.'

'But you didn't scream or call out?'

'I was so surprised—'

'You mean shocked.'

'Yes, shocked. I couldn't do anything.' Joanne hadn't screamed or called out because a version of the fantasy she had conjured in the cinema had come true and she could hardly believe it. She hadn't been frightened. She had been thrilled.

'What did he do next?'

'He squeezed. I didn't like that.' Maureen's eyes narrowed and Joanne realised she had made another slip. She'd said she hadn't liked 'that', implying she had liked the rest of what he had done. Joanne hurried on. 'I heard a car. He must have heard it too because he let go of me. I pushed him away and told him to leave me alone. I told him I would scream and call the police if he didn't.'

'And what did he do?'

Joanne shrugged. 'He went.'

Maureen's face fell. 'Is that it?'

'What do you mean, is that it?' Joanne cried, slamming her hands on the eiderdown in irritation. The action made her collar fall away from her throat. 'Isn't that enough?'

Maureen's eyes narrowed. 'You have bruises on your neck.'

Joanne put her fingers to her throat, wincing as they pressed against the black marks. 'I know.'

'My God, Jo,' Maureen cried. 'He must have really grabbed you to leave those. Why were you hiding them?'

'Why do you think?' Joanne said desperately. 'I can't let Laurence see them. He might think I encouraged him.'

'But you didn't.'

'I know I didn't.' *How easily the lies come,* Joanne thought. 'But you know how people think.'

Maureen nibbled her bottom lip. 'You know what I think? I think you should go to the police.'

'Oh no. I couldn't bear to tell a roomful of men what I just told you.'

'But this man hurt you—'

'Not really. It was my fault. I should have said something in the cinema. I probably gave him the wrong idea.' Joanne grabbed Maureen's hand. 'No one must know, Maureen. Remember you promised me you wouldn't tell anyone.'

'I know what I said but—'

'You promised, Maureen.'

Maureen frowned and shook her head. 'I don't know.'

Chapter Fourteen

Monckton smiled at the bespectacled librarian on duty at the front desk and headed for the Classic Fiction section at the rear of the library.

An elderly woman was browsing the section with the Ds and he had to pretend interest in Anthony Trollope while he waited for her to move on. After an excruciating few minutes, she selected a title and headed for the front desk.

Monckton moved along and grabbed three volumes of Dickens and pulled them out, stuffing the brown envelope he took from his inside jacket pocket at the back of the shelf. He put the books back, making sure the envelope was out of sight behind them. His palms were sweating as he stared at the books. For the first time in years, he was worried about leaving the envelope, for it contained only the usual twenty pounds, not the fifty his blackmailer had demanded. He gave the spines of the books he had replaced a little poke, making sure they were sitting back on the shelf and not likely to fall off. He bit his lip, wondering if he was making a mistake, then hurried away, past the librarian and out to his car.

He climbed behind the steering wheel and started up the

engine. *This is no bloody way to live*, he thought angrily as he pulled away from the kerb.

Miss Grace McKenna waited until the library was almost empty before making her way across the room to the Classic Fiction section. She didn't think of herself as a particularly nosy person, but she just had to find out what that man was doing. She'd been working at the library for more than a year now and he always came in on the fourth Wednesday of the month. He never brought any books back, never took any out. So what was he doing in the Classic Fiction section? Come to that, what was he doing in the library at all if he wasn't interested in the books?

She looked up and down the shelves, wondering which one to begin with. It was impossible to tell which shelf the man had visited, so she started at the As. Austen was pulled out and examined, the pages of each novel flicked through. Nothing. R. D. Blackmore was rifled through, as were Bronte and Burney, Carroll, Collins and Conrad. Defoe was next, and then Dickens. *Bleak House* proved fruitless, as did *Dombey and Son.* But *Great Expectations* gave up its secret!

Miss McKenna's mouth curved upwards in excitement. An envelope had been put behind the book and had fallen down when she took it out. Tucking *Great Expectations* under her arm, she reached in and took out the envelope, noting that nothing was written on the front and that it was sealed. She made a noise of annoyance. If only the flap had been merely tucked in, she could have seen what was inside.

Hearing a cough on the other side of the bookcase, Miss McKenna hurriedly returned the envelope to the shelf, stuffing *Great Expectations* back in to hide it. Dreading the thought of being caught snooping, she hurried back to the

front desk and stamped the returns with more than her usual
vigour.

Wilf banged on the front door, letting the holdall he was
carrying slip from his shoulder to his hand. He winced as the
silverware inside clanked. The front door opened and Stanley
Tompkins stood in the doorway, looking him up and down
with suspicion.

'I'm after Frank,' Wilf declared.

'Oh, yeah?' Tompkins said. 'And who are you?'

'A friend of his. You going to let me in or what?'

'All right, all right.' Tompkins stepped aside and Wilf
entered. 'He's upstairs. Room at the front.'

Wilf bounded up the stairs. As he reached the landing, the
front bedroom door opened and Crowther grinned at him
from the doorway. 'I thought I heard your dulcet tones.'

Wilf pushed him back into the room and closed the door.
He put the holdall on Crowther's unmade bed. 'I got a job for
you.'

'About time.' Crowther peered over Wilf's shoulder as he
opened the bag and pushed back the sides so he could see
what was inside. 'Now that's a lovely sight. How many
houses did you have to turn over to get all that lot?'

'Just the one,' Wilf said and was pleased to see
Crowther's eyebrows rise in admiration. 'Can you get rid of it
for me?'

'Easy. What's my cut?'

'Five per cent. Agreed?'

'Agreed.'

They both spat into their hands and shook on the deal.

'When can you do it?' Wilf asked.

'I can manage it this afternoon,' Crowther said, lifting the holdall off the bed and putting it by the door. 'I'll get the money to you tomorrow. How's that sound?'

Wilf nodded. 'Sounds all right. But don't come to the house. I'll meet you in the park near the fountain at noon.' He raised a warning finger. 'Don't get greedy, though, Frank, and think you can help yourself to any of that or try to diddle me.'

'Wilf! What do you take me for? We're partners, aren't we?'

'I suppose so,' Wilf said doubtfully. 'Right. I'll be off.'

'You're not staying for a drink? Pub's only at the end of the road.'

'Nah,' Wilf said. 'Got things to do. I'll see you tomorrow, Frank, with the money.'

It was nearly five o'clock and the library would be closing soon. Miss McKenna shoved the stack of books at the schoolgirl with irritation. The schoolgirl, unsure what she had done to warrant such treatment, gave the woman a bewildered look which the librarian entirely failed to notice.

Miss McKenna made her way to the Classic Fiction section and removed *Great Expectations* from the shelf. The envelope was still there, stuffed at the back. Disappointed, she returned to the front desk.

The library door squealed on its hinges and Miss McKenna turned to see Edna Gadd waddling towards the front desk laden with shopping bags.

'Afternoon, love,' Edna said, putting down her shopping bags and delving into one of them to pull out two hardback books. She banged them down on the counter. 'Thought I wouldn't make it before you shut. I didn't want to get a blooming fine.'

'Yes, there's a few minutes left,' Miss McKenna said,

slipping the tickets back into the books and setting them aside for re-shelving.

'Have I got time to get a couple more?'

'If you're quick.'

Edna headed for the Romantic Fiction aisle and Miss McKenna looked up at the clock on the wall. It was two minutes to five. Whoever was coming to pick up the envelope didn't appear to be coming tonight. She put the books on the returns trolley as Edna came back to the desk with her selection.

'That was quick,' Miss McKenna said, stamping the books.

'I knew what I wanted.' Edna slipped the books into one of the shopping bags. 'Thanks, love. See you next week. Take care.'

Miss McKenna watched her go, then took another look at the clock. Five o'clock on the dot. Time to go home. Sighing, she locked the library door, deciding that before she left, she would take one last look.

Back at the Classics, Miss McKenna took down *Great Expectations* and let out a cry. The envelope had gone.

Edna shut the front door with a shove of her hip and called out, 'I'm back.'

'Kitchen,' Wilf replied. 'Do you want a cuppa?'

Edna put a hand to her chest, trying to press the pain away. When it had eased, she waddled down the passage to the kitchen.

'I said, do you want a cuppa?' Wilf called over his shoulder as she entered.

Edna heaved her shopping bags onto the kitchen table. 'Yes, I do.' She fell into the chair. 'My feet are killing me.'

Wilf put a cup and saucer on the table before her. 'Did you get it?'

'In the bag.'

Wilf rummaged in the bag and fished out the envelope. He was grinning as he ripped it open, but the smile vanished as he took out the notes.

'The bastard!' he snarled.

'What's up?' Edna asked.

Wilf handed her the money. 'There's only twenty. He hasn't paid the rest.'

Edna counted the notes. 'I said you shouldn't push it.' She winced as Wilf kicked the table leg, making the tea slosh out of the cup into her saucer. She studied the envelope Wilf had tossed aside. There was something poking out and she picked it up. 'There's a note.'

Wilf snatched it out of her hand and read. 'Here's the twenty pounds as usual. I can't afford more. You're asking too much. I really can't give you any more. I beg you. Please leave our agreement as it is.'

'I told you he wouldn't pay,' Edna said.

'He can afford it.'

She pointed at the note. 'He says he can't.'

'Says,' Wilf scoffed. 'He can afford to have a nice big house, though, can't he? And send his kid to a posh school and for his wife to have her clothes made in France and all that? He's got the money. He just don't want to part with it.'

Edna sighed. 'But if he won't pay—?'

'Oh, he'll pay, Ma,' Wilf assured her. 'He ain't getting away with this.'

Chapter Fifteen

Matthew opened the door of the private waiting room and smiled at the woman sitting at the table. She sat up a little taller and watched him as he took a seat opposite.

'Mrs Baxter? I'm Detective Inspector Stannard. I understand you wanted to report an assault?'

'That's right,' Maureen said.

'I'm very sorry to hear that.' For someone who had been attacked, Matthew thought Mrs Baxter was extraordinarily composed. 'When were you assaulted?'

'Oh, no, *I* wasn't,' she said, putting a hand to her breast. 'It was my friend who was assaulted.'

'And why is your friend not reporting this assault herself?'

'She absolutely refused to. And she made me promise not to tell either. So, you see, inspector, she doesn't know I'm here.'

Matthew frowned. 'Why doesn't she want to report the attack, Mrs Baxter?'

'She's embarrassed and worried what you will think of her. Joanne has this absurd idea that she led the man on. That she wanted him to do what he did.'

'I see,' Matthew said, wondering whether that was the truth, that it was an encounter that had gone too far for the lady's comfort, and the interview would prove a waste of time. 'Can I have your friend's name?'

'Mrs Joanne Cooper,' Maureen enunciated clearly as Matthew wrote the name down in his notebook.

'And when did the assault occur?'

'Tuesday night. Joanne and I had gone to the cinema. *The Rescue* was showing. Ronald Colman,' she said with a dreamy smile, then shook herself back to the matter in hand. 'Apparently, this man sat behind Joanne in the cinema and stroked her neck. Joanne, the silly thing, let him do it. If he'd done it to me, I'd have turned around and given him a talking to like he'd never had before, I can tell you.'

'I'm sure. But that's not what you're here to report?' Matthew asked hopefully. Stroking a woman's neck hardly counted as assault.

'Oh no,' she shook her head. 'What he did in the cinema was nothing compared to what he did later.'

'What did he do later?'

'He manhandled her into a bus shelter and grabbed her around the neck.'

'Did you see the man? Can you describe him?'

Maureen shook her head. 'I'm afraid I didn't see him at all.'

'But you are certain this assault occurred?'

'Joanne's neck was covered in bruises, inspector,' Maureen said, giving Matthew a stern look. 'I don't think she put them there herself.'

Matthew smiled an apology. 'You realise I am going to have to talk to Mrs Cooper about this, and that I will have to tell her it was you who told me about this attack?'

'Of course,' Maureen said matter-of-factly. 'Joanne won't be pleased I've broken my promise, but I just couldn't let this lie. I mean, this man could do the same to another woman, couldn't he? And she might not be as lucky as Joanne.'

Matthew rang the bell of No. 23 Rutland Avenue and got his warrant card ready. The door opened a few inches and a woman peered around the edge. 'Mrs Cooper?' he asked.

'Yes.'

He showed Joanne his warrant card, and her brown eyes widened in fear. 'I'm sorry to disturb you, Mrs Cooper, but your friend, Mrs Maureen Baxter, reported you were assaulted the other night. I'd like to talk to you about it, please.'

'What? No... I....' Joanne looked back over her shoulder. 'My husband's here. And Maureen promised she wouldn't tell anyone.'

'Mrs Baxter came to me because she's concerned for you and the safety of other women,' Matthew said smoothly. 'May I come in?'

Joanne hesitated only a moment longer. 'Yes,' she said resignedly, and opened the door wider. 'I'm sorry if I was rude. Come in.'

'Who is it, Jo?' a male voice called from somewhere in the house.

'Just someone for me, darling,' she called back. She gestured Matthew into the sitting room and he settled himself into a comfy armchair. 'I don't want my husband to know,' Joanne said, closing the sitting-room door carefully.

Matthew took out his notebook. He wasn't about to promise Mr Cooper wouldn't learn of his wife's encounter. 'Mrs Baxter told me you'd been assaulted, but she didn't give me the details you can. So, I need you to tell me exactly what happened. Please don't leave anything out.'

Joanne squirmed in her seat. 'Do I have to? It's all so... so embarrassing. And I don't want to get anyone into trouble. It may have been my fault.'

'Why do you say that?'

'I may have encouraged him. Not intentionally,' she hastened to add.

Matthew thought he understood. 'Mrs Cooper,' he said, 'do you know the man? Is he a friend of yours?'

'No,' she cried in indignation. 'Oh, I knew this would happen. This is why I didn't want Maureen to tell. I'm not having an affair, inspector, or whatever else you're thinking. I have no idea who he was.'

'But you think you encouraged him?' Matthew pressed. 'Because of what happened at the cinema? I understand this man stroked your neck?'

Joanne's face flushed crimson. 'I know now I should have said something or called the manager. But I was just so shocked that someone would touch me like that. And I didn't want to make a fuss or draw attention to myself.'

'So, he followed you after you and Mrs Baxter parted company?'

'I heard his footsteps behind me.'

'And?'

'And he grabbed me and pulled me into the bus shelter.'

'How did he grab you?'

'What do you mean?'

'Did he put his arms around you and drag you into the shelter? Did he pull at you?'

'Oh, I see. Well, he grabbed my arm and sort of turned me into the bus shelter.'

'So, you didn't resist?' Matthew tried not to make it sound like an accusation.

'No, not then,' she said sheepishly. 'I didn't know what he was doing, you see?'

'And it was then he put his hands around your neck?'

'That's right.'

'I understand he left bruises.' Matthew pointed to the scarf she wore. 'May I see?'

Biting her lip, Joanne unwrapped the scarf and revealed the bruises. Matthew's idea of what had happened changed instantly. If it had been a lovers' tiff and Mrs Cooper had changed her mind about an intimate encounter, then the man hadn't taken the rejection well and had most certainly gone too far.

'Those look painful,' he said.

'They are a bit,' she admitted.

'Did you feel he meant to hurt you?'

Joanne considered. 'I don't think so. I mean, why should he? I expect he just didn't know his own strength. And he did let go of me, inspector.'

'Do you know why he did that?'

'A car came down the road.'

'So, he was frightened off?'

'I suppose so.' Joanne's eyes widened as the implication of Matthew's words dawned on her. 'Oh, my God. Do you think he would have strangled me if that car hadn't come?'

Matthew couldn't answer this question in any way that would make her feel better, so he chose not to. 'Can you describe this man?'

'No,' she groaned. 'That's the ridiculous thing. I can't. It was so dark, and he had his cap down and a scarf over his face.'

'How old was he?'

'I couldn't tell.'

'What about his voice?'

'He didn't say anything.'

'What else was he wearing?'

'A dark overcoat. It came down to his knees, I think.'

'You said you heard his footsteps. Shoes or boots?'

'I don't know,' Joanne sighed.

'But going by the clothes you did see, he was a working man?' Matthew suggested.

Joanne cringed as she nodded. 'I think so.'

Matthew flipped his notebook shut. He had enough to believe a genuine assault had taken place. 'I'd like you to come to the station and make a formal statement, Mrs Cooper.'

The frightened look came back into Joanne's eyes. 'Oh, no, I can't do that.'

'I can't make you, Mrs Cooper,' he said, giving her his understanding smile, 'but Mrs Baxter was right when she said she was concerned for other women. He might do to another woman what he did to you.'

'But that's not my fault,' Joanne cried.

'No, but if by acting you could prevent it from happening again...?'

Joanne's defiance drained away from her. 'That's not fair,' she whimpered.

'No,' Matthew agreed. 'It isn't.'

'I'll have to tell my husband,' she said miserably.

'I'm sure he'll be upset when he learns of what happened to you, Mrs Cooper.'

Joanne shook her head. 'You don't know Laurence, inspector.'

Chapter Sixteen

Matthew put Mr and Mrs Cooper in Interview Room Three, then returned to the CID office, glad to be out of their company. The atmosphere had been decidedly cool between husband and wife, and he suspected Mrs Cooper hadn't been wrong about her husband's lack of understanding.

Pinder stuffed the magazine he had been reading in his desk drawer and slammed it shut as Matthew entered. 'I was just having a break, sir,' he said, getting to his feet.

Matthew eyed the drawer with irritation. 'There's a couple in Interview Room Three. The lady was assaulted the other night. I want you to take down her full statement. Be patient with her, Pinder. She's not happy about being here and her husband's probably going to give her a hard time. Then get it typed up and leave it on my desk. Now!' he added when the detective didn't move.

Pinder grabbed a pen and paper and hurried out.

'Bloody waste of space,' Matthew muttered as he went into his office and rooted around in his desk drawer for the new packet of cigarettes he'd put there earlier.

'What's a waste of space?' Lund asked, hanging up the telephone receiver.

'Pinder.' Matthew lit a cigarette and tossed the smoking match in the ashtray. 'He's a lazy sod.'

'Gary's all right.'

'He was reading a magazine when I came in.'

'So what?'

'So what?' Matthew cried. 'He's supposed to be working, not reading magazines.'

'He was taking five minutes, Stannard. It's not as if we're run off our feet, is it?'

'There's plenty he should be doing,' Matthew gestured at the outer office. 'There's a filing cabinet out there stuffed with leads that need following up.'

'Cases that will go nowhere,' Lund countered. 'You know as well as I do, some cases will never be solved. Like your red paint vandal or the burglary Denham's got. That's a prime example. The stuff that was taken has either been melted down or passed through so many hands by now that we've got no hope of tracking it down. Are you saying we should be running around trying to find a couple of candlesticks?'

'It's what we're paid to do, unless you've forgotten.'

Lund's expression hardened. 'Don't you lecture me, sunshine. We all know the powers that be think the sun shines out of your arse, but don't come the big I am in here, telling everyone what to do.'

Matthew slammed his desk drawer shut. 'If anyone wants me, I'll be at the cinema on the high street.'

'Oh, yeah. Taking it easy, are we?' Lund called after him as he strode out of the office.

'No,' Matthew shouted over his shoulder. 'Interviewing the staff.'

Wilf threw away his cigarette when he saw Crowther approaching through the trees. 'All done?' he asked, taking the empty holdall Crowther held out to him.

'All done,' Crowther nodded and dipped into his over-coat's inside pocket, drawing out a wad of notes held together with a red rubber band. He held the wad out to Wilf. 'There you go.'

'I hope you got the best price,' Wilf said, counting the notes.

'I got the best on offer,' Crowther assured him.

Wilf nodded as he finished counting. 'It's not bad.' He eyed Crowther suspiciously. 'If it's all here?'

Crowther put a hand to his chest. 'It's all there, swear to God. I'll have my five per cent, though, if it's all the same.'

Wilf slipped a few notes out of the rubber band and handed them to Crowther. 'Who'd you use?'

Crowther counted the notes before putting them in his pocket. 'Why do you want to know?'

'Just wondering if I know him.'

'You won't,' Crowther sniffed. 'When's your next job?'

Wilf shoved his hands in his pockets and shrugged. 'Dunno. Maybe tonight. Maybe not. I haven't decided.'

'Sticking to Craynebrook, are you? I just come through there. Posh place, that.' Crowther grinned lasciviously. 'And it has all those stuck-up ladies I like.'

'Don't do anything stupid, Frank,' Wilf warned him. 'I don't want the police knocking on my door because of you.'

'You don't have to worry about me, Wilf,' Crowther said. 'I ain't getting caught again.'

The cinema manager hurried out of his office into the lobby where Matthew was waiting. 'You wanted to see me, inspector? Is there a problem?'

'No problem, Mr Fairweather,' Matthew assured him. 'I just need to ask you and your staff a few questions.'

'Has someone made a complaint about the cinema? I can't think—'

Matthew held up his hand to halt the manager. 'Nothing like that. Are all the staff here?'

'Yes. They're in the back room, having their tea break. I'll take you to them. Follow me, please.'

Mr Fairweather led Matthew down a dingy, narrow corridor to an equally shabby door. Mr Fairweather opened it and stepped aside so Matthew could enter. He stepped into a small room containing several uncomfortable-looking chairs, a rickety table and a gas ring with a dented kettle upon it. By the kettle was a mixed selection of chipped cups and saucers and a souvenir biscuit tin printed with a picture of the king's coronation.

Mr Fairweather clapped his hands to get their attention. 'Everyone, this is Detective Inspector Stannard. He wants to ask some questions.'

Five faces looked at Matthew with curiosity. One belonged to a young man in uniform, an usher. Two belonged to young women in usherette uniforms and the other two belonged to a middle-aged man and woman. The man was wearing a militaristic-style overcoat with gold trim and Matthew took him to be the doorman. The woman probably sat in the booth at the front and sold the cinema tickets.

'Inspector Stannard? I've read about you,' the young man said, wagging his finger at Matthew. 'You caught the woman who killed all those men from the Empire Club, didn't you?'

Matthew gave him a tight nod. 'I'm sorry to disturb your tea break,' he said, doing his best to ignore the admiring glances the girls were casting his way. 'But I'm enquiring about a man who was here between seven and ten o'clock on

Tuesday evening. He would have been on his own, wearing a flat cap, scarf and a dark overcoat. Do any of you remember seeing a man fitting that description?'

The older man and woman shook their heads. The usher frowned, trying to remember. One of the usherettes held up her hand.

'There was a man like that,' she said. 'He was sitting by himself in the cinema, over by the wall. I remember thinking he was a bit strange because he kept his coat and cap on during the film and it was really quite warm that night.'

'You didn't speak to him?'

'Only at the start of the picture. I asked if he wanted ice cream or cigarettes, but he just ignored me, so I didn't bother with him again.'

'Can you tell me what he looked like?'

She made a face. 'I really couldn't say. He didn't look up, you see, and it's dark in the cinema.'

'Had you seen him before?'

'I've never noticed him before.'

'Did you see him leave?'

'No, I don't remember seeing him go. But if he left when the picture finished, then I wouldn't have noticed him. Everyone would have been moving about, getting up to go, and all I would have been worried about was how much clearing up I'd have to do. People leave so much rubbish behind. You wouldn't believe it.'

Matthew appealed to the others. 'Can anyone tell me anything else about this man?' They shook their heads. 'Then I'll let you get back to your tea.' He put his notebook away, disappointed. 'But if you do see him again, any of you, please telephone the police station and let us know.'

'Should we detain him, inspector?' the doorman asked, squaring his shoulders.

'There's no need for that,' Matthew said quickly. 'Just let us know if he comes back.'

The doorman nodded, clearly unhappy with the answer, and Matthew left, pretending to listen to Mr Fairweather's assurances that the cinema's clientele were all decent people all the way to the front doors.

Chapter Seventeen

Matthew had barely got through the station door when Police Sergeant Alan Turkel called to him from the front desk.

'Sorry to bother you, sir, but there's a lady in there,' Turkel pointed to the door of the lobby's private waiting room, 'who claims she was flashed in the park. Would you see her? She's been waiting half an hour.'

'Why didn't you get Inspector Lund to see her?' Matthew demanded irritably. 'He was here when I left.'

'I did ask him, sir, but he's in the canteen and said he'd see her after his break. He's, er, still in there, sir,' Turkel added sheepishly, checking his wristwatch. 'And I thought as you're back and she's still waiting—'

Matthew banged his fist on the front desk in annoyance.

'The lady would probably rather see you, anyway, sir,' Turkel went on encouragingly. 'Inspector Lund isn't exactly the most tactful of men, if you don't mind me saying so.'

'All right, Turkel,' Matthew sighed. 'I'll see her. What's her name?'

'Mrs Angela Plumton,' Turkel said with relief. 'She has her little boy with her.' A series of barks came from the waiting room. 'And a dog. The boy wouldn't be parted from it.'

'I hope it's house-trained.'

'Thank you, sir,' Turkel called as Matthew headed for the waiting-room door.

'Mrs Plumton.' Matthew nodded at the woman sitting at the table. A boy, perhaps four years old, was on her lap, held tightly against her chest and making faces at the Yorkshire Terrier sitting by his feet. 'I'm Detective Inspector Stannard. I'm sorry you've been kept waiting.'

'That's all right,' Mrs Plumton said, her polite reply made automatically. 'I'm sure you're very busy.'

Some of us are, Matthew thought angrily. First Pinder, now Lund, taking the piss. One look at Mrs Plumton made him even angrier. He noted the white knuckles on her hands as she clutched her son and the eyes that blinked a little too often to keep back tears. She shouldn't have been made to wait, all alone save for a child and a dog, in the impersonal waiting room. Matthew cursed Turkel for not even giving Mrs Plumton a cup of sweet tea to calm her.

'I understand you had a rather unpleasant encounter this afternoon?' he said, taking a seat.

Mrs Plumton stared at him for a long moment, then burst out crying. The boy, frightened by his mother's sobbing, cried too, and the dog, alarmed by the sudden noise, barked loudly.

Matthew fished inside his pocket for his handkerchief. He handed it to Mrs Plumton without a word. He had no idea what to say to a crying woman and figured it was best to let her get on with it until her tears reached a natural end.

She wiped her eyes, smearing mascara across the clean white cotton. Kissing her son's forehead, she said, 'Mummy's just being silly, Bobby. There now,' and rocked him until his crying ceased. The dog looked up at the pair, its head on one side. 'Get down and play with Buster.' Easing the boy off her lap, Mrs Plumton wiped her nose and offered Matthew his handkerchief back.

'Keep it,' he said. 'I'm sorry to distress you, Mrs Plumton, but I need you to tell me what happened in the park.'

'Yes, I know. I'm sorry about this.' She gestured at her blotchy face. 'But it was just so horrible.'

'I'm sure it was.' Matthew took out his notebook and pen and waited.

Mrs Plumton took a deep breath. 'I'd taken Bobby to the park to have a runabout with the dog. They were playing a little way off and,' she lowered her voice, 'I went to have a cigarette. I don't like him to see me smoking, so I went where he couldn't see me, but I could still see him. I'd been there for a minute or two when I heard a rustling behind me and I turned to see a man...' She broke off and wiped her nose again.

'Yes?' Matthew prompted.

Her face reddened, and she cast a worried look at her son, who was now sitting cross-legged on the floor, ruffling Buster's fur. 'His trousers were open, and he was...' she gestured with her hands. 'I can't say it.'

'You don't have to,' Matthew said. 'I know what you mean. Please go on.'

'I couldn't believe it, him doing that. You hear about these sorts of things happening and you think you'd shout or scream or something, but I just froze.' Another wipe of her nose. 'He finished what he was doing and grinned at me. Then he buttoned himself up and just walked away.'

'When did this happen?'

She looked at her watch. 'It must have been almost two hours ago.'

'Two hours?' Matthew frowned. 'But the desk sergeant said you came in half an hour ago. It did happen in the park just over the road?'

'Yes,' she said with a groan. 'I know what you're thinking. What was I doing all that time? But I told you, I just froze. After that man had gone, I fell down on one of the park benches and just sat there, going over it and over it. I don't think I could quite believe what had happened. But then Bobby came over to me and, seeing him, I just became so angry. I mean, what if that man had done what he did in front of him or even done it to him instead of me? Bobby would have been terrified. And I thought something should be done about him. I am right, aren't I?'

'Absolutely right,' Matthew nodded, realising that telling Uniform to keep an eye out would be pointless as the flasher would be long gone by now. 'Can you describe this man?'

'He had a cap on, one of those flat things. I couldn't see what colour his hair was. He was wearing a dark-coloured coat.'

'But you saw his face?'

'Oh yes, I saw his face. He had dark eyes and a long, straight nose. His lips were rather full.' She gave a wry smile. 'In different circumstances, I would have thought he was rather a handsome young man.'

'How young?'

'Early to mid-twenties, I think. Sorry, but I'm not good at ages.'

'But not in his thirties?' Matthew asked.

'I don't think so.'

'Did he speak at all?'

She shook her head. 'No, he just laughed when he'd done.'

Matthew closed his notebook. 'I'd like you to look at some photographs, Mrs Plumton, to see if you recognise the man from the park.'

'But what if I don't recognise him?'

'Then we'll have to find him some other way.' He rose and gestured for her to go with him.

She grabbed her son's hand and pulled him to his feet. 'You think you will find him, then?'

'I will certainly do my best,' he promised as the dog jumped around his legs.

Matthew installed Mrs Plumton in Interview Room One and put CID's mugshot books before her. She looked at every photograph of every criminal ever arrested by Craynebrook Police Station, but she couldn't find the man who had exposed himself to her. Disappointed, Matthew had shown her, Bobby and Buster out of the station.

Pinder was back in the office when Matthew walked in. 'Mrs Cooper's statement is on your desk, sir,' he said, following Matthew into his office.

'Everything all right with Mrs Cooper?' Matthew asked, reading the statement.

'So so. The husband was a bit put out by what she said and he was giving his wife some strange looks, but it's all done. They've gone.'

Poor Mrs Cooper, Matthew thought, as his eyes read the description she had given of her attacker. It sounded remarkably similar to the description Mrs Plumton had given him of the flasher. 'All right, Pinder. You can get on.'

'Yes, sir,' Pinder said, backing out of the office.

'Watch what you're doing,' Lund scolded as he came in, balancing a file on top of a cup and saucer in one hand and holding a plate with an Eccles cake in the other. He spotted Matthew as he shuffled around his desk. 'Turkel said you dealt with that woman who said she got flashed.'

Matthew murmured an affirmative.

'Did you show her the mugshots?'

'Yes,' he sighed, 'I showed her the mugshots.'

'Pick anyone out?'

'No.'

Lund frowned at Matthew. 'What's up with you?'

'Nothing.'

'Come on, spit it out. What's got your goat now?'

'All right, if you really want to know.' Matthew glared at him. 'You kept her waiting. A woman with a young son who's been subjected to a gross indecency and you leave her sitting in the waiting room while you stuff your face.'

'I'd only just sat down,' Lund protested. 'And Turkel was outside if she wanted anything. Besides, it's all a lot of fuss over nothing. So what if some bloke waved his willy at her?'

Matthew stared at him. 'I can't believe you just said that. What if it had been your daughter he'd flashed?'

'That's different.'

'Why is it different?'

'Because my daughter's just a girl. This fella flashed a married woman, didn't he? So, it's not as if she hasn't seen it all before, is it? Probably gave her a thrill.'

'You really are a pig, Lund. I don't know how your wife puts up with you.'

'She don't go on at me as much as you do,' Lund said, unrepentant. 'First you're moaning about Pinder, now you're having a go at me. I never thought I'd say it but,' he raised his eyes to the ceiling and gestured with his hands, 'come back, Barry Carding, all is forgiven.'

Chapter Eighteen

The kitten had been trying to climb on Georgina's lap all evening and she'd spent most of it pushing the animal away. She had eventually persuaded it to settle in front of the fire, putting down one of her cushions for it to lie upon. It had been asleep for a while, but it lifted its head, ears pricked, at the sound of the front door opening.

Georgina stuffed her knitting needles down the side of her armchair and kept her eyes on the door. Would Dominic go straight up to bed or would he come in? she wondered. A slight feeling of dismay trickled through her as the sitting-room door opened and Dominic entered.

'You haven't been waiting up for me, have you?' he asked.

'No,' she said. 'I've been listening to the wireless. Have you had a pleasant evening?'

'Not bad,' Dominic said, going to the kitten and scooping the little wriggling creature up in his arms. He plumped down on the sofa, planting kisses on its fluffy head.

'Will you take it back to India with you?' she asked, hoping to make him understand he couldn't leave it with her to look after.

'Maybe.'

Georgina's jaw tightened. She was getting a little tired of Dominic's terse responses to her questions, as if he didn't want to talk to her at all. 'Have you given it a name yet?' she tried again.

'It's not an it, Grandma. It's a he.'

'Well, whatever it is,' she snapped. 'At this rate, you'll be back in India before you know what to call it.'

'Why do you keep going on about India?'

'I don't,' she protested.

'Yes, you do. Every time we talk, it's India this, India that. I swear it's all you think about.'

'I didn't realise I mentioned it so often. It's just that you like it so much—'

'Not so much. And besides, I've been thinking.'

'What have you been thinking, Dom?' Georgina asked warily.

'I suppose I might as well tell you,' he said, tickling the kitten's chin. 'I've decided to chuck India and stay here.'

'You're not going back?' Georgina cried, a part of her mind trying to work out exactly what he meant by 'here'. Here as in England? Or here with her? 'But what about your job?'

'I've resigned.'

'But—' she broke off in astonishment. 'Why didn't you tell me? You should have written and told me you were planning to resign.'

'If I had written, you would have talked me out of it. And if that didn't work, you would have got all your friends over there to pressure me into staying. But most of all, I didn't tell you, Grandma, because it's none of your business.'

'Dominic!' Georgina cried, shocked by his rudeness.

'Anyway,' he shrugged, smiling a little, 'it's done now.'

'But what are you going to do?'

'I'll get a job here.'

'What sort of job?'

'I don't know. Can't you stop interrogating me?'

'But you've got to think about these things. What are you going to do about money? I hope you're not planning to rely on me?'

'There you go again. Money, money, money.'

'Money is important, Dom.'

'There are more important things, Grandma.'

'Oh, are there?' she demanded. 'Like what?'

'Like family,' he said, glowering at her. 'But you don't understand about family, do you?'

'What do you mean by that?'

Dominic looked away, pouting as he scratched behind the kitten's ear a little too roughly. It turned its head and sank its teeth into a finger. He murmured 'Sorry' in its ear and stroked more gently.

'Dom?' Georgina said. 'I asked you what you meant.'

'It doesn't matter,' he said sulkily.

'Obviously, it does. So, kindly tell me what you mean.'

Dominic had the decency to look a little ashamed of himself. 'I just don't see why Father has to live in that place.'

Not that again! 'I have told you, Dom. Your father's happy in the care home.'

'Father didn't look happy. He looked miserable, being locked up with all those loonies. He'd be happy with us.' Dominic glanced at her out of the corners of his eyes. 'I know he'll be happy with me when I find a place for us both.'

'Dominic,' Georgina said, taking a deep breath to steady herself, 'your father has to stay where he is.'

'Why does he have to?'

'Because I say so.'

Dominic's mouth tightened. He kissed the kitten savagely,

making it mew. 'I think I'll call him Mussmer,' he said, holding the kitten up before his face. 'What do you think?'

'Very nice,' Georgina said, no longer caring about the damned cat.

Her lack of interest seemed to annoy Dominic. 'I'm going to bed,' he said, and left the room, not even bothering to say good night.

Georgina heard his footsteps on the stairs and sank back into her chair, squeezing her eyes shut. Oh God, what was she going to do?

Denham bent down and turned on his torch to look at the back door lock. It was a good lock, strong. Difficult to pick. Whoever got in by picking it was definitely a professional.

'Denham? Where are you?'

'Kitchen,' Denham called, straightening as Lund entered. 'I wasn't expecting you here, sir.'

'I was passing,' Lund said, looking around. 'Saw the bobby on the door and thought I'd pop in and make sure everything is being done properly. Apparently, I'm supposed to keep an eye on you lads.'

'I wasn't aware we needed keeping an eye on,' Denham said.

'Nor was I,' Lund muttered. 'So, what have we got here?'

Denham pointed at the back door. 'Burglar got in by picking the lock. Moved through the house, bagging all the silverware. Left pretty much everything else, though he did take the few notes he found. He was very selective.'

'And tidy,' Lund observed. 'You'd hardly know a burglar had been through here.'

'If it wasn't for the mirror,' Denham agreed.

'Mirror?'

'In the hall.' Denham led Lund out of the kitchen and into

the hall. He pointed at the mirror on the wall behind the front door. 'See? It's been smashed like the dressing-table mirror at the Haydens.'

'Looks like the same man, then. Anyone in mind?'

Denham tugged unhappily at his ear. 'I did think Alan Young, but he has an alibi for the Hayden burglary. I'll talk to him again, but I'm pretty sure it's not him.'

Lund grunted. 'Anyone in when it was burgled?'

'No. The owners had gone out for the evening, but the wife had a headache and they decided to come home early. They came home and found they'd been burgled.'

'So, what do we have? A professional burglar who prefers to pick a lock rather than breaking and entering. And maybe someone who seems to know when the owners are out?'

'Do you think he keeps a watch on the house?' Denham suggested.

'It's possible,' Lund shrugged, 'or he's just lucky. But you do know he's someone who likes to smash a mirror before he goes. That should narrow it down. Something for you to think about, anyway, Denham.' He checked his wristwatch. 'Well, as you seem to know what you're doing, I'll be off.'

'Sir?' Denham asked as he opened the front door for Lund. 'Have I done something wrong, and that's why you're checking up on me?'

'No, lad,' Lund assured him with a sigh. 'It's just certain people at the station think I'm not pulling my weight and that you lot are getting away with murder.'

'I see,' Denham said, understanding who Lund was getting at. 'I like to think I do know how to do my job.'

'Lad,' Lund said, patting his shoulder, '*I* never doubted it.'

Chapter Nineteen

'Another nice lot,' Crowther said, sorting through the holdall
Wilf had deposited on his bed. 'I thought you said you
weren't doing another job so soon?'

'I said I hadn't decided,' Wilf said, leaning against the
door and taking out his tin of tobacco. 'It's not a problem,
is it?'

Crowther lifted out a pair of candlesticks and examined
them. 'It might be if you keep getting stuff of this quality. My
man will worry someone will notice. You might want to think
about slowing down a bit.'

'Yeah, all right,' Wilf nodded ruefully. 'Maybe just one or
two more.'

Crowther put the candlesticks back in the holdall and slid
the bag under the bed. He sat down on the bed and took the
roll-up Wilf offered him. 'What is it?' he asked, tucking it
into the corner of his mouth and lighting it. 'You look like
you want to say something.'

Wilf toed a cigarette stub he'd found, pushing it into the
crack between two floorboards. 'There is. I'm not sure it's a
good idea, though.'

'You can trust me.'

'Can I?' Wilf asked seriously.

'You've trusted me with this lot,' Crowther said, giving the holdall a nudge with his heel.

'This is different.' Wilf thought for a moment longer, then nodded to himself. 'I want you to do something for me. I'll pay you.'

'I'm listening.'

'You remember that bloke I told you about? Monckton? Well, I told him I was upping the money he owes me and he hasn't come through. I need him to know I mean business.'

'What do you want me to do?'

'Just pass on a message,' Wilf said. 'Tell him he's got to pay up or else.'

'Or else what?'

'Never you mind what. Just tell him. Can you do that?'

'How much do I get?'

'A fiver.'

Crowther nodded. 'I take it I have to give him this message face to face? So, I just go up to his front door?'

'I don't care how you do it.' Wilf dug into his trouser pocket and pulled out a grubby piece of paper. He handed it to Crowther. 'That's his address.'

Crowther smiled as he read. 'Craynebrook. My favourite place.' He tucked the paper into his pocket. 'When do you want me to do it?'

'Today. I ain't waiting any longer. Tell him to leave the extra thirty quid in the usual place by next Friday. No more excuses. You got that?'

'I got it. You've upped it by thirty quid, eh? So, how much you getting in total?'

'None of your business.'

Crowther held up his hands. 'Fair enough. You don't want to tell me. I'm just thinking a fiver ain't a fair share.'

'I told you before, Frank,' Wilf said, 'don't get greedy. A fiver's plenty for what I'm asking.'

Crowther met Wilf's eye for a long moment. Maybe he saw something in it he didn't want to mess with, but whatever his reason, he nodded and said, 'All right. A fiver it is.'

Dickie wiped his dripping nose and stuffed his handkerchief back in his pocket. He looked at his wristwatch and shook his head. He'd give it five more minutes, then he was leaving.

He pulled out his copy of that morning's *Chronicle* and read the article he'd written for the Great War feature. He'd interviewed a Mr Ernest Porter for this week's piece, a man in his late fifties, a widower, whose only son had been killed in the war.

Mr Porter had shown him a photograph of his son taken in 1914. In the picture, Jeremy Porter wore his army uniform, a feeble excuse for a moustache adorning his upper lip, and a wide-eyed expression of optimism and anticipation Dickie remembered so well from that time, when all the young men were falling over themselves to go to war. The picture of Jeremy in his army uniform and a photograph of his father standing outside his house accompanied the article.

The interview had left Dickie feeling flat. Jeremy Porter had been killed in 1915, just a few days after his nineteenth birthday. It had not been a noteworthy death. Jeremy had performed no great feat of heroism and Dickie had got the sense his father had been disappointed, that Ernest Porter would have preferred his son to die in glory. Dickie had asked him if the death of his son had changed how he felt about the war, whether he had come to think of it as a senseless slaughter and a waste of young lives. Ernest Porter had looked appalled at the very idea.

'My son died fighting for his king and country, Mr Waite. No father could ask more.'

Dickie had not made the retort that was on the tip of his tongue. That, as a father, surely Mr Porter would have preferred to see his son live a long and happy life? He had merely thanked him, flipped his notebook shut and shook the old soldier's hand.

The slats on the bench dipped beneath his backside. A man had sat down and was stretching his legs out in front of him.

'Twenty minutes,' Dickie said, folding up the newspaper.

'Eh?' Pinder said.

'That's how long I've been sitting here.'

'Yeah, sorry. First chance I've had to get away.' Pinder grinned at a young woman walking past. She smiled back, her cheeks dimpling.

Dickie pulled out his pipe and lit it. 'What do you have for me?'

Pinder turned, resting his arm on the back of the bench. 'If the DI found out I was talking to you, Mr Waite—'

'DI Lund wouldn't care.'

'I don't mean him. Stannard will have my guts for garters if he knew.'

'How will he find out?' Dickie asked, knowing Pinder was right. 'I'm not going to tell him.'

'I just think that for the risk I'm taking, my information is worth more than a few bob.'

'How much more?'

'Make it five quid.'

Dickie laughed out loud. 'You are joking? For the rubbish you give me?'

'I've given you some good stuff,' Pinder protested. 'There was that drunken councillor who started that fight outside The King George. The kid who went missing. The—'

'All right.' Dickie held up his hand, not wanting to hear the complete catalogue of Pinder's gossip. 'I can make it a quid, but that's all.'

'Make it two.'

'Forget it,' Dickie cried, growing annoyed. 'I'm not paying you any more than that. If you don't like it, we'll call it a day.'

Pinder tutted and turned back around on the bench, folding his arms over his chest.

'So, what do you have for me?' Dickie asked again.

'There have been two burglaries in the past week,' Pinder said sulkily.

'I already know about those. Silverware taken at each. Work of a pro. Is that all you've got? Burglaries? They're not going to set the world alight, are they?'

'All right. How about this? There's been a flasher in the park and a fella who nearly strangled a woman in a bus shelter. You heard about those?'

Dickie took out his notebook and scribbled. 'Was the woman badly hurt?'

'Nah. Lot of fuss over nothing, if you ask me. I'll bet you anything you like she was up for a bit of the other, led him on, then changed her mind and he got the hump. You can't blame him.'

'Who's working on the case?'

'Stannard.'

'Does he think that's all it is? A bit of How's-Your-Father got out of hand?'

Pinder made a face. 'Like he tells me what he's thinking. But he's treating it as serious. He's on the flasher, too. Denham's on the burglaries.'

'Is Lund on anything?'

Pinder chuckled at the sarcasm. 'He keeps himself busy.'

'Yeah. Busy doing nothing. That everything?'

'That's it.' Pinder rubbed his thumb and forefingers together suggestively.

Dickie pulled out his wallet, took out a pound note and handed it to Pinder.

'Ta very much, I don't think.'

'It's better than nothing, Gary,' Dickie said as he got up and walked away.

Pinder stuffed the note in his pocket. 'Not much better.'

Monckton watched the two men vacate the park bench and made his unsteady way over to it.

He'd had another heavy night on the booze and was paying the price for it this morning. Ordinarily, he would have slept off his hangover, but Felicity had played Wagner in the room below his at a ridiculously loud volume and he would rather brave the day than have to listen to that racket. He suspected she'd done it deliberately, just to annoy him, knowing his head was splitting in two.

He crashed down onto the bench and leaned back, raising his face to the sky, keeping his eyes closed. If only Felicity was someone he could talk to, someone he could confide in. That's what he needed, to unburden himself. How much better he would feel if he could tell her everything and know she would understand. If he could say to Felicity, 'I know I've been rather a brute to you of late, but I can explain. The fact is, my dear, I'm in rather a spot of bother. You see, I did something very foolish a few years back and someone found out about it and has been blackmailing me all this time to keep it quiet', then maybe she could help him get out of this mess.

But no, he couldn't say that to Felicity. She never wanted to know about other people's problems and she would probably despise him even more than she already did for being so weak as to do something foolish in the first place, let alone pay to cover it up. She might even go to the police and tell them everything. No, he couldn't tell her. He couldn't tell anyone. He just had to go on.

The bench creaked as someone sat down beside him. Monckton snapped his head upright and glanced at his new companion out of the corner of his eye. It was nobody he knew; that was something, at least.

'The sun's out,' Crowther said, squinting at the sky, 'but it's still a bit chilly today.'

'Yes,' Monckton said, hoping his new companion wasn't about to draw him into conversation.

'A bit too chilly to sit this long on a park bench, if you ask me. You must be getting cold.'

The words took a moment to register. Monckton turned his head.

Crowther grinned. 'That's right, old chum. I've been watching you.'

'Who are you?' Monckton asked, his blood running cold.

'Don't matter who I am. What matters is that you listen to me.'

'I don't underst—'

Crowther put a finger to his lips. 'Just listen. You have business with a friend of mine. You know who I mean. Well, you were supposed to keep your end of the bargain and you haven't. That's made my friend very angry. So, he's asked me to have a word.'

'But I explained—'

'I ain't interested, chum. I'm just here to pass on a message. Pay up or you'll get what's coming to you. Now, you understand that, don't you?'

Monckton nodded. He could hardly breathe.

'Good. So, you put the rest of the money in the same place by the end of Friday and everything will be all right. If you don't, then my friend's going to have to get nasty. And you don't want that, believe me.' Crowther rose, stuffing his hands into his overcoat pockets, and grinned down at Monckton. 'Cheerio, old chum.'

Monckton watched Crowther walk away, feeling as if he was about to throw up. What the hell was he going to do now?

Chapter Twenty

Dickie raised his hand in greeting to the man sitting at the back of the restaurant and manoeuvred his way around the tables.

'Running a little behind, are we, Dickie?' Tony Blake said as Dickie hung his coat over the back of a chair and sat down.

'Sorry,' Dickie said. 'I got held up. Have you ordered?'

'Yeah. The usual. That all right?'

'It's fine.' Dickie flicked a napkin over his lap.

'Held up on a story?' Blake asked, taking a sip of his wine.

Dickie shook his head. 'I was kept waiting by a source. One who thinks he's a lot more valuable than he is.'

'We've all got sources like that,' Blake said understandingly. 'I had one the other day who telephoned to say he had a cracking story. I make the trip all the way up town and it turns out to be a story I covered in the *Gazette* last week. I gave him an earful for wasting my time. I don't expect I'll be hearing from him again.'

A waiter appeared at the table with two soup bowls. He set them down and both men picked up their spoons.

'So,' Dickie slurped at his soup, 'what's happening in your neck of the woods?'

Blake ripped apart a bread roll. 'Not much, to be honest. It's all gone a bit quiet. The only story worth repeating is a couple of attacks on prostitutes. My editor didn't want to put the story in the 'paper. Said people didn't want to read about tarts over breakfast, but in the end, he had to agree to let me write it up, otherwise there would have been nothing to report.'

'Do you have it on you?'

Blake reached beneath the table to the seat of one of the spare chairs. He drew out a copy of *The Graydon Heath Gazette* and handed it to Dickie. 'Bottom of page two.'

Dickie flipped to page two and found the article that took up no more than half a column inch. The article's headline stated: TWO WOMEN ATTACKED. He read the article aloud. 'Two women were attacked this week in Graydon Heath in the latter part of the evening. The women, who were out alone, reported that a man put his hands around their necks and tried to strangle them. In both instances, the man was disturbed, and the women were, for the most part, unharmed.' He set the newspaper to the side. 'That's all you got out of it?'

'I told you, my editor didn't want me to write it at all.'

'Couldn't the police have given you more information than that?'

Blake snorted. 'They didn't want to know either. Prostitutes being attacked by punters? What's in it for them?'

'That's what they think, is it? Over-enthusiastic punters?'

'I'd say that's their general idea.'

'It's interesting,' Dickie said thoughtfully. 'Craynebrook had something similar. A woman was assaulted in a bus shelter. That man allegedly tried to strangle her.'

'Was she a tart?'

'I don't think so. At least, my informer didn't say so.'

'Something to chase up on, then,' Blake said, scraping his spoon across the bottom of the empty bowl. 'What have you got other than that?'

'A flasher and a couple of burglaries,' Dickie shrugged.

Blake wiped his mouth. 'We had a flasher, too.'

'Well, Graydon Heath's not all that far from Craynebrook,' Dickie said, as the waiter cleared the bowls away. He frowned thoughtfully. 'I wonder if the Craynebrook police know about the Graydon Heath attacks. It could be the same man, I suppose. '

'I wouldn't be surprised if they didn't,' Blake said sourly as the waiter brought over their steak and kidney puddings. 'They're not like us, Dickie. We talk. We tell each other things. The Graydon Heath police like to keep it all to themselves. I'm lucky if they so much as let a fart squeak out.'

Dickie chuckled. 'Craynebrook isn't much better. Superintendent Mullinger's got even worse since the Empire Club murders. He's so worried about looking bad, he hardly dares open his mouth anymore.'

'Except when there's good news, eh?'

'Except when there's good news,' Dickie nodded. 'But for all that, I might have a word with CID about these attacks.'

'Make sure they know you're doing them a favour, then,' Blake said, licking his lips as he cut into the soft suet crust and thick brown gravy oozed out. 'Let them know they owe you.'

Monckton slammed the front door shut, making him flinch, and he put a hand to his forehead. His head swam and black spots danced before his eyes. Christ, he needed a drink.

Staggering into the sitting room, he headed straight for the drinks cabinet and poured himself a double whisky, closing his eyes in pleasure as he chucked it down his throat. He gasped as the whisky warmed him and turned to fall into his armchair. He froze when he saw Felicity sitting on the sofa.

'What a surprise,' she said, staring contemptuously at the glass. 'Straight for the booze.'

'I fancied it,' he said defiantly. There was no way he was going to apologise for having a drink after the shock he'd had.

'Of course you did,' she said with a shrug of her bony shoulders. 'And must you slam the front door like that? You made the whole house shake.'

Monckton slammed the glass down on the cabinet. 'Anything else?'

Felicity looked at him with cool, disinterested eyes. 'What?'

'I said, is there anything else you want to complain about? Because if there is, could you say it all now and get it over with?'

Felicity's eyes returned to her magazine. 'Where have you been?'

Monckton fell into his chair and stretched his legs out in front of him. 'I went to the park and had a chat with a stranger.'

'How nice for you.'

'Not really.' Monckton stared at his black brogues thoughtfully. He knew he had no choice but to ask her. 'Felicity,' he said, 'it seems I've overspent a little this month. I wonder if you could see your way to letting me have—'

Felicity flicked a page. 'I refuse to pay your drinking bills.'

'It's not drinking bills.'

'Then what is it? Gambling debts?'

'I've just overspent, that's all. Just a temporary cash flow problem. Christ, I'm not asking for much—'

'No. Just my money. You're not getting your hands on it, Andrew. Your first wife may have been stupid enough to indulge you, but don't expect me to do the same.'

Monckton's expression hardened. 'Don't you dare speak of Annie like that.'

A plucked eyebrow rose. 'Oh, I mustn't speak ill of the dead, even if they were stupid?'

His chest was heaving, his heart knocking hard against his ribs. Anger swelled in him and Monckton leapt up from the chair. His arm swung in an arc, bringing his hand to smack hard against Felicity's cheek. The blow knocked her sideways, slamming her face into the arm of the sofa. She cried out and Monckton took pleasure in the sound. He bent over her, put his hands around her neck and squeezed. Her sharp heel jabbed into his thigh and Monckton cried out in pain. Losing his grip, he stumbled backwards, only just keeping his balance. Felicity, coughing and gasping for breath, fell onto her hands and knees, and crawled around the sofa towards the door. She was crying, a loud, retching mewling that brought the maid running.

'Madam!' she cried, and helped Felicity to her feet. She stared at Monckton for help or an explanation, he couldn't tell which, but Felicity pushed and pulled the girl out of the room. The sitting-room door closed upon them.

Monckton heard their footsteps clambering up the stairs. He rubbed at the spot on his thigh where Felicity's heel had stabbed him and knew what he needed to numb the pain. Snatching up his glass, he filled it to the brim with whisky, then fell down on the sofa and drank the lot in two gulps. Monckton laid his head back and closed his eyes.

Chapter Twenty-One

Matthew was reading Dickie's article in *The Chronicle* when Lund came into the office.

'We've got another one,' Lund said, running his hand through his thinning hair.

'Another what?' Matthew asked.

'Another indecent exposure.' Lund slurped lukewarm tea from the cup on his desk. 'There's a woman down in the lobby waiting room, crying her head off, saying a man's attacked her in the park.'

'Did you get a description? He might still be over there.'

'I can't get anything out of her. She's hysterical.' Lund fell into his chair with a loud sigh. 'Besides, it's your case. You go. See if you can get her to stop snivelling.'

Matthew rose and hurried down the stairs to the lobby. He could hear crying even before he'd reached the waiting-room door. The room's occupant jumped and cried out in alarm as he entered.

'It's all right,' Matthew said, holding out his hands. 'I'm Detective Inspector Stannard. You're quite safe.'

Her sobs subsided. Matthew pulled out the spare chair and sat down at the table. Pulling out his handkerchief, he handed it to her, and she wiped her eyes and nose while Matthew sized her up. In her mid-thirties, a little plain, a little on the thin side. No wedding ring. Quality tweed suit, perhaps a couple of years old. A respectable, middle-class spinster, he decided.

'Can you tell me your name?' he asked, taking out his notebook and a packet of cigarettes.

'Grace McKenna,' she stammered, shaking her head at his offer of a cigarette.

He lit one for himself. 'Can you tell me what happened, Miss McKenna?'

Her cheeks flooded with colour. 'I don't think I can. It's so embarrassing.'

'There's no need to be embarrassed with me, Miss McKenna,' he assured her. 'And it's only us here.'

Miss McKenna nodded at him gratefully, then took a deep breath. 'I was walking through the park, going back to work after lunch. I work in the library just over the road. A man jumped out from behind a bush, blocking my way.' She looked away, down at her hands. 'His trousers were unbuttoned, and he had his… his thing in his hand. I didn't know what to do. I couldn't think.' She put her head in her hand and sighed.

'And then what did he do?' Matthew prompted.

'He lunged at me and grabbed my hand. He tried to make me touch him. I struggled and then I screamed. He called me a name and ran off. I couldn't stop screaming. People were coming over to me. I don't really know what happened after that. It was all such a blur. Someone, I don't know who, brought me here.'

Matthew wondered where that someone was. Whoever it had been hadn't been eager to stick around. 'What did the man call you?'

'He called me a bitch. No one's ever called me that before.'

'Can you describe him?'

'Youngish, younger than me, anyway. Dark hair. Long nose. Red mouth. I don't know what colour his eyes were.'

'Build?'

'I don't know. But the overcoat he wore seemed too big for him.'

'Was he wearing a hat?'

'Yes. A flat thing. A cap.'

'Would you say he was working class?'

'I suppose so. Gentlemen don't do that sort of thing, do they?'

It was a rhetorical question, but Matthew had to bite his tongue to stop himself from telling her he'd known plenty of so-called gentlemen who had done equally disgusting things.

'Would you recognise him if you saw him again?'

Her eyes widened in alarm. 'I don't want to see him again.'

'I understand that,' Matthew said, smiling kindly. 'But would you?'

'I suppose so. Yes.' She sighed, calmer now.

'Good. Well, that will do for now, Miss McKenna,' Matthew said, putting his notebook away. 'I'll send an officer in here to take some details from you and then you can go.'

'Will I have to tell him what I've told you? I don't think I could bear to tell it again.'

Matthew thought she would cry again if he said yes, so he shook his head. 'Just give him your contact details. I will need you to come in and sign a statement at some point, but that can wait until you're feeling better. Don't worry.'

'And no one at work will know, will they?'

'This is a confidential matter, Miss McKenna. No need for anyone not involved in the investigation to be told.'

'Thank you,' she said, managing a feeble smile. 'You've been very kind.'

Matthew arranged for a constable to escort Miss McKenna home, then hurried up to his office. He wanted to compare the description Miss McKenna had given him of her assailant with that given by Mrs Plumton.

Lund was still at his desk as he entered. 'Did you get anything out of her?'

Matthew delved into his In tray for Mrs Plumton's statement. 'Yes, she told me what happened.'

'Huh. Knew she'd talk to you,' Lund said grumpily. 'Well, what did she say?'

'That she was walking through the park back to the library when a man jumped out in front of her and exposed himself. Then he grabbed her and tried to make her touch him.'

'Filthy bugger. And did she?'

'No. She struggled and screamed and he ran off.'

'Good for her.' Lund pointed at the paper Matthew was reading. 'What's that?'

'Mrs Plumton's statement,' Matthew said, running his finger down the lines of typed text. 'Overcoat. Flat cap. It's got to be the same man.'

'Of course it's the same man. How many flashers do you want in Craynebrook?'

Matthew's telephone rang and he snatched up the receiver. 'Stannard.'

'Front desk, sir,' Sergeant Turkel replied. 'Sorry to disturb you again, but I have Mr Waite here asking to see you. That's Mr Waite of *The Chronicle*, sir.'

Matthew heard Dickie say, 'Tell him it's important.'

'Mr Waite says it's important, sir,' Turkel relayed.

'All right,' Matthew said. 'But I'm not coming down again. Send him up.'

'Send him up, sir?' Turkel's tone was incredulous at the Press being allowed into the private sanctum of CID.

'That's what I said.' Matthew hung up and kicked his chair out from beneath his desk to sit down. From his In tray, he pulled out the file marked 'Mrs Joanne Cooper'. He read the description she had given of her attacker and scratched his head.

A shadow fell over the page. Lund had come round and was standing over him. 'What's the matter?'

'Both flasher victims have given a description that's similar to the one Mrs Cooper, the woman who was nearly strangled in the bus shelter, gave.'

'So? It's him again. An all-round nasty piece of work.'

'I don't know.'

'You don't know what?'

'Do flashers normally get that close to their victims? Close enough to try and strangle them?'

'You said this one just now grabbed hold of the woman.'

'I know,' Matthew admitted unhappily. 'But strangling and flashing just don't seem to go together to me.'

Lund groaned. 'You're thinking too much about it.' He looked up and caught sight of Dickie through the partition window. 'What's all this? Since when do the Press get to just walk in?'

Dickie came into the office. 'And it's nice to see you too, inspector.'

'What you doing here, Waite?' Lund growled.

'He's here to see me, Lund,' Matthew said. 'So, be polite. I know it's difficult.'

'Up yours,' Lund muttered, glaring at Dickie as the reporter took a seat. 'The Super won't like it.'

'The Super needn't know.' Matthew waved Lund back to his desk. 'What is it you want to see me about, Mr Waite?'

'About the attack on the woman in the bus shelter. A man tried to strangle her, yes? Well, I've just had lunch with a friend of mine from *The Graydon Heath Gazette*.' Dickie handed Matthew the newspaper Tony Blake had given him and pointed. 'Read that.'

Matthew's eyebrows rose with interest at the headline and he quickly read the article.

'Did you know about those incidents?' Dickie asked when Matthew had finished.

'No,' Matthew said with irritation. 'I didn't.'

'What is it?' Lund asked.

'There have been similar attacks to the one on Mrs Cooper in Graydon Heath.' Matthew tossed the newspaper to Lund.

'The women who were out alone,' Lund read. He smirked. 'That means they were prossies.' He threw the newspaper to Dickie. 'They had unhappy punters, that's all.'

'That's what the Graydon Heath police thought,' Dickie said. 'That's why they haven't bothered to investigate.'

'How do you know that?' Matthew asked.

'Because a reporter told me so.'

'Yeah, because reporters always tell the truth, don't they?' Lund scoffed.

Dickie ignored him. 'He said Graydon Heath's also had a flasher.'

Matthew's eyes narrowed at Dickie. 'How do you know about the attack? Or about the flasher, come to that? We haven't told the Press about them.'

'Don't you think you ought to have done?'

'Answer the question.'

'You should know better than to ask, Matthew.'

'Matthew?' Lund cried. 'That's 'inspector' to you, Waite.'

'Look,' Dickie said, angry with himself for making the slip, 'I'm just saying you and Graydon Heath should be swapping notes on these cases. That's all.' He glared at Matthew. 'I thought you'd be grateful.'

Matthew glanced at Lund, who was watching him with interested suspicion. 'Thank you for bringing this to my attention, Mr Waite,' he said.

'That means you can go,' Lund growled.

Dickie looked from Lund to Matthew, and Matthew knew he was expecting him to rebuke Lund for his rudeness, but now wasn't the right moment. Dickie had already aroused Lund's curiosity and Matthew didn't want to give him anything else to wonder about.

Dickie scraped back his chair and got to his feet. 'I'll be reporting these cases in the 'paper. Just so you know,' he said, and strode out of CID.

'I'm not kidding,' Lund said. 'You shouldn't get too pally with the Press. The Super really wouldn't like it.'

'The Press can be useful,' Matthew said. 'We wouldn't know about these other attacks if it weren't for Waite.'

'They might just be coincidences.'

'And they might not. I think I'll drop in to Graydon Heath station in the morning. See what they have.'

'Be polite, then,' Lund smirked. 'I know it'll be difficult.'

Chapter Twenty-Two

Matthew arrived at Graydon Heath Police Station before eight the next morning. He introduced himself to the front desk sergeant and asked to speak with someone in CID. A young detective constable came down a few minutes later, a little bleary-eyed and yawning.

'Morning, inspector,' he said, holding out his hand. 'I'm DC Owen Lowell. Were we expecting you? Only it's just me at the moment.'

'You'll be able to help me, I'm sure,' Matthew said. 'I understand you've had a couple of attacks on women lately?'

Lowell nodded. 'A few weeks back, but they weren't anything. Just a couple of tarts with an axe to grind.'

'I'd like to see what you have on them, constable.'

Lowell's nonchalant expression faltered. 'Yes, of course. If you come with me to the office, I'll show you the files.'

Matthew followed him up a flight of stairs and through a door marked CID. Graydon Heath's CID looked much the same as Craynebrook's. There same paper-laden desks, the smell of stale cigarette smoke hanging in the air, the windows in desperate need of a clean. The only difference was the map hanging on the wall; Graydon Heath instead of Craynebrook.

Lowell went straight to the bank of filing cabinets against the wall. He opened a drawer and flicked through the files, pulling out a blue folder and bringing it to his desk where Matthew was sitting. 'The first complaint was made by a Mrs Margaret Longford,' he said. 'The second by a Miss Agnes Trent.' He handed the relevant pages to Matthew.

Matthew read the reports. 'Mrs Longford said she was walking home when the man attacked her. Not that she was soliciting.'

'That's what she said.'

'But you didn't believe her?'

Lowell gave him a lopsided smile. 'She's a tart, inspector. She just didn't want to admit she was out looking for punters.'

Matthew switched his attention to the second complaint. Miss Trent made no secret of being on the game, nor that she had been working when she was attacked. 'Can I see their arrest records?'

Lowell flicked through the folder and pulled out a sheet of paper. 'That's Miss Trent's record.'

'And Mrs Longford's?'

'She doesn't have one.'

Matthew frowned. 'But you said she was a prostitute. So, she's been arrested for soliciting, yes?'

'No, sir. We've never actually arrested her.'

'So, what makes you think she's a prostitute?'

'She was out late at night all on her own.' Lowell gave a hollow laugh. 'Decent women don't go out by themselves late at night, do they, sir?'

Matthew fixed the detective constable with a hard stare and held out his hand for the file. Reluctantly, Lowell gave it to him. 'Are there papers missing from this file?' Matthew asked. 'There's no follow-up beyond the initial statements.'

'The complaints weren't followed up, sir.'

'Because?'

'Inspector Wheeler's orders. He said the tarts were probably getting their own back on some punters and that we had better things to do with our time. Sir.' Lowell licked his dry lips. 'It's a dangerous trade. The tarts know it. They can't expect to do what they do and not get a rough customer every now and then.'

Matthew shook his head. He'd encountered this kind of attitude before and it always annoyed him. He couldn't understand why so many of his fellow policemen believed that what a victim did for a living made a difference to the crime perpetrated upon them.

'Are these the only attacks of this kind reported?' he asked.

'Just those two.'

'I understand you've had a flasher, as well?'

Lowell couldn't hide his surprise at Matthew knowing about the flasher. 'Yes, sir. A couple of complaints.'

'Have those been investigated?'

'Yes,' Lowell said, brightening at being able to answer in the affirmative. 'But we haven't got anywhere with them. Not yet, at least. If I may ask, sir, why the interest in these cases?'

Matthew closed the file. 'Your attacker may have shifted his activities to Craynebrook.'

'He's attacked a prostitute?'

'No. He's attacked a respectable, middle-class woman who has a husband and two children.'

Lowell swallowed. 'I'm sorry to hear that.'

Matthew got to his feet. 'As you're not investigating these cases, I'll take the file.'

'I don't know if I can let you do that, sir,' Lowell said, following Matthew to the door. 'I'll have to ask my DI—'

But Matthew had already gone.

Matthew knocked on the door and got his warrant card ready. 'Mrs Longford?' he asked when the door opened.

Maggie eyed the warrant card warily. 'What do you want?'

'I'd like to speak to you about the attack you reported to Graydon Heath Police.'

'Oh, so now you want to talk to me?' She shook her head. 'Forget it.' The door began to close.

Matthew put out a hand to stop it. 'Mrs Longford, I'm from Craynebrook CID. I'm aware you got short shrift from Graydon Heath and that you're under no obligation to talk to me, but I'm hoping you will.'

'Craynebrook?' She frowned. 'What have you got to do with what happened to me?'

'It's possible the man who attacked you has also attacked a woman in Craynebrook.'

Maggie hesitated only a moment longer. 'All right. Come in.'

She pointed Matthew into a front room furnished with a lopsided sideboard, a small, round dining table covered in ringmarks and a threadbare armchair. He pulled out a dining chair and sat down while she lit a cigarette and settled into the armchair.

'Did he hurt her?' she asked. 'The woman in Craynebrook?'

'He bruised her neck. She was very shaken up by the attack.'

'So was I,' Maggie said sourly.

Matthew nodded. 'I know the officers at Graydon Heath didn't take your attack seriously—'

'They didn't take it any way,' she snapped. 'They didn't want to know.'

'Forgive me, Mrs Longford, but I must be blunt,' Matthew said. 'The officers at Graydon Heath believed you were soliciting the night of the attack. Is that so?'

She tutted and shook her head. 'You lot are all the same.'

'Were you?' Matthew persisted.

'What if I was? It doesn't mean he had a right to do what he did.' She sucked noisily on her cigarette. 'Yes, I was working, but I only do it when I need the money. I've got kids to feed and my husband's buggered off. What else am I supposed to do?'

Get a respectable job, Matthew felt like replying, but said instead, 'Did you approach him or did he come up to you?'

'He was following me. I turned around and asked him if he wanted business. He nodded, and I took him to an alleyway. He started stroking my neck. I wasn't in the mood to be there all night, so I told him to get on with it. Then he put his hands around my neck and tried to strangle me.'

'It wasn't—' Matthew broke off, not knowing how to put his question.

'Wasn't what?'

'What he was paying for?' he settled on.

'I don't do anything kinky, inspector,' Maggie declared, glaring at him, and Matthew felt himself reddening. 'If a man wants that sort of thing, he can go elsewhere. I know he meant to kill me.'

'So, why didn't he?' Matthew wondered.

'A light came on in the house above us,' she said. 'It scared him off.'

'Can you describe him?'

Maggie shook her head. 'Not what he looked like. Only

what he was wearing. A flat cap, overcoat. He had a scarf round his face.'

'Did he say anything?'

'Not a thing.'

'Young or old?

'I couldn't say.'

'You must have sensed that, surely?' Matthew asked in exasperation. 'You saw his hands, didn't you? They can be a giveaway of age.'

'I wasn't looking at his hands, inspector. I just saw his eyes. They were dark and...' Her face paled. 'They frightened me.'

Matthew nodded understandingly. 'Is there anything else you can tell me, Mrs Longford?'

'Only that you need to catch him,' she said. 'Because a man like that won't stop until he's killed someone. So you find him, you hear me? You find him and you lock him up and throw away the key.'

Chapter Twenty-Three

Pinder kicked open the door leading into the front desk office and sighed. 'God, I'm bored upstairs.'

Sergeant Turkel folded up his *Daily Mirror* and got to his feet. 'Fancy a cuppa? I was just going to have one.'

'Go on then,' Pinder nodded and picked up the newspaper.

'Nothing on?' Turkel asked.

'Not a thing. I hate doing the night shift. I either get them when nothing happens or I'm run off my feet dealing with all the drunks after chucking-out time.'

'You can't have it both ways.' Turkel handed Pinder an enamel mug. 'Personally, I like it when it's quiet. Gives me a chance to catch up on paperwork.'

'Sod paperwork. I didn't join the police to do the filing.'

'I thought you had those attacks to look into?'

Pinder made a face. 'The DI's dealing with those. He doesn't trust me to do a proper job.'

'Don't talk rubbish.'

'I'm not. He's been over to Graydon Heath today to find out about their attacks. I could have gone there and found out what he wanted. But no, he has to do it all himself.'

'You should have said something.'

'Like he's going to listen. And you know what he's gone and done now? Only given me the vandalism case.'

'The war memorial?'

'That,' Pinder nodded, 'and the other one.'

Turkel frowned. 'What other one?'

'Haven't you heard? A Mr Ernest Porter over on Ellesmere Gardens had red paint thrown all up his front door. Stannard's given me that. It's not good enough for him.'

'Oh, stop your moaning, Gary. Vandalism like that isn't a DI's job, especially when he's got these attacks on. He's right to give it to you.'

Pinder waved two fingers at Turkel as the door from the downstairs cell area opened and Sergeant Copley walked in.

He saw Pinder. 'What you doing down here?'

'He's just come down for some company, Tom,' Turkel said.

'Yeah, I was lonely,' Pinder grinned.

Copley grunted and moved to the front desk, taking out a large ledger from the shelf beneath. He flicked through its pages.

'So, how are things going with Mavis?' Pinder asked.

Turkel winced. It was well known that Pinder had tried his luck with Mavis Halliwell when he'd first arrived. She had rebuffed his advances, but that he had tried it on still rankled with Copley, who had long had an understanding with the secretary.

'That's none of your business,' Copley said.

'That bad, eh?'

'It's going fine, actually,' Copley said, rising to Pinder's bait. 'In fact, we're talking about getting married.'

'Is that right? Just shows you can't believe everything you hear, don't it?'

'What have you heard?'

'Ignore him, Tom,' Turkel said. 'He's just winding you up.'

Copley slammed the ledger shut. 'What have you heard?'

Pinder shrugged. 'Oh, nothing really. Nothing for you to worry about anyway. Just gossip.'

'Gary,' Turkel said warningly.

'What gossip?' Copley growled.

'I just heard Mavis is keen on the DI, that's all,' Pinder said. 'And no, I don't mean Lund.'

'Who told you that?'

'Just something I heard. Why? It's not true, is it?'

'Course it's not true,' Turkel said, patting Copley on the arm. 'Don't pay any attention, Tom.'

Copley, still smarting, turned back to the ledger.

Pinder took a few mouthfuls of tea, his mischievous eyes glancing from Copley to Turkel and back again. 'So, where is Mavis tonight?'

'She's gone to the cinema with her mother, if you must know,' Copley said.

'Oh, I see.'

Copley turned back to him. 'You see what?'

Turkel groaned.

Pinder shook his head innocently. 'It's just I heard the DI say he was going to the cinema tonight. Maybe he'll see her there. Maybe he'll take her out afterwards and—'

'Gary,' Turkel said sharply. 'That's enough.'

But Pinder was enjoying himself too much to stop. 'Just think, sarge. Mavis could be dropping her knickers for the DI right now—'

'Tom!' Turkel cried as Copley lunged at Pinder.

Copley grabbed Pinder by the collar and yanked him off the desk. Drawing back his arm, his fingers curled into a fist, but Turkel grabbed hold of him and pulled him away. Copley tumbled onto the floor.

'Pack it in, the pair of you,' Turkel yelled. 'I'm not having this. If you're going to behave like kids, you can both bugger off. What if someone came in here now and saw you two fighting? Now, are you going to calm down, Tom?'

'Tell him to shut up,' Copley snarled, getting to his feet and dusting off his backside.

Turkel shook his fist at Pinder. 'Gary, button it.'

'I was only having a joke,' Pinder said sulkily. 'I didn't mean it.'

'Say you're sorry,' Turkel said. 'Say it.'

'I'm sorry,' Pinder said, holding his hands up to Copley.

'Just watch it,' Copley warned.

The telephone on the front desk rang. With a last warning glance to Pinder, Turkel answered it. 'Craynebrook Police Station.' His eyes widened as he listened to the caller at the other end of the line. 'I'll get an officer down there straight away,' Turkel said and hung up the receiver. He turned to Copley and Pinder. 'There's been another attack. This one's bad. The lady's been taken to the hospital. Gary, you need to get down there. Sharpish.'

Matthew hurried along the hospital corridor, adjusting his hastily knotted tie.

He'd spent the evening at the cinema (Pinder had been right about that) but he hadn't met anyone there, Mavis Halliwell or otherwise. He'd been alone and had gone purely on the off-chance the man in the flat cap would turn up. He hadn't, and Matthew had gone home, wondering what on earth he could do to find this mysterious assailant.

The telephone had rung just before midnight, and Matthew hurried down the stairs, hoping to reach it before it roused his cantankerous neighbour, Mr Levitt. It was Pinder calling, and the detective constable had apologised without

137

conviction for disturbing him and telling him about the attack in the certain knowledge Matthew would want to know. Matthew told Pinder he was on his way.

Matthew entered the ward and saw Pinder hovering outside a curtained-off bed at the far end.

'Mrs Baker,' Pinder told him in a voice barely above a whisper, nodding at the curtains. 'Her husband's with her.'

'Has she made a statement?' Matthew asked.

'Not yet, sir. She's pretty badly beaten up and talking's difficult for her. I thought it best to wait until you got here rather than make her go through it twice.'

'But you got a description?'

'From the husband. It sounds like our man.'

'Where was she attacked?'

'Falconer Close. It's a cul-de-sac off Osprey Drive.'

'Get down there and see what you can find out. And have Barnes and Denham called in. Barnes is to help you with the house-to-house enquiries. Denham's to question all the cab and bus drivers to see if any of them picked up a fare that matches the description we've been given. I'll question the Bakers and get a statement. We'll meet back at the station later. Got all that?'

Pinder confirmed he had and hurried off.

Matthew parted the bed curtains. A man sitting by the bed looked up, then glanced at the woman in the bed. She might have been aged anywhere between thirty and sixty. Matthew couldn't tell her true age because her face was swollen and bruised and there were two large black marks on either side of her windpipe. She stared at Matthew through red, puffy slits.

'Mr Baker?' Matthew asked, dragging his eyes back to the man at the bedside, who nodded mutely. Mr Baker had evidently dressed in a hurry, for his hair was unbrushed, stubble showed dark on his jaw and he hadn't thought to put on a tie. 'I'm DI Stannard. I'll be investigating the attack on your wife.' He sat down in the chair on the other side of the bed and addressed Mrs Baker. 'I'm afraid I'm going to need to ask you questions about the attack.'

'My wife can't open her mouth without pain, inspector,' Mr Baker said angrily. 'You can't expect her to—' His wife's trembling hand reached up from the blanket and touched his clenched fingers. He cradled her hand with both of his own and nodded before looking across at Matthew. 'I'm upset, inspector. You'll have to excuse me.'

'It's quite understandable, sir,' Matthew said, 'and I appreciate your wife will find it difficult to talk. But the sooner I know what happened, the sooner I can catch him.' He smiled encouragingly at Mrs Baker, and she gave the faintest of nods back. 'I'll try to be as quick as possible,' he promised.

Matthew took out his notebook and flicked to a clean page. 'I understand you were attacked in Falconer Close?'

'About a hundred yards from our house,' Mr Baker said bitterly. 'She was almost home.'

'What time was this?'

'Around ten forty-five. Jane was late. I'd been expecting her no later than ten-thirty, so I went out to look for her. Thank God I did or he would have killed her.'

'Where were you coming from, Mrs Baker?'

'She'd been at her mother's,' Mr Baker said in a tone that suggested his mother-in-law was at least partly to blame for his wife's attack. 'She lives about twenty minutes' walk away on the other side of Craynebrook.'

'And did you take your usual route home?'

Mr Baker looked at his wife. She nodded, and her husband told Matthew the route that would have been.

Matthew noted it all down. 'Can you tell me what happened when you were attacked?'

Mr Baker seemed to realise he couldn't answer this question for his wife and fell silent.

'I didn't see him at first,' Mrs Baker rasped, and Matthew winced inwardly at the sound of her voice. There was no doubting she was in a great deal of pain. 'He stepped out of the shadow of a tree and just stood in front of me. I stopped and stared at him. He didn't move, so I tried to step around him and he moved to block my way again. Then he lunged at me and put his hands around my neck. He squeezed.' Her eyes closed. 'So hard I couldn't breathe. I struggled. I hit out at him. He squeezed even tighter. I tried to scream but...' she shook her head. 'I made him angry, struggling. He let go and started hitting me about the head. I fell to the ground and just hoped he would stop.' Tears fell from her eyes and Mr Baker leant over and stroked her hair.

'No more talking, Jane,' he said and turned to face Matthew. 'That was when I came across them. I heard a noise, and I turned into the cul-de-sac and saw him standing over Jane, kicking her. I shouted and he stopped kicking her and stared at me. Then he ran off down the alley. I hurried over to Jane and found her in this terrible state. I shouted for help. A man came out of a house and I told him to telephone for an ambulance.'

'You gave a description of the man to DC Pinder?'

'That's right,' Mr Baker nodded. 'He was about five foot nine, five foot ten. Not fat. He had a hat on and an overcoat.'

'Was it a long overcoat or knee-length?'

'Knee-length, I think.'

'And what kind of a hat?'

'A flat cap.'

'Did he have a scarf tied around the lower part of his face?'

'Yes, he did.' Mr Baker's eyes widened. 'Do you mean you know who he is?'

'I don't know his name, Mr Baker,' Matthew said. 'But I will catch him. I promise you that.'

Chapter Twenty-Four

Monckton's first sensation upon waking was a pounding in his head. His second was the noise of car engines and the chatter of people. He winced as he shifted, not daring to open his eyes just yet. Putting out his hand, palm down, Monckton felt grit and water on his skin, and he wondered where the hell he was.

He took a deep breath, feeling rawness in his throat, and pulled his eyelids apart. They strained and tugged before submitting. Pain shot through his skull as daylight entered his pupils and stabbed the back of his eyes. He squeezed them shut again.

Monckton waited a full minute before daring to open them again. The pain was still there but less intense, and he forced himself to keep his eyes open. He looked onto a wall, damp streaks from rainwater staining the red London bricks. He groaned as he realised where he was. Sitting on his backside in the alley next to The Green Man. Again.

First things first. Monckton fished in his inside jacket pocket and cursed. His wallet was gone. He probed his trouser pocket and his fingers felt the jutting metal of his keys. That was something, at least.

There was movement at the end of the alley. He'd soon be discovered if he didn't get moving. Monckton clambered to his feet, propping himself up against the wall, not bothering to dust himself down. He knew he looked a sight without even having to check. In fact, he'd made sure of it. Monckton had decided long ago that he didn't want to be recognised as Andrew Monckton, Liberal Party candidate for Craynebrook in the dives he visited. So, when he went drinking, he'd swap his Savile Row suit for a collarless shirt and hard-wearing trousers, his black Oxford brogues for a pair of working boots, and a cap he could pull low to shadow his face.

Where was the car? Monckton dug the knowledge out of his memory and pushed away from the wall. Reaching the alley entrance, he peered out and saw people hurrying to work, intent on minding their own business, and Monckton made a dash for the end of the street where his car was parked. Keys ready in his hand, he fitted them clumsily into the lock, not managing it on the first or even the second attempt. The scratched paint that would have bothered him when sober didn't even register now, and he yanked the door open and climbed into the driver's seat with a long sigh of relief.

There was a rap on the window, making him jump. His eyes fixed blearily on the old man peering in.

'You all right, mister?' the old man asked.

Monckton fumbled his keys into the ignition and started up the engine. He held a hand up to the glass and mouthed a thank you at the old man. Pulling out into the road, ignoring the blare of a horn from a car he almost hit, Monckton drove home, trying to remember what he'd got up to the night before.

Matthew paced up and down in Miss Halliwell's office. He needed to see Mullinger, but the superintendent hadn't yet arrived. Miss Halliwell had offered him tea and biscuits and tried to engage him in conversation, but Matthew wasn't in the mood for small talk and his monosyllabic replies persuaded her to stop trying. She was typing when Mullinger's footsteps were heard on the stairs.

'Stannard?' Mullinger said as he caught sight of Matthew. 'What are you doing here?'

'I need to speak to you, sir. It's urgent.'

'Urgent? Oh, very well. Come in. Coffee, Miss Halliwell.'

'One cup or two, sir?' she asked.

'Just the one,' Mullinger called as both men entered the superintendent's office. 'Now, Stannard, what is it?'

'There was another attack on a woman last night,' Matthew began. 'The assailant was disturbed, but not before he beat the woman up so badly she's now in the hospital.'

'Good God,' Mullinger said, sinking into his chair. 'She's not going to die, is she?'

'The doctor said she will recover. But it's clear this man isn't going to stop. I need your permission to print posters to put up on the high street, warning women to be on their guard.'

Mullinger frowned. 'I don't like the idea of that, Stannard. It will be as good as admitting we can't catch this man. We'll appear incompetent.'

'With all due respect, sir, that shouldn't be our main concern,' Matthew said. 'Women need to know to take care if they're out alone. We also need the public's help if we're to catch him. We have nothing to go on. An appeal for information might give us the lead we need.'

'Oh, very well,' Mullinger waved Matthew silent. 'Print

the posters, but only enough for the high street and be sure to get a receipt.'

'Yes, sir,' Matthew said, heading for the door.

'Before you go.' Mullinger crooked a finger to bring Matthew back. 'I had a telephone call yesterday. At home.' Matthew guessed what was coming. 'It was from my opposite number at Graydon Heath. It seems you paid the station a visit yesterday?'

'I did, sir. They have incidents that may be related to the assaults.'

'Something to do with prostitutes, apparently,' Mullinger said with distaste.

'Both women were soliciting the nights of the attacks,' Matthew admitted, 'but that might not be relevant. The women attacked here certainly weren't prostitutes.'

'Have you established a connection between our cases and the others?'

'I believe there is a strong connection. The descriptions each woman gave is an exact match, as is what he did to them. And in all four incidents, he was disturbed. Both Graydon Heath victims believe he meant to hurt them, if not kill them.'

Mullinger groaned. 'Not another killer.'

'And then there is the matter of the flasher,' Matthew said.

'What flasher?'

'There have been reports of a flasher twice here and twice at Graydon Heath. The descriptions are very similar to the man committing the attempted stranglings.'

'You think they could be the same man?'

'It's possible, but there is a significant difference. The flasher doesn't cover his face. The strangler does. And besides, I'm not convinced a flasher attacks his victims. The two MOs seem a little too different to me.'

'You're not a psychologist, or a psychoanalyst, or whatever the term is,' Mullinger scoffed. 'Who's to say what goes on in a deviant's mind?' He waved his hand. 'And all of this is by the by. It doesn't alter the fact you trespassed on another station's authority, Stannard.'

'There was a failure to investigate, sir,' Matthew protested. 'DI Wheeler ordered his men not to follow up on the complaints simply because the victims were prostitutes. We don't get to pick and choose which crimes we investigate simply because we don't approve of the victims.'

'Don't lecture me, Stannard,' Mullinger cried indignantly. 'I'm well aware of our duty to the public. But the fact is you're not aware of the many factors that go into deciding which cases should be afforded priority. You have the luxury of not having to concern yourself with budget constraints or crime statistics. I do, and I can tell you, sometimes we have to decide which cases deserve our attention and which do not. Now, I've smoothed the matter over and no formal complaint will be lodged, but be advised, Stannard. I will not accept conduct of that kind again from you. Do I make myself clear?'

Matthew nodded. 'Perfectly, sir.'

Pinder, Barnes and Denham were waiting for Matthew in CID. Pinder jumped up from the desk from where he had been slouching, Barnes stifled a yawn and Denham put down his mug of tea.

'Well?' Matthew demanded.

'I've got the statement from the man who called the ambulance,' Pinder began. 'But he didn't see the assailant or hear anything useful.'

'The same goes for the houses nearby,' Barnes put in. 'No

one saw or heard anything until after the man had run off. And no one's noticed anyone hanging around.'

'None of the cab or bus drivers remember picking up a fare that time of night resembling the assailant's description,' Denham finished.

Matthew banged his fist down on the filing cabinet. 'So, he just vanished into thin air. Is that what you're telling me?'

The three men looked at one another, shamefaced.

'Yes, sir,' Denham said. 'Sorry, sir.'

'Wonderful!' Matthew strode into his office, snatching up the piece of paper he had been working on before going to see Mullinger. 'Pinder,' he shouted, and the detective constable came running. 'Get over to the printers. I want this printed on twenty posters straight away. When they're done, get them pinned up all along the high street, wherever they're likely to be seen. And get a copy of the invoice,' Matthew shouted after Pinder as he hurried out. 'Denham! Telephone Graydon Heath station and speak to DC Lowell. Tell him about this attack and that if he gets any information relating to it or the ones they've had, he's to pass that information on to me.'

'Yes, sir,' Denham said, snatching up his telephone.

'What do you want me to do, sir?' Barnes asked eagerly.

'You're going to help me go through all our records on violent offenders,' Matthew said. 'Maybe our man is in our files somewhere.'

Chapter Twenty-Five

Monckton jiggled on the balls of his feet as he waited in the queue. He could feel sweat on the palms of his hands, taste it on his top lip. He felt sure every person in the bank knew what he was planning to do and they were just waiting for him to make his move before wrestling him to the ground like a common criminal.

When he'd got home, he found Felicity had left and the maid wasn't anywhere to be seen. It was just as well they had both gone. It made things easier. For the past hour, Monckton had been sitting at the bureau, practising Felicity's signature. Hers wasn't a difficult one to copy and he reckoned he'd got it down pat. Putting her real signature and his side by side, he hadn't been able to tell them apart.

So, he'd taken out her cheque book from the bureau drawer and signed one of the cheques. Before he could think twice, he'd written the word CASH on the payee line and ONE HUNDRED POUNDS ONLY beneath, resisting the temptation to make it two. He figured one hundred pounds would see him through the next two months. Give him a bit of breathing space.

The queue moved forward. Only one person before him

now, and once he was at the counter, that was it. He wouldn't be able to back away, not without looking suspicious. He wiped his hands on the tails of his jacket.

The queue moved forward again. Monckton's heart was banging so hard in his chest he thought it was going to burst through his ribs. *You're not up to this*, he told himself. *Get out now before you make a mistake. Another mistake to add to all the others you've made.*

But then the person in front of him finished their transaction and suddenly, Monckton was at the counter and it was too late to run away.

'Good morning, sir,' the cashier greeted him. She looked at him expectantly, the smile faltering a little as he stared back at her. 'What can I do for you?'

He pushed the cheque beneath the bars and watched, not breathing, as the cashier took it up and read what he'd written. He studied her face. It didn't alter its business-like expression. Delving into the box to her right, she counted out ten ten-pound notes, licking her finger to flick through them with ease. A bang of her inked stamp. The placing of the cheque in a box with others. The pushing of the notes beneath the grill towards him.

'There you are, sir,' she said.

Monckton snatched up the notes and tucked them inside his jacket pocket. 'Thank you,' he whispered and hurried out of the bank, expecting a hand to be laid on his shoulder at every step.

A man was standing on his doorstep when Monckton got home.

'Henry?' he said. 'What are you doing here?'

His father-in-law turned and looked Monckton up and

down with undisguised contempt. 'I'd like a word with you, Andrew.'

Oh God, Monckton thought. *Felicity's been on at him and he's come to give me a ticking off.* He took out his keys and unlocked the front door. 'Go in.'

Henry went through into the sitting room but didn't take a seat. He stood, hands clasped behind his back, and waited for Monckton to join him.

'Can I get you a drink?' Monckton asked.

'No, thank you. I won't beat about the bush, Andrew. I've come because Felicity asked me to. The fact is, she's filing for divorce.' Henry tutted in impatience as Monckton stared at him. 'Oh, come now, you can't be surprised. Not after the way you've treated her.'

'She wants a divorce?' Monckton said disbelievingly.

'She told us what happened,' Henry went on. 'And if I'd been here, I can tell you, you would have got a punch on the jaw. What kind of man are you, hitting a woman? No, don't answer that. I know the kind of man you are.'

Monckton moved to the sideboard and poured himself a double whisky. He would never have believed Felicity would want to divorce him. That she would leave him, that they would officially separate, yes, he had expected that. But a divorce? How would Felicity bear the shame?

'Your daughter hasn't exactly been the angel in the house all these years, Henry,' he said, draining half the glass in one go.

'I don't want to hear your excuses, Andrew,' Henry declared.

'Well, you're going to hear me. You think I'm the only one to blame? Now, I'll admit, I haven't been the best of husbands, but she hasn't been even a halfway decent wife.'

Henry put up a hand. 'Andrew—'

'She's mocked me, belittled me, denied me everything.'

'Don't be vulgar. I don't want to hear about that side of your marriage.'

Monckton laughed. 'I wasn't talking about sex, Henry. I was talking about her making me beg her for everything. But as you brought it up, yes, let me tell you about our sex life. Or the lack of it, I should say. Did you know your daughter is a frigid bitch?'

Henry headed for the door.

'And what about how she treated my son?' Monckton cried, hurrying to block his exit. 'Your daughter wouldn't know a maternal instinct if it slapped her in the face. She sent Sebastian away at Easter without even asking me because she didn't want him getting in the way of her bridge parties and her friends. She sent him away when she knew how much I was looking forward to seeing him. And now she wants to divorce me, does she? Well, that suits me. I'll be glad to be rid of the bitch.'

Henry's lips tightened. 'You won't contest the divorce, then?'

'She'd love that, wouldn't she?' Monckton grinned drunkenly. 'Make it look as if I couldn't live without her.'

'I'm glad you're being reasonable. My solicitor will work out the money side—'

'What money side?'

'The money you will pay to Felicity to keep her.'

Monckton snorted. 'You're not serious? Why should I keep her?'

'You have a duty to provide for her.'

'You provide for her, she's your daughter.'

'So, you're not going to be a gentleman about this.' Henry nodded as if he expected nothing less.

Moncton laughed humourlessly. 'I can't afford to be a gentleman. I'm cleaned out, Henry, old man. The cupboard is bare. You can tell that grasping bitch of a daughter of yours that.'

Henry pushed Monckton out of the way and strode towards the doorway. He paused and turned back. 'I'm sorry you've chosen to be like this, Andrew, but I can't say I'm surprised. We warned Felicity about you when she told us you were to marry. If only she'd listened to us then. Still, there's no point going over that. You will receive a letter from my solicitor and you will have to pay for what you've done. Good afternoon.'

He strode out of the room, and a moment later, Monckton heard the front door close. He picked up the bottle of whisky and tipped it up. Nothing came out and he slammed it down on the sideboard. Damn all women! Bitches, all of them!

Chapter Twenty-Six

Marjorie Kirby winced as she shovelled coal into the bucket for the front room fire and straightened. There was the pain in her back again, shooting up the left side of her spine. She got it every time she bent down. She'd gone to the quacks about it and all the doc had done was prescribe her a bottle of lineament and told her to avoid bending down. What good was that advice when she had the floors to clean and the beds to make, the front step to scrub, the chicken house to clean out…? Honestly, men had no idea.

Marjorie set the bucket down by the kitchen door, wondering if she'd done enough housework to earn herself a cup of tea and a sit-down. She decided she had, and filled the kettle from the dripping tap in the sink and set it on the ring. While the water boiled, Marjorie bustled around the kitchen, putting things away, wiping down the countertop and was just wondering whether she should finish off the seed cake in the biscuit tin before it went stale when the kettle whistled and the front doorbell rang.

'Always just as I'm about to put my feet up,' she muttered, pouring the boiling water into the waiting teapot.

Then she headed down the narrow hall and opened the front door. 'Yes?'

'Here to read your meter, love.'

Marjorie frowned, looking the man in the brown overall up and down. 'You're not the usual fella. What's happened to Larry?'

'He's off sick today, so, you've got me.' He gave her a smile. 'Aren't you lucky?'

She returned the smile. 'You're a cheeky one, aren't you? All right. Come in, then. I was just about to have a cup of tea. Do you want one or you on the clock?'

'I'd kill for a cuppa,' he said, closing the door behind him. 'Under the stairs, is it?'

'That's right.' She opened the under-stairs cupboard door. 'I'll make the tea while you're doing that.'

Marjorie returned to the kitchen and stirred the tea leaves in the pot, then took out another cup and saucer from the cupboard and put it beside the pair she'd set out for herself earlier. Placing the strainer over the cups, she poured the tea and reached up into the cupboard for the biscuit tin with the seed cake. Her fingers had closed around the tin when she felt the man come up behind her.

'Oh,' she said, spinning around and backing up against the counter. 'You made me jump, coming up behind me like that.'

'Did I?' he asked innocently. 'Thought you knew I was here.'

'Well, of course I did,' she said, embarrassed at his close-ness, 'but all the same.'

'All the same, what?'

She paused, not quite knowing what to say. Worried about making a fool of herself? She shrugged one shoulder. 'Nothing. Do you want a slice of seed cake?'

'Now you're spoiling me,' he said, smiling.

His smile soothed her. 'Some men are made to be spoiled,' she said, a trifle coquettishly.

'Is that right?' he said, frowning. 'What would your husband say to that, I wonder?'

'I don't mean anything by it,' Marjorie said, embarrassed by her words, adding brusquely, 'Well, do you or not?'

'Do I what?'

'Want a slice of cake?'

'Let me see.' He took the tin from her and opened the lid. 'That looks nice,' he said, setting it on the counter behind her. 'But not right now.'

He stared at her face. It felt as if his eyes were travelling over every mound and indentation. Mrs Kirby felt her skin growing hot under such scrutiny. She didn't like it and put her hands on his forearms to persuade him to move away.

His hands went to her throat. She felt their dry hardness against her skin as the fingers tightened. She tried to cry out, to protest, to scream, but she couldn't make a sound. Her hands flailed at him. She struck him across the face, but he took the blow without a sound and squeezed harder. She tried to kick at him, but her legs were turning to jelly and the room was darkening.

The last thing she saw was his eyes, dark and fierce, as she slumped to the ground.

A small crowd had gathered outside No. 9 Wellington Road, and Matthew saw Dickie among the gawpers as he climbed out of the police car. He acknowledged the reporter with nothing more than a tight nod and made his way up the garden path. PC Rudd was standing guard on the door, and he let Matthew into the house with the grimmest of expressions.

'In here, sir,' Denham greeted him from the kitchen door.

Matthew entered the kitchen, his eyes immediately drawn

to the body on the floor. Mrs Marjorie Kirby's legs were splayed, rumpled stocking tops showing where her skirt had rucked up. Her head was propped up against the base of the kitchen cabinet.

'Who found her?' he asked.

'Her daughter when she came home from school,' Denham said. 'She's six.' There was a note in his voice that gave away just how unsettled he was by the sight of Mrs Kirby and that a little girl had discovered her mother's dead body.

'Have you searched the house?'

'Yes, sir. No forced entry and nothing else appears to have been disturbed. Apart from the front room, that is.' Denham gestured for Matthew to follow and showed him the mirror above the fireplace in the front room. 'Smashed. Just like at the burglaries I'm working on.'

'This doesn't strike me as a household that would have a great deal of silverware,' Matthew said. 'That's what your burglar takes, isn't it?'

'It is, sir,' Denham nodded. 'That's what's odd about it. Nothing's been taken as far as I can tell.'

'Make sure the mirror's dusted for prints. Where's Bissett?'

'On his way,' Denham said, returning with Matthew into the kitchen. They both stared at the body, not wanting to look at it but unable to look away. 'Did you see the tea cups, sir?'

Matthew nodded. 'Two cups and saucers. Is there tea in the pot?'

'It's full up, sir.'

'So, she had time to make the tea, but not to pour it out. And a biscuit tin.' Matthew pointed to the tin on the worktop with its lid half off.

'There's a quarter of a cake in there, sir.'

'The tea and cake seem to indicate she was entertaining a

guest. So, maybe she let her killer in, not seeing him as a threat.'

'Someone she knew, then?'

'Possibly. Make sure Bissett dusts all this.' Matthew gestured at the tea cups and biscuit tin. 'Have you questioned the neighbours?'

'Only the bloke over the road and the lady next door to the left so far, sir. She was the one who called us. And she's got the daughter with her. I thought it best to leave her looking after the little girl for the time being. The husband's in no fit state.'

'Where is he?'

'In the front room. I haven't questioned him yet, sir.'

'I'll do it,' Matthew said. 'What did the neighbours say?'

'The lady next door heard the doorbell ring about eleven-thirty. Heard the door open and close, but didn't see who was at the door. The bloke over the road, though, passed a man he hadn't seen before and wearing brown overalls round about the same time walking down the street, but he didn't see if he stopped at any of the houses.'

'A man in overalls makes sense as to why she would let him in,' Matthew said thoughtfully. 'A carpenter or builder, perhaps? Is there any work being down here? Upstairs or out the back?'

'None, sir.'

Matthew tutted, then pointed at the cooker. 'It might have been a gas man to read the meter. Have the meter dusted, just in case.'

'Yes, sir. Do you think it's the burglar? The smashed mirror?'

'It's possible, although I'd expect a burglar to help himself to whatever took his fancy. There might not be silver-ware, but surely, he'd find something worth taking, even if it was only a couple of quid?'

'Unless he got scared after killing her?' Denham suggested.

Matthew considered this for a moment, then shook his head. 'It doesn't make sense. Mrs Kirby made tea and was going to give someone cake. She didn't do that, so common sense says she was killed before she could. She wouldn't be offering a burglar tea, would she?'

'What if she had a visitor and they were going to have tea, but something stopped them? The burglar, maybe? The visitor runs away, doesn't say a word to anyone?'

'That's hardly likely, Denham. And why would a burglar kill her? Or come to a house like this in the first place? It wouldn't be worth his trouble. Not to mention it would have been in broad daylight.'

'I see what you mean, sir. So, we're going with the visitor being the killer?'

'Until a more likely explanation crops up.' Matthew turned towards the door at the sound of voices in the hall. A moment later, a tall, elegant man carrying a Gladstone bag entered the kitchen. 'Afternoon, Dr Wallace.'

Wallace's eyes were on Mrs Kirby as he returned the greeting. He set his bag down by her legs and knelt at her head. 'No need to tell you the cause of death, inspector. Strangulation.'

'Time of death, doctor?' Matthew asked after Wallace had made a quick examination.

'Within the last four to six hours, at a very rough estimate.' He lifted the chin to expose the neck. 'No sign of a ligature. I'd say strangulation was manual.'

'Was he facing her or did he strangle her from behind?'

'Difficult to say without further examination,' Wallace said. 'But from the position of the body, it's most likely he was facing her when he strangled her. She might have been looking straight into his eyes all the time.'

Matthew could have done without this extra speculation. It didn't help to imagine the poor woman's last moments.

Wallace got to his feet. 'There's nothing more I can say until I've got her on the slab. If you can make the arrangements to transport the body to my mortuary, I'll book the post-mortem for 9 a.m.'

'Thank you, doctor,' Matthew nodded. 'I'll see you at nine.'

The doctor left the kitchen as Detective Sergeant Bissett entered with his dusting equipment.

'Can I make a start, sir?' he asked Matthew.

'Go ahead,' Matthew said, and took another look around the kitchen while Denham pointed out the areas Bissett was to make sure to dust for prints. When Denham had finished, Matthew jerked his head towards the door. 'Time we talked to the husband.'

Mr Kirby was seated in an armchair, his hand propping up his head as he stared at the empty grate in the fireplace. He looked broken, Matthew thought, signalling for Denham to close the door behind him.

'Mr Kirby, I'm Detective Inspector Stannard. I'm very sorry about your wife,' Matthew said as he took a seat on the settee opposite.

'Thank you,' Mr Kirby said without lifting his head.

'I realise this is a very upsetting time, but I do need to ask you some questions.'

This roused Mr Kirby. He looked up at Matthew, eyes struggling to focus, then straightened. 'Yes, of course you do. What do you want to know?'

Matthew glanced at Denham to make sure he had his notebook ready to take down what was said and Denham nodded his readiness. 'Was your wife expecting any visitors this morning? Anyone at all?'

'I don't think so. She didn't say any of her friends were coming round.'

'What about other callers? The milkman? Window cleaner? Anyone who would have knocked on the door?'

'The milkman would have left the milk this morning, but I don't think he would have had any reason to knock. And we don't have a window cleaner.'

'Any workmen? One who might be expected to wear a brown overall?'

Mr Kirby frowned. 'Not that I know of, but I don't know what's usual, inspector. I'm not here during the day.'

'I understand,' Matthew nodded. 'Was your wife the kind of woman who would let a stranger into the house?'

'She wasn't silly, inspector,' Mr Kirby said a trifle defensively.

'I don't mean to imply she was,' Matthew said quickly, 'but would she have let in a man she didn't know if she believed him to be calling to carry out a job? A coal man, for example, or a gas meter man?'

'Oh, I see what you mean,' Mr Kirby nodded. 'Yes, I think she probably would have done.'

'Do you know when your gas meter is normally read?'

'I'm not sure. You'll have to ask Mar—' He broke off as he realised what he'd been about to say. 'Next door would know when the meter's read. They would have the same man. Do you want me to ask them?'

'No, we'll do that.' Matthew nodded at Denham and he silently exited the room. 'Had your wife mentioned anyone following her in the last week or so? Had she noticed a man acting strangely at all?'

'No, she never said anything like that.'

'And she would have told you?'

'If a man had been following her, yes. Marjorie would have wanted me to do something about it. She wouldn't have liked that kind of attention.'

'She hadn't received any threats, written or verbal?'

'Of course not. Everyone liked Marjorie. She was a wonderful wife and mother.' Mr Kirby put his head in his hands. 'I don't know what I'm going to do without her.'

Mr Kirby burst into sobs and Matthew knew he would get nothing more out of him. He rose, thanking Mr Kirby for his time and expressing condolences once more. He didn't think Mr Kirby heard him. He exited the room and met Denham in the hall.

'The gas meter gets read on a Thursday, sir,' Denham said. 'The gasman normally comes around noon. Always the same man. Fella called Larry. Don't know the surname.'

'Get onto the gas board. Tell them we want to talk to him. Get his details. Find out where he was today. Then knock on all the doors on this street. See if anyone's been acting suspiciously the last week or so.'

'Very good, sir. Just so you know, there's a reporter outside.'

'I know,' Matthew said, opening the door and stepping out. 'Dickie Waite. I saw him on the way in.' Dickie had seen him and Denham come out and was pushing through the crowd to the front. 'Get on those house-to-house enquiries.'

'Inspector?' Dickie called and waved his notebook.

Matthew went over to him. 'Good afternoon, Mr Waite.'

'Afternoon,' Dickie said, and Matthew didn't miss the rancour in his friend's eyes. 'What can you tell me?'

'Mrs Kirby's body was found a little more than an hour ago by her daughter. We are treating it as a suspicious death.'

'How was the lady killed?'

'I can't tell you that.'

'Is the husband suspected?'

'Mr Kirby is not a suspect at this time.'

'Who is?'

'I can't tell you that, either. A statement will be made later. That's all for now.' Matthew stepped away from the crowd and made a show of lighting a cigarette. He caught Dickie's eye and jerked his head to get him to come closer.

'What is it?' Dickie said.

'Thanks for the other day,' Matthew said. 'The information you gave me was useful.'

Dickie huffed. 'A thank you back then wouldn't have gone amiss.'

'Lund was there,' Matthew offered as an explanation.

'Right,' Dickie said, and Matthew was relieved to see him unbending a little. 'Is that it?'

'No. I want to ask you something, but this isn't for your rag,' Matthew warned him. 'I just want to know. You've covered the burglaries for your 'paper, yes?'

'That's right.'

'Did you mention anything about mirrors being smashed?'

Dickie frowned. 'No. Why?'

'Just something that doesn't make sense.' Matthew tutted and shook his head. 'Never mind. I've got to go.' He climbed into the police car and told the driver to take him back to the station.

'I'll be waiting on that statement,' Dickie called as the car pulled away.

Chapter Twenty-Seven

The front door slammed shut behind Georgina and she grabbed the newel post of the staircase, taking deep breaths, willing her heart to slow down.

She'd made an exhibition of herself in the shop, Georgina knew, but the news the shop assistant had told her had come as such a shock. A woman had been strangled in Craynebrook. Again.

'Grandma?'

Startled, Georgina gasped and looked up. Dominic was standing at the top of the stairs, looking down at her with concern.

'What's wrong? Are you ill?' He hurried down the stairs and grabbed hold of her arm. 'Should I call the doctor?'

'I'm fine, Dom,' she said. 'I just had a bit of a turn, that's all. I need to sit down.'

Dominic helped her into the chair beside the telephone table. 'You look terrible, Grandma. I really do think a doctor should take a look at you.'

'No,' she said, smiling and patting his hand. 'I'll be all right in a minute. I just heard some news that rather shocked me.'

'What news?'

'A woman died.'

'Someone you knew?'

'It doesn't matter. I'm better now.' She took a deep breath and noticed his clothes. 'You look very smart. Are you going out?'

'Just out with Daniel,' Dominic said, buttoning up his cuffs. 'But if you're not feeling all that, I'll stay with you.'

'Nonsense. Of course, you must go out with your friend. Lucy's here if I need anything.'

'You're sure?'

'Yes, Dom,' she smiled again, touched by his solicitude. He did care about her, after all. 'Go.'

He kissed her cheek and left. Georgina stared at the front door for a long time, trying to work out what, if anything, she should do. She picked up the telephone receiver and asked the operator to connect her.

When the connection was made, Georgina said, 'Dr Avery, please.'

The Press were invited to the station at eight o'clock to hear the official police statement Matthew had promised Dickie. The murder had attracted a great deal of attention, and Matthew recognised reporters from *The Graydon Heath Gazette, The Colmbridge Recorder* and *The Trentwood Mercury*, all crowding into the station's small lobby. Mullinger was to speak to the Press, but he'd ordered Matthew to be present, and Matthew was currently standing with his back pressed up against the front desk counter, dying for a cigarette.

'It is with deep regret,' Mullinger began, hands clasped behind his back, 'that I can confirm Mrs Marjorie Kirby was killed in her home earlier today by an as yet unidentified assailant. Her body was discovered by her six-year-old daughter upon her return to the family home after her school day. The daughter is currently being cared for by a friend of the family.'

'How was Mrs Kirby killed, Superintendent?' a voice called out.

'Mrs Kirby was strangled.'

'What was the motive for the murder?'

'There is no apparent motive.'

'Was she violated?'

'I cannot comment on that until after the post-mortem.'

Tony Blake raised his hand. 'Is the husband a suspect, Mr Mullinger?'

Mullinger shook his head. 'We have no reason to believe Mr Kirby was in any way connected to the murder of his wife.'

'Do you have any suspects?'

'We are following up several leads,' Mullinger said, and Matthew cringed at the untruth. They had nothing and Mullinger knew it.

'Inspector Stannard,' Blake called. 'Are you in charge of the Kirby case?'

Matthew straightened. 'Yes, I am.'

'Do you think the murder of Mrs Kirby and the recent attacks on women in both Graydon Heath and Craynebrook are connected?'

'We have reason to believe so.'

'So, are you working with Graydon Heath Police on these cases?'

Matthew slid a glance at Mullinger. The expression on the superintendent's face told him clearly that he didn't want the lack of cooperation between the two stations to become public knowledge.

'We shall certainly be in communication with Graydon

165

Heath should any leads take us in that direction,' Matthew said carefully. He caught Dickie's eye. *The Chronicle* reporter was giving Matthew a highly sceptical stare. 'And we shall keep them fully informed of our developments to aid them in their own investigations.'

'What leads are you following up?' another reporter asked.

'As Superintendent Mullinger said, we have several,' Matthew said, hating to repeat the lie. 'In particular, we are interested in speaking with a man wearing brown overalls who was in the vicinity of Wellington Road this morning. We ask that anyone who can provide information about this man come forward. Any information given to us will be held in the strictest confidence.'

'That's the second appeal for information Craynebrook Police have made,' Blake said, and Matthew saw Mullinger stiffen. 'Posters were put up on the high street yesterday regarding a man indecently exposing himself to women. What response have you had from that appeal?'

'We've had a great number of responses from members of the public who have seen a man in a flat cap and overcoat and who we believe is responsible for those incidents.'

'Have you made an arrest?'

'No arrests have been made at this time,' Matthew said. 'Each report has to be thoroughly investigated and that takes time, but we are confident that the man responsible will be apprehended.'

'And apprehended very soon,' Mullinger declared loudly.

'Are the indecent exposures and this murder connected, Superintendent?'

'We cannot comment on that at this time.'

'Are you going to make it three in a row, inspector?' the *Colmbridge Recorder* reporter grinned. 'The Marsh

Murderer, the Empire Club Murderess and now the Crayne-brook Strangler?'

Before Matthew could reply, Mullinger clapped his hands. 'Thank you, gentlemen, but that's all for now. We will, of course, update you as soon as we have news.' He made shooing gestures towards the doors.

'Inspector?' Dickie's voice rang out, halting Mullinger as he was about to return to his office and the other reporters as they prepared to leave.

Matthew tensed. There was a look on Dickie's face that he couldn't quite read. What was it? Excitement? No, not quite that. Interest? Yes, perhaps, but there was something more. Matthew realised suddenly what it was. Smugness.

Dickie met Matthew's eye. 'Is there any connection between the killing of Mrs Kirby and the murder of Hannah Moore?'

The reporters had gone and Mullinger was fuming.

'Of all the nerve,' he growled, his hands curling into fists at his side while Turkel was making himself as inconspicuous as possible behind the front desk.

'Who is Hannah Moore?' Matthew demanded.

If Mullinger was angry, Matthew was furious. Mostly at Dickie for asking a question he knew Matthew wouldn't be able to answer, but also at his colleagues. What did Dickie know that he didn't and why had none of the others told him about a previous unsolved strangling?

'Hannah Moore is a six-year-old murder case,' Mullinger said. 'It can't possibly have a bearing on the Kirby killing.'

'Then why is Waite asking about it?'

'He's trying to stir up trouble, Stannard. That's what the Press does.'

'But what happened to her?' Matthew persisted.

Mullinger shook his head. 'I don't remember the details.'

'Mrs Moore was strangled in her bed, sir,' Turkel put in warily. 'The killer was never found.'

Matthew turned to Turkel. 'Suspects?'

'A burglar, I think. The house had been turned over. The file should be in the Records room.'

'No,' Mullinger cried out, halting Matthew as he headed for the door. 'I don't want you wasting time on an old murder, Stannard.'

'But it sounds like it might have a bearing, sir,' Matthew said.

'How can it? It happened in 1924, for heaven's sake.'

'I need to read the file.'

'Because a damned reporter thinks there's a connection?'

'To avoid being accused of not investigating properly, sir,' Matthew said. 'The question's been asked in a room full of reporters. If I don't at least look into it, we're going to be accused of—'

'Yes, yes, all right,' Mullinger waved Matthew quiet. 'Look into it. But if there's no connection, you leave it alone. Is that understood? I don't want all our failures dragged out for public scrutiny.'

Matthew switched on the light in the Records room. The dented green shade illuminated a room crammed full of book-cases and shelving, all stuffed with boxes of files. Every few years, the boxes would be reviewed and any closed cases would have their paperwork archived. He hoped the Hannah Moore case file was still on the shelves.

There didn't seem to be much of a filing system. Boxes were shoved in anywhere, so that case files beginning with M were sitting alongside boxes marked A, B, C or D and so on. Matthew got to work, pulling out every one until he came to a box file labelled 'MOORE, HANNAH'. He carried it up to CID, demanded a coffee from Pinder and sat down at his desk.

Inside the box was the usual buff-coloured file Craynebrook Police Station used for all their records. The first page was the crime report of the finding of Hannah Moore's body, signed off by DI Barry Carding. Hannah Moore had been a thirty-six-year-old woman, fairly well-to-do, living with her husband and sixteen-year-old son in a semi-detached house on Craynebrook's Ambourne Crescent. The murder had taken place on 9th April 1924 and her body had been discovered by her mother-in-law the next morning. Matthew read the post-mortem report next, which told him Hannah Moore had died from asphyxiation by manual strangulation, that heroin had been found in her body, and that in every other respect, she was perfectly healthy.

Hannah Moore had given a party the night of her murder. The party had been quite a raucous affair, and the guests none too particular about the havoc they wrought. So much so that it wasn't until two days after the discovery of the body that the mother-in-law realised items were missing from the house and that a burglary had taken place. This discovery had immediately altered DI Carding's approach to the investigation. Until then, he had assumed one of the guests had killed Hannah Moore. Once the burglary was discovered, his primary suspect became the burglar.

'What about the husband?' Matthew wondered. He flicked through the file until he came to Oliver Moore's statement.

Oliver Moore had not attended his wife's party. He had left Craynebrook in the afternoon and stayed with a friend at his flat in town for the next two days. He had told no one where he was going, so no one had been able to contact him to tell him of his wife's murder. He had returned to the family home to discover his house had become a crime scene and his wife was lying in the mortuary. Carding had never considered him a suspect because his friend with whom he had stayed, a Major Leslie Kirwin, had corroborated his alibi.

Matthew turned to another report dated four days after the murder. "*Several of Mrs Moore's friends allege she was carrying on with a man, but that they didn't know who he was,*' Carding had written. *'It was thought Mrs Moore had ended the affair and that the man had taken it badly. It is my opinion that this unknown lover should also be considered a suspect, along with the burglar.*"

'With no evidence to back either opinion up,' Matthew muttered as he reached for his cigarettes.

Chapter Twenty-Eight

Marjorie Kirby was laid out naked on the slab when Matthew arrived in the mortuary's examination room.

'Good morning, inspector,' Leo Wallace greeted Matthew from the other side of the slab. 'We've got her all ready for you. Her clothing is on the side if you'd like to take a look.'

Grateful for any reason not to have to look at the corpse, Matthew turned to the metal tray that had all the clothing Mrs Kirby had been wearing when she died: a cream blouse, woollen skirt, girdle, chemise, knickers and stockings. All were shop-bought and well-worn. None showed any signs of damage.

Dr Wallace said, 'Let's begin, shall we?' and nodded at his assistant, who stood nearby with a clipboard and pen. 'We have here the body of a well-nourished woman of thirty-eight years. Height is five foot five. Weight is ten stone three pounds, a little on the plump side. No external trauma to the body except for the bruising around her throat, which extends to the nape of her neck. No sign of a ligature. No defensive marks on hands or arms.' Wallace nodded to his assistant, who put down his clipboard and helped turn Marjorie Kirby over. 'There is a long, thin horizontal bruise at the top of the buttocks.'

'What would cause that?' Matthew asked.

'Possibly she was pushed back against something,' the pathologist suggested.

'The kitchen worktop?'

'Yes,' Wallace nodded. 'That would certainly cause such a bruise. I shall now begin the internal examination.' His assistant handed him a scalpel. 'Ready, inspector?'

'Don't worry about me, doctor,' Matthew said, steeling himself. He closed his eyes as Wallace's scalpel punctured Marjorie Kirby's skin.

While Wallace called out his findings, Matthew occupied himself with re-reading the Hannah Moore case file he had brought with him. He was so absorbed he barely noticed Wallace conclude his examination.

'Your attention, please, inspector,' Wallace called.

Matthew closed the file. 'Sorry.'

'To confirm what I said at the house, she died from strangulation, inspector. The hyoid bone is fractured.' Wallace pointed to the red gash that had been Marjorie Kirby's throat.

'Any sign of sexual assault?'

'No. At least the poor woman was spared that.'

'Then why kill her?' Matthew wondered, shaking his head. 'If he doesn't get a sexual thrill out of it?'

'That's for you to find out, inspector.'

Matthew nodded. 'Anything else I should know?'

Wallace looked over the body he had cut up. 'All her organs were in perfectly good shape for her age. There is a slight curvature of the spine, possibly early onset osteoporosis. She would have been in some pain from that, but otherwise, there is every reason to suppose that she would have lived to a ripe old age had not some brute robbed of her that. There now. All done, inspector. You shall have my full report by the end of the day.' Wallace moved to the sink and washed his hands.

'While I'm here, Dr Wallace,' Matthew said, 'would you mind reading a post-mortem report and giving me your opinion?'

'I don't mind at all,' Wallace said, drying his hands on a towel and holding his hand out for the report. 'What in particular do you want my opinion on?'

'Whether the strangling of Hannah Moore is similar to Mrs Kirby's? If the same man could have killed both women?'

Wallace returned his gaze to the report. 'Hyoid bone fractured. That is common in strangulation, so nothing unique there. Manual strangulation, though, is something of a unique identifier of a killer, I'd say. In the majority of strangulations, or at least, those I'm aware of, the killer uses a ligature. A rope, cord, scarf or stocking, that sort of thing. To kill with one's hands in this way is, I'd say, unusual.' He tapped his finger against the physical details of Hannah Moore. 'Thirty-six years old. Mrs Kirby was thirty-eight, so similarity in age. Mrs Moore was nine stone eleven pounds and five foot six compared to Mrs Kirby's ten stone three. Ah,' he raised his eyebrows. 'Needle marks found on the arms and thighs and heroin in the blood. Alcohol too. I found neither of those in Mrs Kirby. I'm afraid I can't tell you if they were murdered by the same killer. All I am prepared to say is that your victims shared a similar age and manner of death.' He held the report out for Matthew. 'Is that of any help, inspector?'

Matthew took it and stuffed it back into the case file. 'Not really, doctor. But thank you, all the same.'

Matthew left the mortuary and made his way to Ambourne Crescent, curious to see the house where Hannah Moore had lived and died.

He studied the house, trying to imagine how it would have looked on a summer night six years earlier. Trees lined the road; they would have created shadows between the street lamps. The house had a large porch; a burglar breaking into the house there would probably have not been visible from the pavement at night, especially if there hadn't been a porch light on. There was a narrow alley between the Moore house and the house next door, barred by a gate. The gate was low, no obstacle to a determined intruder, assuming it hadn't been changed in the past six years.

'What are you doing there?'

Matthew turned. A woman, aged perhaps forty-five, was staring at him with suspicion from behind her front garden gate. She wore a patterned scarf around her frizzy, grey hair and a heavy beaded necklace hung from her neck.

'Police,' Matthew said, digging out his warrant card and holding it up for her to see. 'Detective Inspector Stannard.'

She squinted at it. 'I see. Sorry if I was a little abrupt. It's just with all that's happened lately, a woman has to be careful.'

Matthew returned his warrant card to his pocket. 'May I ask your name, madam?'

'Miss Ellen Jernigan.' Her gaze shifted to over Matthew's shoulder. 'What were you doing?'

'I was just looking at the house,' Matthew said, pointing over the road and wondering why the name Jernigan rang a bell. It took a moment for him to work it out. Ellen Jernigan was one of the guests at the party the night of the murder. 'You knew Hannah Moore, didn't you?'

Miss Jernigan smiled sadly. 'We were best friends, inspector.'

'And you were at the party on the night she was killed?'

'I was. How do you know that?'

'Your statement's in the case file. I'd like to talk to you about that night, if I may?'

Miss Jernigan's fat lips broadened into a grin. She opened her gate and waved him through. 'Please do come in.'

Chapter Twenty-Nine

Miss McKenna handed the books over to the young woman with a weary smile. She was feeling tired. In fact, she'd felt tired ever since that horrible day in the park. She wasn't sleeping properly, waking up in the middle of the night in a sweat because of a nightmare she kept having where a man jumped out from behind a bush and tried to kill her. As it was, she was suspicious of every man she encountered, watching the men she served in the library with a wariness she'd never known before, wondering if he was the one who had molested her.

No one at the library knew of what had happened. She'd been too ashamed to tell Mr Slater and too embarrassed to tell her fellow librarian, Mrs Bishop, who had been married twice, widowed twice, and wasn't afraid of any man. She had a feeling that if she had told Mrs Bishop of what had happened, she would have laughed at her innocence and inexperience and told her what she would have done if the man had exposed himself to her.

Miss McKenna glanced up at the clock on the wall. Four-forty. Just another twenty minutes to go and she could scurry back to her flat, lock the door and be safe for another twelve hours.

The library's doors opened and her wariness turned to a frown. The dark-haired man who always came in on the fourth Wednesday of the month had just walked in. He did as he always did and made for the Classic Fiction section. Her previous interest in him, borne out of curiosity, intensified out of suspicion.

Careful to keep at a safe distance, Miss McKenna hurried around the desk and tiptoed after him. Peering around the end of the long bookcase, she saw him take out two Dickens' novels and put an envelope in their place before putting the books back with a heavy sigh. His head drooped, his shoulders sagged. His whole aspect told her this was not something he wanted to do or enjoyed, so why, she wondered, did he keep doing it?

He abruptly straightened, as if resolved, and turned in her direction. She hurried backwards, out of his way, out of his notice. He headed for the doors, yanked one open and passed through. Miss McKenna waited a minute, perhaps two, before she traced his steps to the bookshelf. Her heart beating fast, she took out the novels and stared at the envelope sitting on the shelf. It was all just as before, except that he'd come on the wrong day. What was going on? With a sigh of irritation and a little frustration, she stuffed the book back, just as someone turned into the aisle.

The newcomer stared at her.

She stared at him. She couldn't breathe. For it was him! The man from the park.

Miss McKenna ran.

Outside the library, hiding around the corner, Monckton lit a cigarette and kept his eyes on the library doors.

He'd done it; he'd left the extra money as instructed. The money that wasn't his to give away. The money he'd committed a crime to get his hands on.

If only this was a one-off, he felt he could have borne it. Pay fifty pounds and never hear from his blackmailer again. But he wasn't a fool. He knew this wouldn't be the only time. And knew too that the cost of silence would undoubtedly rise again and again, and what would he do then?

Don't think about that now, he told himself as he sucked on his cigarette. *Think about it when it happens.* That had become his mantra, pushing away unpleasant thoughts until the next day, or the one after that.

Monckton took another drag and almost choked on the smoke as he saw a man go into the library, a man he recognised, a man wearing a flat cap and a knee-length overcoat. He came out less than five minutes later without any books, tapping his coat where an inside pocket would be, and Monckton knew his envelope had been collected.

So, it had been a lie. The man on the park bench hadn't just been passing on a message for a friend. It was him all along. It was an odd feeling, Monckton thought, to be able to put a face to his tormentor at last.

Chapter Thirty

When Matthew accepted Miss Jernigan's offer of tea, he hadn't expected to be given nettle tea. He sipped gingerly at the unappealing green-brown liquid and grimaced. Hoping his hostess hadn't noticed, Matthew set the home-made earthenware mug down on the paint-splashed table and took out his notebook and pen.

'So,' he said, 'how long had you and Mrs Moore been friends?'

'Ever since she and Oliver moved here in 1920,' Miss Jernigan said. 'Hannah and I clicked at once. We understood each other, you see. We were both—'

'The party,' Matthew interrupted with a polite smile. 'What can you tell me about that?'

'Well, it was one of Hannah's usual get-togethers. She invited the crowd—'

'Who were?'

Miss Jernigan held up her hand and curled a finger towards the palm as she recited the names. 'Reggie and Sidney Barlow, Salome Baird, the Ketchell girls, David Mason, Fenella and Arthur Irwin. Kenneth and Mary Chase.

And oh yes, Freddie Tamblin. There were other people there as well, but I didn't know them. Hannah's friends brought their friends and so on. That's how it always was.'

Matthew looked at all the names he had written down. He recognised the Barlow names from the file – Carding had interviewed them, as well as the other men on the list – but he hadn't seemed to bother with the women.

'These people you've named. They were all close friends of Mrs Moore?'

'Not as close as Hannah and I were, but yes, they were good friends of hers. I'm still in contact with a couple of them, but you know how it is. People drift apart. And after Hannah was killed... well, it was rather painful to get together after that.'

Matthew nodded as if he understood. 'What happened at the party?'

'We played music and talked. Salome read some of her poetry to us.'

Matthew stopped himself from rolling his eyes. 'Were you drinking?'

'Of course we were,' Miss Jernigan laughed. 'What's a party without a drink?'

'Taking drugs?'

The smile dropped off her face. She snatched up her mug of tea. 'No.'

'Was Mrs Moore?'

'I don't know why you would even think such a thing.'

'Because the post-mortem found needle marks on her body and heroin in her blood.'

She cleared her throat.' Yes,' she said, playing with the handle of her cup. 'Hannah sometimes used drugs. It helped her to relax.' She put her hand to her heart. 'But I never touched them.'

'Did Mrs Moore need to relax often?'

'Quite often, because of Oliver.'

'Why because of him?'

'He was a burden, inspector. There,' she held up her hands, 'I've said it. It's unkind but true. Poor Hannah had such a lot to put up with.'

'Why was he a burden?'

'The war affected him badly. Sometimes, he'd wake up in the middle of the night screaming. I could hear him all the way across the road here. He'd wake up the neighbours and they would complain but there was nothing Hannah could do about it. And then there were the accusations he made against her.'

'What accusations?'

'Oh, all sorts of terrible things. That she didn't love him. That she wished he'd been killed in the war. He even doubted Dominic was his son. I honestly don't know how she put up with him.'

'Was he violent towards her?'

'Oh, yes. He'd throw things at her and shout. He kicked in a door once when she'd locked herself in a room to get away from him. Hannah was frightened of Oliver, inspector. She would even send Dominic over to me when she and Oliver were having one of their set-tos because she was worried what Oliver might do to him.'

'Did that happen often? Her sending the son to you because they were rowing?'

'Often enough. It got so I had to tell Hannah I wouldn't take Dominic anymore and that she would have to send him to his grandmother and let her deal with him.'

'Deal with him? Was Dominic a handful, then?'

Miss Jernigan's expression became pained. 'I've never been very fond of children, inspector. I admit I find them rather trying. And Dominic would go on at me to let him go back to the house so he could stop his parents fighting. I would tell him that it wouldn't make any difference, that they'd argue whether he was there or not, but...' she shrugged.

Matthew nodded, remembering his own parents' arguments and understanding how Dominic must have felt. 'Going back to the party. I understand Mr Moore wasn't there?'

'No, thank God,' she said, lighting a foul-smelling cigarette. 'He got out of the way.'

'Mr Moore got out of the way, or his wife got him out of the way?'

Miss Jernigan blew out a plume of smoke as she considered. 'I couldn't say for sure. But I wouldn't be surprised if Hannah had told him to leave. She knew he would have spoiled our fun if he had been there.'

'That was usual?'

'Oh yes. Oliver didn't like us. He'd either lock himself away if he knew we were coming or leave altogether.'

'So, what else happened at the party besides the drinking and the talking and the poetry recitals?'

Miss Jernigan's eyes danced with amusement. 'What do you mean, inspector?'

Matthew's jaw tightened in irritation. 'I don't mean anything in particular, Miss Jernigan, even if you think I do.'

Her face hardened at his rebuke. 'Nothing else happened. The party didn't go on all that long. Hannah threw us out.'

Matthew's irritation with Miss Jernigan vanished instantly. There had been no mention of the party ending early in the case file. 'Why did she do that?'

'Well, she said she had a terrible headache, but we didn't believe that for a moment. We all knew Hannah just wanted us out of the way so she could have her chap over.'

'She was expecting him that night?'

'I suppose so.'

'Who was he? Did you know his name?'

'No. Hannah kept him very close to her chest.'

Matthew tutted in frustration. 'What time did the party end?'

'Ten, ten-thirty.'

Matthew tapped his pen against his notebook thoughtfully. 'If she was expecting her lover that night, why have a party?'

The thought obviously hadn't occurred to Miss Jernigan. Her mouth opened to reply, then it closed again as she realised she didn't have an answer.

'Did she receive a telephone call or message?' Matthew asked. 'Anything that might change her plans?'

'Not while we were there.'

'How was Mrs Moore that evening?'

'How do you mean?'

'Well, was she in a good mood? Or was she annoyed or upset in any way?'

Miss Jernigan tilted her head back and stared at the ceiling as she searched her memory. 'Now you ask, I remember Hannah was very grumpy that night.'

'Was she often like that?'

'No. Hannah usually enjoyed her parties.'

'So, her behaviour that evening was unusual?'

She shrugged. 'I suppose so.'

Matthew made a note. 'When you left Mrs Moore's house, where did you all go?'

'Most of the others went to Freddie's place, I think. David and I came here.'

Matthew flicked back a page in his notebook. 'That would be David Mason? And what time did he leave?'

'Oh, around seven.'

He looked at her, eyebrow raised. 'Seven? In the morning?'

'Yes, inspector. Seven in the morning.' She stared at him, daring him to say something.

Matthew could feel himself colouring. 'And did you see or hear anything from Mrs Moore's house that night?'

'I was otherwise occupied, inspector,' she said, her mouth twisting in amusement at his embarrassment.

Her amusement at his expense annoyed him. 'So, you don't know if Mrs Moore's lover did go to the house after you all left?'

'I'm afraid not.'

'Is it possible her lover was one of the men friends who had been at the party?'

'Very unlikely. It wouldn't have been a secret if it was one of them.'

'Why would she have kept his identity a secret from you?' Matthew wondered. 'If you were such close friends? I thought women told each other everything.'

'I asked her to tell me about him,' she said sulkily, 'but Hannah said she'd promised not to talk about him. I supposed he was married and didn't want his wife to find out, so he swore Hannah to secrecy.'

'Did Mr Moore know she was having an affair?'

'I've no idea. But I wouldn't be surprised if he did. It would have been like Hannah to tell him so she could rub his nose in it.'

'You say Mrs Moore had a lot to put up with from her husband,' he said, 'but it sounds like she was just as bad. Carrying on with men, taking drugs, drinking—'

'What do you know of it?' Miss Jernigan snapped. 'What does any man know what women have to endure? Cosseted slaves, that's what women are, inspector. That's why I've never married. Ask your wife what she really thinks about men. If she tells you the truth, you'll be shocked.'

She suddenly rose and hurried from the kitchen. Matthew stared after her, taken aback by her tirade and wondering what she was doing and whether he should follow. But a moment later, she returned carrying a folio-sized notebook.

'You should read this,' she said, handing it to him.

'What is it?' he asked.

Miss Jernigan resumed her seat. 'Hannah's manuscript. She was writing a book. Semi-autobiographical. She changed the names of the characters, but everything she wrote was true to life. She wrote about her and Oliver. You read that, inspector. Their life is all in there.'

'Why do you have this?' Matthew asked, flicking through the pages with their rounded, almost childlike script.

'I didn't steal it, if that's what you're thinking. Hannah gave it to me to read so I could critique what she'd written. She wanted to know whether it was any good before she sent it to a publisher. She gave that to me two days before she was killed. I never got the chance to give it back to her.'

'Did you show DI Carding this?'

She shook her head. 'I saw no reason why I should help him. He made it very clear he didn't want anything from me. But if you're actually going to investigate Hannah's murder – and God knows it's about time someone did – then you should have it.'

'From that, do I take it you don't think the original investigation was thorough?'

'Thorough?' she snorted contemptuously. 'That other detective couldn't care less about Hannah. She was just another woman who got was coming to her.'

From reading Carding's case notes, Matthew couldn't disagree with that assessment. 'Just one last question, Miss Jernigan. Who do you think killed Mrs Moore?'

Miss Jernigan replied without hesitation. 'Oliver killed Hannah, inspector. I'm as sure of that as if I'd seen him do it.'

'There you go.' Frank Crowther handed the envelope to Wilf.

Wilf checked the seal. It was still stuck down. 'You haven't opened this?'

Crowther gave him an affronted look. 'What do you take me for?'

Wilf didn't bother to answer. He tore the envelope open and took out the notes. He broke into a wide, toothy grin. 'I knew he'd pay up.'

'All there, is it?' Crowther eyed the notes greedily.

Wilf stuffed the money back into the envelope and tucked it into his trouser pocket. 'Any problems?'

Crowther shook his head. 'Nah. Picked it up, sweet as anything. But there was something after.'

'What?' Wilf said sharply.

'I think that Monckton fella was watching.'

'He saw you?'

Crowther shrugged. 'I saw someone peering around the corner of the library. I only got a quick look, but I'm pretty sure it was him.'

'Did he follow you? Did he see you come here?'

'Calm down,' Crowther patted the air. 'He didn't follow me.'

'You're sure?'

'Course I'm sure. I know when I'm being followed, Wilf, and I weren't.'

'All right, then.' Wilf moved to the cooker and lit the gas. He banged the kettle down on the ring.

'So, is this going to be a regular thing? Me picking up for you?'

'Nah. This was a one-off. I got our regular pickups sorted.' Wilf cocked his ear at the sound of the front door opening. 'Ma's back. Time you were off.'

'If you say so.' Crowther grinned at Edna as she came into the kitchen. 'Hello, Mrs G. How's tricks?'

'You 'ere, are you?' Edna said, pushing past him.

'He was just going, Ma,' Wilf said, taking the shopping bags off her and putting them on the table. He pushed Crowther into the hall and saw him out.

'What was he here for?' Edna asked as Wilf came back into the kitchen, wincing as her heart fluttered and she put a hand to her breast in the vain hope that would stop the pain.

Wilf didn't notice. He took out the envelope from his trouser pocket and flapped it at her. 'Monckton paid up.'

'You're kidding?' she said, taking the envelope and flicking through the notes inside.

'I told you he would.' The kettle whistled and Wilf took it off the gas. He poured the boiling water into the teapot and put on the lid.

'So, how'd you get it?'

'The same way as usual. The library.'

Edna frowned. 'Did you pick it up?'

'I got Frank to do it.'

She tutted. 'What did you involve that dirty bugger for?'

'Frank's all right,' Wilf said, stirring the tea.

'We can't trust him.'

'We can trust him to help us as long as we pay.' He poured out the tea and put a mug in front of her. 'You don't need to worry, Ma. I know what I'm doing.'

'I know what you'll be doing if it all goes wrong, Wilf.'

'Ma!' Wilf slammed the milk bottle he held down on the counter and turned to Edna. 'For Christ's sake, don't keep on at me.'

Edna's eyes closed. She turned her head away.

'Sorry,' he said, putting a hand on her shoulder and squeezing. 'I didn't mean to shout at you.'

Edna put her hand on his. 'I just don't want you going the same way as your father, Wilf.'

'I won't,' he promised. 'Now, I'm going out tonight, and I want you to have an early night. You're looking tired, Ma.'

Chapter Thirty-One

Detective Inspector Barry Carding had retired to a terraced house in Barking whose façade was in desperate need of a paint job and a front garden overrun with weeds. There wasn't even a doorbell, and Matthew had to bang the letterbox flap to announce his presence.

A woman opened the door. Her hair was wrapped up in a cotton turban, silver hair-clips poking out the front. 'Yes?'

'Mrs Carding?' Matthew asked.

'That's right. Who are you?'

'My name's Matthew Stannard. I took over from your husband at Craynebrook CID. Is he in? I'd like to have a word with him.'

'There's not any problem, is there?' she asked worriedly.

'No, I'd just like to speak to him about an old case. Is he in?' he asked again.

'He's in the back room.'

She opened the door wider and Matthew stepped into the hall and looked around the narrow space. Wallpaper probably hung before the war was peeling from the walls and the smell of damp dog hung in the air.

Mrs Carding opened a door at the end of the passage. 'A Mr Stannard to see you, Barry.'

Matthew entered the back room to see a bald, jowly man in a burgundy cardigan sitting at a dining table covered with an oil-cloth.

'Good afternoon, Mr Carding,' Matthew said.

'Shall I make tea?' Mrs Carding offered as her husband's eyes narrowed at Matthew and a dog barked somewhere in the house.

'That would be nice,' Matthew said, and Mrs Carding backed out of the room, closing the door to. 'Southwark Cathedral, isn't it?' He pointed at the matchstick model Carding was working on.

'That's right,' Carding said. 'Well, you going to sit down? Just be careful pulling the chair out. This has taken me three months so far and I don't want it falling to bits.'

Matthew carefully pulled out a dining chair opposite and sat down.

'I've heard of you,' Carding said. 'Made quite a name for yourself, haven't you?'

'I've been lucky,' Matthew said. 'How are you finding retirement?'

'I'm bored out of my skull, Mr Stannard,' Carding said with a heavy sigh. 'Still, I suppose it's better than dealing with criminals day in, day out. How are you finding Craynebrook?'

'Busier than I expected,' Matthew said.

Carding took a packet of tobacco out of his cardigan pocket and rolled a cigarette. 'How's Ray?'

'Lund? The same as ever, I expect.'

Carding nodded. 'So, what are you doing here, Mr Stannard? Don't tell me a man like you needs help with something?'

'In a way,' Matthew said. 'I've been looking into a murder case you worked on six years ago.'

'That would be Hannah Moore,' Carding said, his eyes narrowing.

Matthew was impressed. 'That's quite a memory you have.'

'It's a case I'm not likely to forget.'

'Because the killer wasn't caught?'

'Because it was a nasty business. And thanks for reminding me I didn't catch the bugger who did it.'

The door opened and Mrs Carding came in with two cups and saucers, holding them aloft while her husband carefully lifted his model and put it on the sideboard. She put the cups on the table, asked if everything was all right, received an affirmative from her husband and a polite smile from Matthew and left.

'You had your suspects?' Matthew prompted, taking a sip of his tea. He winced at the amount of sugar Mrs Carding had added.

'The burglar or the bloke she was seeing on the side,' Carding said, tipping some of his tea into his saucer and slurping at it. 'We never found either of them. But the burglar was my main suspect.'

'You didn't consider the husband a suspect?'

Another slurp. 'Well, of course, in a case of murder, your first suspect is the spouse, but not this time. Oliver Moore had a watertight alibi. He was in town with a friend from that afternoon to two days later. Didn't even know his wife was dead until he was told.'

'What did you think of Oliver Moore?'

'He was a decent bloke, I suppose. Been a captain in the army during the war. Did a good job, but was never the same since, according to his mother. The marriage was a bit rocky, but when you knew what his wife got up to, you could understand why.'

'Got up to?' Matthew asked innocently.

'Drink. Drugs. Putting it about like a tart. Well, you only had to talk to her friends at the party that night to know what sort of people she mixed with.'

'And what sort were they?'

'A load of layabouts and deviants who liked to make themselves seem more interesting than they were.'

'I've met one of them. A Miss Ellen Jernigan.'

Carding shook his head. 'Don't remember her.'

'She was there the night of the party. Best friend of Hannah Moore, so she told me.'

'Oh, well, then I would have questioned her. Probably didn't tell me anything of interest.'

'Who told you about the man she was seeing?'

'Can't remember. One of the friends, I expect.'

'But you never found out who he was?'

'No.'

'How hard did you try to find him?'

Carding's eyes narrowed. 'It was the burglar who killed her, Mr Stannard. I weren't going to waste my time looking for some limp-wristed poet Hannah Moore was having it off with.'

Matthew set his cup back on the saucer. 'Moore's alibi.'

'Major Kirwin.'

'Yes. Major Kirwin confirmed Moore was with him all that time.'

'That's right.'

'And you had no reason to doubt him?'

'No, I didn't. He was a gentleman, Mr Stannard, and an army officer. When a man like that tells you something and swears it's the truth, you believe him.' Carding picked up the cigarette he had left smouldering in the ashtray while he had his tea and took a puff. 'Why are you asking about this murder anyway?'

Matthew pushed his cup and saucer to the side. 'There's been a series of attacks on women over the past few weeks in Graydon Heath and Craynebrook, all attempted stranglings. And yesterday, a woman was strangled in her kitchen. A mirror was broken in the front room. A mirror was smashed in Hannah Moore's bedroom. Seems an odd coincidence.'

'You think whoever did Hannah Moore's at it again, eh?'

'It's possible,' Matthew said.

'It was the burglar, Mr Stannard,' Carding said, pushing both cups and saucers to the far edge of the table and bringing his model back to the table. 'The burglar broke in, Hannah Moore caught him and he killed her to shut her up. Then he did a runner back to wherever he came from and that's why we didn't catch him. Don't waste your time looking for anyone else.'

Matthew got back to the station just as Denham and Barnes were calling it a night.

'Anything on the house-to-house?' he asked, stifling a yawn.

'Afraid not, sir,' Denham said. 'Larry Barker was reading meters on the other side of Craynebrook at the time of the murder. That's been confirmed by multiple residents. And the gas board has confirmed they didn't send anyone to read the meter at the Kirbys today.'

'And no other house on the road had a visit from anyone unusual today,' Barnes said. 'Certainly no one wearing an overall. And no one's been noticed lurking around.'

Matthew sighed. 'Fingerprints?'

'We've had a bit of luck there, sir,' Barnes said. 'Bissett's put his report on your desk, but there's a set of prints on the biscuit tin that doesn't match either Mr or Mrs Kirby. I've been going through our records, but I haven't turned anything up yet. Gary... er, DC Pinder said he would carry on checking.'

Matthew looked around. 'Where is Pinder?'

'Call of nature, sir,' Barnes said, giving a sideways glance at Denham that Matthew caught and knew meant Barnes was covering for Pinder. The detective constable was probably in the canteen. 'I've also sent a copy of the prints to the Yard in case we draw a blank.'

'Good. All right, off you two go.' Matthew moved to the tea urn to pour himself a mug.

'You're not knocking off yourself, sir?' Denham asked.

'Not just yet,' Matthew said, picking up a couple of biscuits from the tin that, though a little on the stale side, would go some way to filling his empty stomach. 'I have some reading to do.'

'I can stay on for a while, if you need me?' Denham offered as Barnes headed for the door.

Matthew shook his head. 'There's not much you can do until we match those prints or we get some more information. Go home. But bright and early in the morning, please.'

'Yes, sir. Goodnight.' Denham left as Pinder walked in.

'Evening, sir,' Pinder said awkwardly as he saw Matthew. 'I didn't know you were back.'

'I only just got here,' Matthew said, too tired to ask where he had been. 'I'm told you're checking fingerprints?'

'Yes, sir.' Pinder tapped a tall stack of files on his desk. 'Going through them now.'

'Good. Carry on.'

Matthew entered his office and slumped in his chair. He lit a cigarette, closing his eyes, and the nicotine worked its magic and soothed his tired brain. When he opened them again, his eyes fell upon Hannah Moore's manuscript. He opened it to the first page.

He was about a third of the way through when someone coughed. Matthew looked up to see Dickie standing in the doorway.

'Sergeant Turkel said it was all right for me to come up.'

'Sergeant Turkel shouldn't presume,' Matthew said, but waved Dickie in, glancing through the partition window to see what Pinder made of the unexpected presence of a reporter in CID. Pinder appeared to be working, but there was a tilt to his head that suggested he was listening. Matthew gestured to Dickie to close the door. 'To what do I owe the pleasure?'

Dickie took a half bottle of whisky out of his pocket. 'Thought I'd pop by and see if we're still friends.'

Despite himself, Matthew gave a half-smile. 'There are glasses in the top drawer of that filing cabinet.'

Dickie pulled the drawer open and took out two glasses, setting them on Matthew's desk. He unscrewed the cap and poured in two measures, handing one glass to Matthew. 'Cheers,' he said, and they clinked glasses. He sank down into a chair with a loud sigh. 'Not that I wouldn't blame you if you did send me packing.'

'I've certainly got good reason to. What was the idea of asking about the Hannah Moore murder like that, in front of everyone, when you knew I knew nothing about it?'

'Getting my own back?' Dickie said with a sigh. 'What can I say, Matthew? I've got the mentality of a five-year-old. My only other excuse is that you can't teach an old dog new tricks. Reporters don't tell the police anything they don't have to.'

'Even if it can help solve a murder?'

'So,' Dickie leaned forward, 'Hannah Moore and Marjorie Kirby are connected?'

Matthew sighed. 'I don't know. Both women were strangled. Both were in their late thirties. There, the similarities end as far as the victims are concerned. The only reason they might be connected is they both had smashed mirrors in the house.'

'That's what put me on to Hannah Moore. You asking about smashed mirrors made me remember her murder. But why'd you ask if the smashed mirrors at the burglaries were in the 'paper?'

'Because if the smashing of the mirrors at the burglaries had been reported in your rag, then it might be someone copying the burglar's MO. But if it hasn't been reported, then...' Matthew spread his hands.

'Then it probably is the same man?' Dickie ventured.

'Possibly,' Matthew toyed with a corner of his blotter. 'I went to see Barry Carding today to ask him about the Moore murder.'

'And what did he have to say about it?'

'Is this off the record?'

'Absolutely.'

'Carding was convinced Hannah Moore was killed by the burglar. So convinced he didn't bother following up any other leads.'

'Which were?'

'The husband and the mystery lover.'

'As I remember it, the husband had an alibi.'

'He did, given to him by an old army friend, a Major Kirwin.'

'What's wrong with that?'

Matthew sighed. 'In most murders, especially murders committed in the home, the prime suspect is the spouse. If I'd been investigating Hannah Moore's murder, I would have wanted her husband's alibi corroborated by more than one person.'

'You think this Major Kirwin may have lied about Moore being with him?'

'I don't know,' Matthew said in exasperation. 'He may have been telling the truth. But the Moores had a bad marriage. Plenty of rows, and according to a friend, violence too. She's sure Oliver Moore killed his wife. If Carding had bothered to listen a bit more and not make assumptions, he wouldn't have been able to ignore Oliver Moore's motive for killing his wife and he wouldn't have taken Major Kirwin's word at face value.'

'Did you say that to Carding?' Dickie asked, his mouth twisting in a smirk.

Matthew shook his head. 'I didn't see the point. He wasn't exactly pleased to see me, as it was.'

'Who was the friend you talked to?'

'She lived over the road to the Moores.' Matthew tapped the manuscript he had been reading. 'She gave me this.'

'And what is that?'

'A semi-autobiographical novel Hannah Moore was writing. She changed the character names, but it's pretty obvious who they represent. There's Sidney Poole, the husband who came back from the war with mental problems. Alistair Moreton, the lover who wants her to get a divorce so they can marry, but of whom she's growing bored. And there's Frederick Poole, the son the writer wishes she didn't have.' Matthew suddenly thought of Georgie, and his throat tightened. He pushed the image away as Dickie spoke.

'So, the husband has a motive. Hannah Moore's bit on the side has a motive. What about Carding's burglar theory?'

'It's not a bad theory,' Matthew admitted, 'and to be honest, the murder of Marjorie Kirby seems to make it more likely.'

'How's that?'

'Because of the smashed mirrors. Suppose whoever did it

197

had a personal reason for killing Hannah Moore. What personal reason can he have for killing Marjorie Kirby? Murders six years apart of two women who didn't know each other, weren't of the same social class and have no other links between them that I can find. So, if I accept there isn't a personal reason for killing them, then I have to consider that they were killed to keep them quiet.'

Dickie nodded. 'I don't envy you having to work all this out. So, are you going to reopen the investigation into the Moore murder?'

'Mullinger doesn't want me to,' Matthew sighed. 'But if there is a connection between the two killings, then the answer probably lies in the first murder.'

'And if there isn't a connection?'

'Then I'm wasting my time and possibly putting other women at risk because I'm allowing myself to be distracted by an old murder that no one cares about. Oh God.' Matthew yawned and buried his face in his hands. 'If I could only make sense of it all.'

'You should call it a night, Matthew,' Dickie said, rising and pocketing the whisky bottle. 'You're no good to anyone if you're dead on your feet. Go home. Get some sleep. I'm sure things will be clearer in the morning.'

Chapter Thirty-Two

Matthew rang the doorbell of No. 23 Boddington Road. When a maid opened the door, he showed her his warrant card and asked if he could speak with Mrs Georgina Moore. She left him standing on the doorstep while she enquired whether Mrs Moore was home, and returned a few moments later to bid him enter, showing him into a neatly appointed sitting room.

An elderly woman was standing expectantly by the fireplace. Her grey hair was elegantly styled in bouncy curls upon her forehead and her rather pudgy face had a fixed, worried smile upon it. Matthew had seen the expression often. It told of concern that something terrible had happened but also of embarrassment that a policeman had come calling.

'Mrs Moore?' he asked, snatching off his hat. He could feel the maid hovering at his elbow.

'Yes, I'm Georgina Moore,' Georgina replied. 'Lucy, take the inspector's hat. Would you like tea, inspector?'

'No, thank you,' Matthew said, handing his hat over. He waited until Lucy had gone before speaking again. 'I'm sorry to call unannounced, but I would like to talk to you about your daughter-in-law.'

Georgina's cheeks paled. 'About Hannah?'

'You may have heard about the murder of Mrs Kirby yesterday?'

'I heard of it, yes, but what has that to do with Hannah? Oh, please. Won't you sit down?'

Matthew obliged. 'There is a similarity between the two murders.'

'But Hannah was killed six years ago, inspector. I don't see—'

'The killer was never found, Mrs Moore.'

'Oh, I see.' Georgina sank into the armchair. 'You think it could be the same man.'

Matthew brushed cat hair from his trouser leg. 'You found your daughter-in-law's body, I understand?'

'Yes,' she said, her eyes dropping to her hands in her lap. 'It was quite horrible.'

'I'm sorry to make you go through it all again but can you tell me exactly what happened?'

Georgina sighed. 'It was mid-morning. I was taking Dominic back to the house. He'd stayed with me the night before.'

'Dominic is your grandson?'

'Yes. Hannah had sent him to me because she didn't want him there while she was having her friends over.'

'Dominic was how old then?'

'Sixteen.'

Matthew made a note and asked Georgina to continue.

'The front door was open,' she said. 'There were bottles all over the pathway. Really, such a mess. Dominic was eager to see his mother. I told him to wait because I had no idea what state she would be in, or...' she paused and looked away, 'or whether she would be alone. He ran up the stairs to the landing and called down that Hannah's door was closed, which was unusual. She usually left her door open. So, I took the door being shut to mean she did have someone with her. I confess it rather annoyed me, not even bothering to hide her infidelity, and I felt so very sorry for my son. It was quite wrong of me to interfere, of course, especially with Dominic there, but...' She shrugged. 'I went up to the door, knocked but received no reply, so I went in. The room was in darkness. I could smell alcohol and other things.'

'What other things, Mrs Moore?' Matthew asked.

'Urine, inspector,' she said with an effort. 'The odour was very strong.'

Matthew knew it wasn't unusual for a person in their death throes to lose control of their bodily functions, but he was annoyed this hadn't been included in the report Carding had written. What else had Carding left out? he wondered.

'I moved to the bay,' Georgina continued, 'meaning to open the windows to let some fresh air in and the smell out. I tugged the curtains open and turned around, ready to complain to Hannah about her behaviour, and...' She put her hand to her mouth as if she was about to be sick. She took a deep breath. 'I saw her, spread-eagled on the bed, her legs tangled in the sheets. Her face was blue and her tongue was poking out of her mouth. It was the most grotesque thing I've ever seen. I heard Dominic coming into the room and I shouted at him to keep out. Then I telephoned for the police.'

It was the same account Georgina had given Carding, save for the omission of the urine smell. 'You said your daughter-in-law was unfaithful to your son. Did she have one lover or several?'

'I imagine Hannah had several. She was that kind of woman.'

'But you don't know for certain?'

Georgina shook her head. 'I never met any of them, if that's what you're asking.'

'So, how do you know she was unfaithful?'

'From things she said.'

'Not from her husband?'

'No. Not from Oliver.'

'He didn't know his wife cheated on him?'

'No.'

'A friend of Mrs Moore's thought it likely your son did know about his wife's infidelity. That your daughter-in-law would have taken pleasure in telling him of it. Does that sound possible?'

Georgina met Matthew's eyes. 'Hannah could be very cruel.'

'And what about your grandson? Did he know about his mother's carryings-on?'

'Certainly not,' she cried indignantly. 'Dominic was… is very innocent about such matters.'

'Where is Dominic these days?'

'He's been in India since shortly after Hannah was killed. I thought it was best he left England for a while.'

'And he's still there?'

Georgina hesitated before answering. 'No. He's back home for a holiday.'

'When did he come back?'

'Let me see. It was the sixteenth.'

'Of this month?'

'Yes. I met him at the train station.'

'I see.' Matthew made a note in his notebook. 'Is he staying with you?'

'Yes.'

'Is he here now? I would like to talk to him, too.'

'No, he's out with a friend.' Her face became pained. 'Must you speak with him, inspector? I'd prefer it if he wasn't reminded of that time. It's very painful.'

'I appreciate that, Mrs Moore, but I'm afraid it's unavoidable, in view of this recent murder. What about Mr Moore? Can you tell me where he lives now?'

Georgina started up from her chair. 'You mustn't talk to Oliver.'

Matthew, too, got to his feet, startled by her reaction. 'Why mustn't I, Mrs Moore?'

'He's not well,' she said. 'If you were to talk to him about Hannah, I don't know how he'd react.'

'As I've said, Mrs Moore, I'm afraid I don't have a choice in the matter. I need to speak to him. So, please, where is he?'

Georgina was wringing her hands. 'Oliver's resident in Driscoll's Care Home, inspector. He's there's because his health is so very fragile.'

'I promise I'll tread carefully with both him and your grandson,' Matthew said, tucking his notebook back in his pocket.

'No,' she cried. 'I can't allow you to speak to either of them.'

'I'm not asking for your permission, Mrs Moore,' Matthew said, as kindly as he could manage. 'A woman has been killed and your daughter-in-law's murder might help me find the killer.'

'But they can't tell you anything I haven't,' she whimpered. 'Please leave my family alone, inspector. We've suffered enough.'

Georgina watched Matthew walk away through the sitting-room window. She bit her nails, wondering what to do. The inspector had insisted on talking with Oliver and God only knew what Oliver would say to him if he did. She cried aloud and hurried out to the hall, snatching up the telephone receiver and asking the operator to connect her to Driscoll's Care Home.

'Doctor Avery, please,' she said when the connection was made. 'It's Mrs Moore.'

She drummed her fingers impatiently on the telephone table while the doctor was located. When she heard a noise at the end of the line, she cried, 'Dr Avery?'

'Yes, Mrs Moore,' Dr Avery replied. 'What can I do for you?'

'I'm so sorry to bother you, Dr Avery,' Georgina said, 'but I need your help.'

'Is something wrong?' he asked. 'You sound upset.'

'I am, rather,' she admitted. 'You see, I've just had a policeman at my house asking questions.'

'About what?'

'A woman was killed yesterday and this policeman thinks my daughter-in-law's murder has something to do with it. He wants to question Oliver. He was very insistent.'

'Was he, indeed?'

'I told him Oliver wasn't well and to question him about his wife wouldn't be good for him, but this policeman didn't seem to care. I think he will be coming to the home. Dr Avery, is there anything you can do to stop him? I'm worried about Oliver.'

'Of course you are,' Dr Avery said. 'And I agree with you. Oliver won't respond well to being interrogated by the police.' He fell silent and Georgina grew impatient.

'Well, doctor?' she cried.

'Now, calm down, Mrs Moore,' he said and Georgina bristled at his patronising tone. 'I won't allow this policeman to see Oliver. For all his bluster with you, he can't insist, especially not if I forbid it.'

'Really?' she groaned with relief.

'Oh, yes,' he said. 'You have to stand your ground with the police, Mrs Moore. They like to run roughshod over people but one just has to remind them of their place. You leave it to me. I'll send this policeman away with a flea in his ear.'

When Matthew had arrived at Driscoll's Care Home and asked to see Oliver Moore, the secretary had instead shown him into an office and told him Dr Avery wanted to see him. Matthew knew what that meant. It meant Georgina Moore had called the care home to prevent him seeing her son.

The door opened and a white-coated man entered. 'Detective Inspector Stannard, I believe?' he said, moving to his desk.

'Yes,' Matthew said. 'I'd like to see Oliver Moore.'

Avery flicked through a file on his desk. 'So I understand. But that's not possible.'

'Why isn't it possible?'

'Mr Moore's state of health is very delicate. The slightest upset can have the most serious consequences. An interrogation is quite out of the question.'

'I don't intend to interrogate him, doctor,' Matthew said. 'I'd merely like to talk to him.'

Dr Avery laughed. 'Forgive me, but I think I have it right with interrogation, inspector. I'm aware of the heavy-handed techniques police use. I simply cannot allow you to question my patient.'

'Well, Dr Avery,' Matthew said, 'I'm not sure you have the authority to stop me.'

Dr Avery drew himself up, affronted. 'I am his doctor, inspector. Even the police must respect my medical opinion.'

'I respect it, doctor. Just as I hope you respect the fact that a woman has been murdered and Mr Moore just might know something that can help me find her killer.'

'Inspector, to question Mr Moore about murdered

women…' Avery shook his head. 'You will do untold damage to his mental stability.'

'I'll do my best not to upset him.'

'I'm afraid you doing your best is neither here nor there. Just confronting him in the aspect of a policeman will be enough to unsettle him even more than he already is.'

'Why is he so unsettled?' Matthew asked sharply. 'Has something happened?'

Dr Avery smiled at Matthew's ignorance. 'You don't understand neurasthenia, inspector,' his voice dripping with condescension. 'Being unsettled is a constant state for Mr Moore. Like so many men, the war did very great damage to his mind. His mental state is exceedingly fragile. The slightest upset could send him over the edge and I think you'll agree the murder of his wife counts as an upset.'

'Encounters with the police always upset people. I can't allow that to interfere with me doing my job.'

'But Mr Moore isn't like the people you're used to dealing with, inspector. He isn't clear-minded. Any statement he made to you could not be relied upon. It would be muddled, confused, almost certainly inaccurate. You would be wasting your time.'

'It's my time to waste, doctor.'

'And it would be my duty to clear up the mess you leave behind. It is quite out of the question, inspector. I will not allow you to talk to Mr Moore.'

'I can get a court order that will allow me to talk to him,' Matthew said.

'Indeed? Well, if you think you can, then by all means do so.' Dr Avery pressed a button on his desk and Matthew heard a faint buzzing noise from the outside office. A moment later, the secretary who had shown him into the office appeared in the doorway. 'The inspector is leaving, Miss Piper. Good day, inspector. I trust you'll see reason and not bother me again.'

Chapter Thirty-Three

Matthew had his driver take him to the Army and Navy Club in Pall Mall. At the club, a steward showed Matthew into the smoking room and pointed out a wheelchair as being Major Leslie Kirwin.

Matthew went over to him. 'Major Kirwin?'

The newspaper that obscured the top half of the major's body crumpled and eyes in a heavily lined face with a bushy white moustache peered up at Matthew. 'Yes? Who are you?'

Matthew flashed his warrant card. 'Detective Inspector Matthew Stannard.'

'A detective?' Major Kirwin said with delight. 'Oh, do sit down. Harry!' he called for the waiter. 'Get this fellow a drink. Brandy? Whisky?'

Matthew held up a halting hand to the waiter. 'Nothing for me.'

'Are you sure?' Kirwin looked puzzled by the refusal of alcohol.

'Yes, thank you.'

'Well, if you're sure. Bring me another, Harry.' He tapped his empty brandy glass. 'So, what can I do for you, young man? I say. You've not come to arrest me, have you?' Kirwin grinned and held up his hands. 'Honest, guv'nor. It wasn't me.'

Matthew smiled politely. 'I want to talk to you about Oliver Moore.'

The grin dropped from Kirwin's face. 'Oliver? Why? Has something happened to him?'

'It's about the murder of his wife.'

'Oh, I see. You're raking that all up again, are you?'

'You told the inspector investigating the murder that Mr Moore was with you from the afternoon of the ninth of April to the eleventh?'

'Yes, yes, that's right. I did.'

'And when you said he was with you on the ninth, that was where, exactly?'

'Oh,' Kirwin's eyes rolled to the ceiling as he searched his memory, 'the afternoon and evening would have been spent here. I'm always here, inspector. I've nowhere else to go. Yes, we would have been here, and then we would have gone back to my flat.'

'At what time would you have left for your flat?'

'Oh, now you're asking, aren't you? Well, I suppose it would have been a little after nine. I don't do late nights. Early to bed, and all that.'

'You both went back to your flat after nine o'clock on the evening of the ninth of April?'

'Correct, inspector.'

'Couldn't Mr Moore have stayed here that night?' Matthew asked. 'Doesn't the club provide rooms for its members?'

'Oh, yes, the club has rooms for its members, but Oliver wasn't a member. He could have stayed as my guest, of course, if he'd wanted, but unfamiliar surroundings troubled Oliver and he preferred to stay with me.'

'Was he troubled that day?'

'He was a little out of sorts, I seem to remember. His wife was having one of her parties and he felt he'd been forced out of the house.'

'From what I've been told, Mr Moore's marriage wasn't a happy one?'

'I'd go along with that.' Kirwin leant forward conspiratorially. 'Between me and you, inspector, Oliver believed his wife was seeing other men.' He leaned back and looked at Matthew as if he need say no more.

So, Oliver Moore did know about his wife's infidelities. Matthew stored that fact away. 'That night, the ninth, you were both here and then you were at your flat. You were together the entire time?'

Kirwin's mouth opened and shut. He shifted in his wheelchair, winced, then settled back in the seat. 'Almost all the time.'

A thrill ran through Matthew's body as he sensed Oliver Moore's alibi was about to collapse.

'After dinner,' Kirwin continued, 'we left to go back to my flat, but then Oliver said he needed to go for a walk. I wasn't in this damn wheelchair then, but even so, my legs weren't up to it. We parted. I went to my flat. Oliver went...' He spread his hands. 'I don't know where.'

'This would have been just after nine o'clock?'

'Yes.'

'And what time did he return to your flat?'

'I'm afraid I have no idea, inspector. I was asleep as soon as my head hit the pillow and I never wake up until the morning. But he was there for breakfast.'

'If you didn't let him in, how did he get into your flat?' Matthew asked.

'Oliver had a key. I'd let him have one the year before. I'd told him if ever he was in town and needed somewhere to stay, he just had to let himself in. I was glad of the company. So many of my friends have gone now and—'

'So, it might have been several hours since him leaving you and coming back to your flat?'

'I suppose it might.'

'Major Kirwin, this wasn't mentioned in your original statement.'

Kirwin hung his head. 'I know. I should have told that other chap then. But the truth is, I didn't want to make things difficult for Oliver. He'd just found out his wife had been murdered and he'd already been through so much. And the other chap didn't ask, so I ...' he shrugged helplessly.

Matthew nodded. 'How was Mr Moore the following morning? The morning of the tenth?'

'He was all right. He wasn't talkative, but then breakfast's not a chatty meal, is it?'

'There was nothing to suggest anything untoward had occurred the night before?'

Kirwin's expression hardened. 'Are you suggesting Oliver had anything to do with his wife's murder? That's absurd. Oliver wouldn't. He couldn't hurt a fly, inspector.'

'You served in the war together?'

'Yes,' Kirwin said, a smile forming on his lips in pride.

'Did you kill anyone?'

The smile dropped away instantly. 'It was war, inspector.'

'Is that a yes?'

Kirwin sighed. 'Yes. I did. Of course I did.'

'Did Mr Moore?'

'I expect so.'

'So, you'd agree he's capable of killing?'

'Only in certain circumstances, inspector. But that's true of anyone, in my opinion. Given the right provocation, anyone is capable of murder.'

Matthew nodded. 'That's exactly my point.'

Chapter Thirty-Four

Mr Slater opened the library doors to Matthew and said in a low voice. 'She's being very difficult, inspector. I really don't know what to do with her. She insisted I call you, but...' he wrung his hands, 'I feel such a fool involving the police in this, especially when you've got more important things to do.' He checked his watch. 'Mrs Slater expected me home an hour ago. Can I leave Miss McKenna to you?'

'I'm afraid I need you to stay on a while longer, Mr Slater,' Matthew said, ignoring the pained expression on the manager's face. 'Where is she?'

'In here.' Mr Slater pointed at a door marked private. 'She locked herself in the lavatory for half an hour. We had to threaten to break the door down before she agreed to come out. She's been acting very oddly for a few days now. I don't know why. Anyway, we sat her down in here and gave her a cup of tea.' He tutted. 'Miss Bishop insisted on leaving, so I had no choice but to stay. But it's not my job to deal with hysterical women, you know.'

'I appreciate that, Mr Slater,' Matthew said, thinking it was unlikely to be in anyone's job description, 'but she's obviously very distressed and perhaps a little understanding might help?'

Mr Slater's mouth puckered at the rebuke. He opened the door and stepped through.

Miss McKenna was sitting in a straight-backed chair set against the wall. She looked huddled up, as if she was trying to occupy as small a space as possible. When Matthew entered, she looked at him with the same red, puffy eyes she'd had during their interview.

'Miss McKenna?' he said. 'Do you remember me?'

She nodded. 'I asked them to call you. I need to tell you something.'

Matthew pulled over another chair and sat down. 'What do you need to tell me?'

Her eyes flicked to Mr Slater, then back to Matthew.

'Would you mind leaving us, Mr Slater?' Matthew said, turning to the manager. 'But I may need to speak to you again, so please, don't leave the library.'

'I wouldn't dream of it,' Mr Slater said indignantly and left the room, closing the door behind him.

Matthew turned back to Miss McKenna. 'What is it?'

Miss McKenna sniffed. 'He was here. I saw him.'

'Do you mean the man who exposed himself to you? He was here in the library?'

'I saw him.'

Matthew took out his notebook and pen. 'When was this?'

'Just before five. I was in one of the aisles and I turned around and there he was, standing right in front of me. Oh God, it was horrible. I thought he was going to do it again.' She buried her face in her hands.

'You're sure it was the same man?' Matthew asked.

She looked up, wiping her eyes. 'I'm certain. He had on

the same cap and overcoat.' Her eyes narrowed. 'You don't believe me, do you?'

'Miss McKenna—'

'You think I'm hysterical. Like Mr Slater. I heard what he said to you before you came in. He just thinks I'm a nuisance and can't wait to be rid of me.'

'I don't think you're hysterical,' Matthew assured her. 'But you've had a frightening experience and I'm concerned you're not thinking clearly.'

'It was him,' she declared. 'I know it was him. I won't ever forget his face. I wish I could. And what's more, he recognised me. I'm sure of that too. I could tell. You must believe me.'

'All right,' Matthew nodded. 'I believe you. Now, tell me. Had you seen him in the library before?'

'No. He's not been in here before. At least, not since I've worked here.'

'Did he borrow a book?'

'I don't think he came here for a book.' Miss McKenna sighed and ran her hand through her hair, dislodging some pins. She shoved them back in distractedly. 'I don't know if this has anything to do with it, but there's another man who comes into the library. He doesn't come in for the books either. He comes in to leave an envelope behind the books.'

Matthew frowned. 'An envelope?'

'Yes. The fourth Wednesday of every month. He comes in, goes straight to the Dickens, and puts an envelope behind the books. Later, the envelope's gone. That man, that horrible man, came in to pick up the envelope. I didn't see him do it, but I'm sure he came in to take it.'

'What's in the envelope?'

'I don't know. It was sealed. But it felt like money. Notes.'

'And this other man, the man who leaves the envelope. Do you know him?'

She shook her head.

'Can you describe him?'

'Dark-haired, dark eyes. Quite good-looking. In his forties, perhaps a bit older. About the same height as you.'

'You'd recognise him if you saw him again?'

'Yes. I've seen him often enough.'

A thought suddenly occurred to Matthew. 'Wait a minute. You said he comes in every fourth Wednesday of the month. It's Thursday, so why was he in today?'

'To leave a second envelope. It's the only time he's come in twice in the same month.'

'Can you show me where he leaves the envelope?' Matthew asked.

Miss McKenna nodded, and he followed her to the Classic Fiction aisle, ignoring Mr Slater who was hovering by the doors. She pulled out the Dickens.

'He put it here and now it's gone,' she said. 'That horrible man took it. He must have done.'

'But you said this was the first time you'd seen him in the library? So, who normally picks up the envelope?'

Miss McKenna took a deep breath. 'I've never actually seen who normally picks it up, but last Wednesday, I think I could tell who did. At least it was gone after she'd been in the library. I didn't actually see her take it. And to be honest, I can't believe she would have anything to do with it.'

'Who, Miss McKenna?' Matthew asked, impatient for her to get to the point. 'Who normally picks up the envelope?'

'An old lady called Edna Gadd.'

Matthew could find nothing on an Edna Gadd in the station's Records room. There was no Edna Gadd listed on the electoral register and there was no Edna Gadd in the telephone directory. But he had her address, courtesy of Miss McKenna, who had flicked through the library's filing system and given him the address in Leytonstone Mrs Gadd had registered with.

He knocked on the door of No. 74 Crompton Road and got his warrant card ready. Nothing happened for more than thirty seconds and Matthew was about to knock again when he heard shuffling from inside and a woman's voice called, 'All right, all right. I'm coming.' A moment later, the front door opened with a loud squeal of hinges.

Edna's eyes narrowed at Matthew, dropped down to his warrant card, flicked over his shoulder to note the police car, then returned to him. 'What d'you want?' she said.

'Mrs Edna Gadd?' Matthew asked, putting his warrant card away.

'What d'you want?' she asked again.

'Detective Inspector Stannard. I'd like to ask you a few questions.'

'What about?'

'Craynebrook Library. May I come in?'

'If you want,' she said after only a moment's hesitation and shuffled backwards to open the front door for him.

Matthew took off his hat and stepped inside. 'Thank you.'

'In there,' she said, pointing him towards the front room. He went in, knowing he wouldn't be offered tea, nor a seat, and remained standing as he turned to face her. She leaned on the sideboard, her breath a little laboured, as she waited for him to speak.

'You use Craynebrook Library quite often, I understand?' Matthew said.

'What if I do?'

'Why not the Leytonstone one? It's closer. More convenient.'

'They have better books at Craynebrook,' she shrugged. 'I like it there.'

'You must do,' Matthew nodded. 'You go there at least once a week and take out several books at a time.' He pointed to a pile of books on the sideboard. 'You've got four this week, I see.'

'I like reading. That ain't a crime, is it?'

'Is that the only reason you go to the library, Mrs Gadd? For books?'

'Nah, I go to 'ave me hair done.'

Matthew didn't smile at the sarcasm. 'I have a witness who says you always visit the library on the fourth Wednesday of every month. Other weeks, you go on other days. But for that week, it's always the Wednesday.'

'Is it?' Edna looked at him as innocently as her face would allow.

'There's another person who always visits the library on the fourth Wednesday of the month. This man is well-dressed, could be said to be good-looking, in his forties. Do you know him?'

'Me? Know a gent?' She laughed derisively.

'Well,' Matthew went on, 'this gent leaves an envelope behind the novels of Dickens that is later collected. My witness says this last Wednesday, you collected that envelope. Is that correct?'

Edna shook her head. 'I don't know what you're talking about. I take books back and I take books out. That's all I go to the library for. Your witness is talking rubbish. Who is it? Who's been talking about me?'

'I'm not at liberty to say, Mrs Gadd,' Matthew said. 'Do you know another man with dark hair and eyes, wears a flat cap, overcoat and boots?'

She snorted. 'Do I know...? You're 'aving a laugh, ain't

you? That could be anyone. Take a look down this street and tell me how many men you see looking like that.'

Matthew tried not to show his annoyance, knowing she was right. The description he'd given her could apply to almost any working man. He glanced around the room. 'Do you live here alone, Mrs Gadd?'

Edna straightened. 'Yeah, I do.'

'Mr Gadd is...?'

'Dead.'

'And who's that?' Matthew pointed to a framed photograph on the mantelpiece of a young man in an army uniform.

'That's my son.'

'What's his name?'

She hesitated before answering. 'Wilfred.'

'And where's he?'

'He's dead, too,' Edna said, looking down at her feet. 'Blown to bits in France. I'm all on me own.'

'I'm sorry.'

'Don't you feel sorry for me,' she ordered. 'I'm all right as long as I'm left alone. So, if you're done with your questions, you can bugger off. I ain't got all day to spend talking to the likes of you.'

Edna slammed the door and put her ear to the wood, holding her breath as she listened to the sounds from outside. She breathed again only when she heard the police car driving away.

Pain gripped her chest, a fist clenching her heart. Edna squeezed her eyes shut as she prayed for the pain to go away. After a minute or two, when the pain had eased, she staggered into the front room and fell into the armchair. She stayed that way until she heard a key turn in the front door lock.

'Ma?' Wilf called, kicking the front door shut.

'Front room,' she replied, hoping he wouldn't notice how weak her voice sounded.

Wilf poked his head around the door and frowned at her. 'What you sitting there like that for?'

'I'm having a sit-down. That's allowed, ain't it?'

'It just ain't like you.' Wilf held up a paper bag. 'I got you a cake for after tea. What we got? I'm starving.' His head disappeared.

'Wilf!' Edna called after him.

He sighed as he put his head back around the door. 'What?'

'The police were here,' she said, and winced as Wilf threw the door open so hard it banged against the wall behind. 'A detective.'

'What did he want?'

'He was asking about the library. He knew about the envelopes.'

'Christ,' Wilf said, throwing the paper bag on the sideboard and running his hand through his hair. 'What did he say? Tell me everything.'

'He knows about Monckton dropping off the envelopes and he knows I picked them up.'

'He said Monckton's name?'

'Well, no,' Edna said. 'He just said there was a gent who dropped off the envelopes and asked if I knew who it was. I said I didn't. But then he asked about a fella who was dark-haired, wore a flat cap and an overcoat. That's that Frank Crowther, ain't it? That's who he was asking about.'

'He knows about Frank?'

'He must do. I told you we couldn't trust that Crowther.'

'Frank ain't snitched on us, Ma,' Wilf said angrily.

'How does that copper know about me, then? Six years I've been doing that collection and nothing. Then you involve that Crowther and suddenly I've got coppers on me doorstep asking questions. It don't take a genius to work out who's to blame, Wilf.'

'Did this copper ask about me?'

'No, not really.'

'What does not really mean?'

'He saw your picture.' She pointed at the photograph on the mantelpiece. 'Asked who you were. I told him you'd been killed in the war.'

'You told him I was dead?'

'I had to tell him something, didn't I? Better he thinks you're dead than you're here and up to no good.'

'What was this copper's name?'

Edna frowned, trying to remember. 'Stannard, I think. Yeah, that's it. Detective Inspector Stannard. From Craynebrook.'

Chapter Thirty-Five

Monckton closed his eyes as his head swam. Opening them again, everything was blurry, and he narrowed them to see better. It didn't work. Everything remained out of focus, and he groaned in frustration.

So much for cutting down on the drink, he thought bitterly. But he just couldn't give it up yet. The news about the divorce, the stealing of Felicity's money, and seeing his blackmailer in the flesh – it was all too much. He needed the booze. He knew he shouldn't be driving, not when he was this drunk, even though he was going slow.

But then, so what if he crashed the car and killed himself? Who would miss him? Not Felicity, obviously. Sebastian would miss him for a month or so, perhaps, but the boy would get over it soon enough. And if he did crash and kill himself, all his worries would be over. So, perhaps it was the best thing all round?

But perhaps not. Monckton didn't want to die. All he wanted was to clear up the mess his life had become. It had all gone wrong when Annie died. She had meant more to him than anything, and she had understood him, knew his weaknesses and managed them, keeping him on an even keel.

Losing her had been catastrophic for him, and when she died, he truly didn't know how he could carry on without her. Until he thought of his newborn son and what his absence at that young age would mean for him. It had been Sebastian's need that had pulled him through that dreadful time. Monckton would have had to find a way to cope without Annie for Sebastian's sake. He and Sebastian would have muddled along together, finding their own way. Everything would have been fine. If only he hadn't met Hannah...

Don't think of Hannah, he ordered himself and shook the thought away like a dog shaking itself awake from a dream. *Just get home, lie down and get some sleep. That's all you need, Andrew. A good night's sleep. Everything will look better in the morning.*

Monckton forced himself to concentrate on the road. But as he peered through the windscreen, his attention was caught by a man walking on the pavement up ahead. His eyes narrowed in scrutiny. The man looked familiar, and he suddenly realised why. It was the man who had threatened him in the park, the same man who had taken his money from the library. Monckton watched as he crossed the road, looking neither left nor right, his attention entirely focused on the cigarette he was rolling.

He didn't stop to think. Monckton floored the accelerator and twisted the steering wheel so he was heading straight for him. The man looked up at the roar of the engine, but it was too late. The front of the car slammed into him. At the impact, Monckton braked, and he watched, open-mouthed, as the man flew through the air and thudded into the tarmacked road about twelve feet ahead.

His breath was coming fast as Monckton released the brake and floored the accelerator again. His head almost bumped the car's ceiling as he ran over the fallen body and crushed it beneath the wheels. He braked again and opened his door to look behind at the damage he had wrought. The man wasn't moving and a liquid leaking from somewhere on the man's body caught the moonlight and twinkled at Monckton.

Monckton pulled his door shut and put his foot on the accelerator one more time and steered his car down the road.

Blood was rushing in his ears. His heart was banging so hard he felt sure it was going to burst free of his ribs and land in his lap. He could hardly believe what he'd done, but dear God, it had felt so good!

Pinder hid a yawn behind his hand as Mr Walsh bustled into the front room and set a tray down on the table.

'Coffee, wasn't it?' he said, handing Pinder a mug.

'Thanks.' Pinder downed half of the black liquid. It was very hot and burned his throat, but he didn't care. He needed the caffeine if he was going to stay awake.

Turkel had burst into CID half an hour earlier to tell him about the accident. Pinder had wondered aloud why the desk sergeant was bothering him with a road traffic accident, declaring it was Uniform's job to attend, when Turkel had told him that the man who had made the emergency call declared it hadn't been an accident at all but that the driver of the car had deliberately run down the victim. His interest only a little piqued, Pinder had agreed he would get down to Cadogan Street straight away.

He'd arrived just as the ambulance men were putting the broken body of a man on a stretcher before loading it into the vehicle. Pinder told them to hold on a minute while he looked the man over, wincing at the damage he'd suffered, astonished he was still breathing, if only just. Turkel had given him the name and address of the man who had made the emergency call and Pinder had duly sought him out, doing his best to ignore the questions of all the other residents who had come out in their pyjamas and nightdresses to gawp.

'Now,' he said, setting the mug down on the table and resting his notebook on his knee, 'you told my colleague you reckon the driver of the car deliberately ran the man over. Is that right?'

Mr Walsh settled into an armchair. 'Yes, that's right. I couldn't believe it when I saw it. I was upstairs in bed and I heard a sort of cry and then a thud. It sounded awful. I jumped out of bed and looked out of the window and I saw that man lying in the middle of the road, all twisted up. A car had stopped. Then it started up again and drove right over him. It stopped again, and I saw the driver door open, someone lean out, then the door close and the car drive off.'

'Can you describe the car?'

'It was large and dark. Black, maybe, or dark blue?'

'Any idea of the model?'

'No. I can't tell one car from another.' Pinder made a face of disappointment, and Mr Walsh arched his body to put his hand in his trouser pocket. 'But I made a note of the registration number. I saw that all right.'

Pinder grinned as Mr Walsh passed over a scrap of paper. Finding the driver was going to be a piece of cake.

Chapter Thirty-Six

It was just before 6 a.m. when Matthew tramped into CID, feeling like death.

He'd hardly slept. There were too many thoughts going round in his head – the sense that he was letting a killer get away chipping away at his conscience – to allow him to rest, and he'd given up trying about four in the morning. He'd made himself a mug of coffee and smoked three cigarettes. He was so tired, he'd cut himself shaving, and the two nicks on his left jaw were stinging as he nodded to Pinder.

'Morning, sir,' Pinder said, getting to his feet. 'I didn't expect to see you so early.'

Matthew picked up the night log and scanned the entries, hoping there was nothing in it about a woman being attacked. 'You've had a quiet night.'

'Not really, sir,' Pinder said. 'I got called out to a road accident.' He yawned and fiddled with his tie, loosening it a little.

'There's nothing in the night log about a road accident,' Matthew said.

Pinder looked guiltily at the book. 'No, I, er... I hadn't got around to entering it yet, sir.'

'Well, when were you going to enter it? You're off shift in five minutes.'

'I was going to do it, sir,' Pinder insisted.

Matthew tossed the log back onto the shelf. 'Tell me about the incident.'

Pinder grabbed a piece of paper from his desk. 'I've got the report here.' He held it out to Matthew.

Matthew snatched it from his hand and read. 'A man hit by a car on Cadogan Street around 11.45 p.m. Witness claims the driver of the car hit him deliberately. Couldn't name the model of the car but did get his registration number. Well, that's something. Have you checked on that?'

'The council offices don't open until nine, sir. I was going to leave a note for DC Barnes to call them and get the driver's name and address.'

Matthew continued reading. 'The man was dead by the time they got to the hospital.'

'Yes, sir. I saw the body. It was a right mess.'

'Do we know who he was?'

'No identification on him. He had a front door key, some coins and a couple of quid. That was all. The post-mortem's booked for nine. I was going to get DC Barnes or DS Denham to attend, if that's all right?'

Matthew nodded and rubbed his forehead where a headache was brewing. 'Have we had anything more from the poster or newspaper appeal?'

Pinder grabbed his notebook, flicking through the pages. 'Yes, sir. A woman who thinks the man is her neighbour, but it sounds like she has a history of disputes with him, so I don't know if it's going to pan out as anything. A man who thinks it might be a friend of his because he wears a flat cap. About a dozen more from people who think they've seen the man around town.'

'Anything from Uniform? Or from Graydon Heath?'

'Nothing, as far as I know.'

Barnes walked in bearing a bacon roll on a plate and a mug of tea. He halted when he saw Matthew and he cast a glance at Pinder, his eyes asking if he was interrupting something he'd rather not be a part of. 'Morning, sir,' he said to Matthew and gestured at his refreshments. 'Can I get you anything?'

Matthew usually fetched his own food, but he was too tired and the smell of the bacon roll too tempting to refuse. 'I'll have the same as you,' he said.

'Have mine,' Barnes said, passing him his mug and plate. 'I'll get myself another lot.'

'Thanks.' Matthew took them and fished in his trouser pocket, pulling out coins to give to Barnes. He headed for his office.

'Is it all right if I go now, sir?' Pinder called after him.

'Yes, you can go,' Matthew replied. 'Just make sure Barnes has everything he needs.'

Kicking his office door shut, wanting privacy and quiet, Matthew sat down at his desk. He rooted in the drawer for his bottle of aspirin and washed two tablets down with the tea. He ate the bacon roll before brushing his fingers clean of crumbs and pulling the files from his In tray over to sit on his blotter.

Indecent exposure. Burglaries. Violent attacks. Murder. And now a manslaughter, if not possibly another murder, to add to the list. Matthew remembered back to the end of the Spencer/Hailes trial – was that really only a few weeks ago? – when he and Dickie had bemoaned the fact that Craynebrook would be dull. His mother would have told him to be careful what he wished for, and she would have been right. All these cases and he wasn't making progress on any of them. The only definite lead he had was Edna Gadd, and he didn't even know what she was involved in. The indecent exposure or something else altogether? He was waiting to hear what, if anything, Scotland Yard had on her. Until then...

Matthew opened the topmost file and began reading, hoping to find something he'd missed that would give him something, anything, to follow.

He'd found nothing new by the time Lund came in just after half-past eight. Matthew mumbled a greeting, not in the mood for conversation, and Lund seemed to understand, sitting down without another word and getting on with his work.

Matthew carried on for another five minutes, then threw the files back into his In tray. It was no good his reading and re-reading the case notes while his head was pounding. Checking his wristwatch, he rose, grabbed his hat and coat, and told Lund if anyone wanted him, he'd be at the mortuary.

'Good morning, inspector,' Dr Wallace greeted Matthew jovially as he entered the examination room. He frowned as he stared at Matthew's haggard expression. 'Or maybe not?'

'It's not a particularly good morning, doctor,' Matthew agreed, leaning against a counter and folding his arms over his chest. He yawned, throwing his head back. 'Excuse me.'

Wallace's eyebrows rose, but he said nothing, stepping to one side as a trolley was wheeled in by two assistants. They lifted the sheeted corpse onto the slab. Wallace picked up a clipboard and read the notes.

'Victim run over by a car just before midnight last night. Pronounced dead on arrival at the hospital. Right ho. Let's whip the sheet off and begin.' One assistant left; the other folded the white sheet back to reveal the body. 'Oh dear. Not a pleasant sight.'

Matthew could only agree. The body was bent and broken like none he'd ever seen before.

'The corpse,' Wallace began, 'is that of a man approxi-mately twenty-five to thirty-five years of age, height five foot nine, dark-brown hair. He's wearing a dark blue, knee-length overcoat, boots, trousers and a striped shirt without a collar.'

Matthew straightened. 'Is there a flat cap, doctor?' he asked.

Wallace looked at him in surprise. 'A flat cap, inspector?'

'Yes. Was he wearing a cap when he was brought in or is there one on him?'

'His personal effects are in a tray behind you,' Wallace said.

Matthew turned to the metal tray on the counter. There were the items Pinder had mentioned and, the brim folded into its interior so it formed a semi-circle, was a flat cap. Matthew snatched it up.

'Found it, inspector?' Wallace asked.

'Yes, I have.' Matthew hurried over to the slab and looked down at the corpse. Dark hair, long nose, full mouth. 'Has he got dark eyes?' he asked.

Wallace pulled open an eyelid. 'Dark brown,' he confirmed.

Matthew's heart was pounding. 'I need a picture of his face.'

'All in good time, inspector.'

'Not in good time, doctor. Now,' Matthew snapped. 'I need it right now.'

Miss McKenna was stamping books at the front desk when Matthew hurried into the library.

'Oh, inspector,' she said, a hand going to her chest. 'You startled me.'

'I'm sorry,' Matthew said, 'but I need you to look at a photograph and tell me if you recognise the man.' He held up the headshot photograph of the hit-and-run victim, watching her expression as it changed from interest to horror. 'Is it the man who came into the library yesterday?'

'Yes,' she said, her eyes filling with tears. 'It's him.'

'This is the man who exposed himself to you?'

Miss McKenna nodded. 'But he looks odd. Is he asleep?'

Matthew refolded the photograph and replaced it at the back of his notebook. 'He's dead, Miss McKenna. He was hit by a car and killed last night.'

She stared at him. 'Dead?'

Matthew nodded.

'Oh, thank God,' she said, putting her hand to her throat. She took several deep breaths. 'I suppose you think that's awful of me? But all I've been thinking about is that he's been coming for me. I mean, him coming here to the library when he hadn't done that before. Every time the door opens, I've expected him to walk in. Every time I leave my flat to come here or leave here to go home, I've been so scared he's going to jump out at me again. It's been dreadful. You can't imagine.'

'Well, you can stop worrying now,' Matthew said, putting his notebook away. 'He won't be bothering anyone ever again.'

Chapter Thirty-Seven

Matthew stuck in the last pin, fixing a larger version of the mortuary photograph to the CID corkboard, and turned to the watching detectives.

'This,' he said, pointing, 'is our flasher. I've just had one of his victims confirm it. He's also our hit-and-run victim.'

'Who is he?' Denham asked.

'I don't know yet. I've got fingerprints from the mortuary examination.' Matthew took an envelope out of his pocket and handed them to the sergeant. 'I want them checked straight away. If we haven't got anything that matches, get on to Scotland Yard and get them checking their records.' He turned to Barnes. 'Have you got anything on the car registration?'

'Yes, sir. The registration is for a 1926 blue Morris Cowley saloon. Owner registered as a Mr Andrew Monckton.'

'Monckton?' Matthew repeated, his brow creasing. He knew that name. Why did he know that name?

'Yes, sir,' Barnes said, checking his note. 'Mr Andrew Monckton of 19 Ambourne Crescent. I've checked our records and we don't have anything on him.'

'Monckton!' Matthew cried and ran into his office. Barnes and Denham stared after him in surprise, watching through the partition window as Matthew grabbed a file from his In tray and rifled through it.

'What is it, sir?' Denham asked.

Matthew brought the file to the doorway. 'Andrew Monckton, neighbour to Hannah Moore, interviewed by DI Carding. He was out the evening of her murder. Didn't see or hear anything.'

'What has that old murder got to do with the hit-and-run, sir?' Barnes asked and Matthew remembered he hadn't told them he'd been looking into the Hannah Moore murder.

He sighed and rubbed his forehead. 'I don't know. Christ, I'm so tired, I can't think straight.' He saw Barnes and Denham exchange curious glances and pulled himself together. 'Maybe it doesn't mean anything. Maybe it is just a coincidence.'

'Do you want me to interview Mr Monckton, sir?' Barnes asked tentatively.

'No.' Matthew threw the file back on his desk. 'I want to speak to him. But you can come with me.'

There was no Morris Cowley parked on the driveway, nor on the road outside 19 Ambourne Crescent, Matthew noted as he climbed out of the police car and walked up the path to the front door. He rang the doorbell.

Barnes cast his eyes over the front of the house. 'All the curtains are pulled, sir. Maybe no one's home.'

Matthew rang the doorbell again and was about to rap the knocker when he heard the latch lift and the door slowly opened. A man, hair unbrushed and sticking up, unshaven, wearing what looked like the previous day's clothes, peered out through a six-inch gap.

'Yes?' he asked.

'Mr Andrew Monckton?' Matthew asked, showing him his warrant card.

Monckton frowned. 'Yes.'

'Can we come in, sir? We'd like to talk to you about an incident last night.'

'Last night?' Monckton's eyes closed. 'I don't understand.'

'If we could come in, sir, we'll explain,' Matthew said. He was prepared to insist as Monckton hesitated, but then the door was opened wide and Monckton gestured him inside.

'Thank you,' Matthew said, smelling whisky and stale smoke coming from Monckton as he entered the hall.

'You can go into the sitting room.' Monckton closed the front door and shuffled after Matthew and Barnes. He dropped down onto the sofa and reached for a cigarette.

Matthew took a seat on the opposite sofa while Barnes took up a position by the door. 'Are you the owner of a blue 1926 Morris Cowley saloon car, Mr Monckton?' Matthew asked.

Monckton released the striker on his lighter and threw it into the corner of the sofa. 'Yes, that's my car. Have you found it?'

'Found it?' Matthew repeated, surprised by the question.

'It was stolen yesterday.'

Matthew's heart sank. It had all seemed so straightforward back at CID. Now, it seemed it was going to get complicated. 'Where was it stolen from?'

'Let me think.' Monckton stared at the ceiling. 'I parked it on Kinley Way about eight o'clock last night, and when I went back there about ten, it was gone.'

'Kinley Way?'

'That's in Graydon Heath, sir,' Barnes supplied.

'Did you report it stolen?' Matthew asked Monckton.

'No, I didn't. I was going to do that today.'

'Why the delay?'

Monckton gave a little laugh. 'I wasn't up to reporting it last night, inspector. I'm afraid I had a little too much to drink.'

'And yet you were planning to drive?'

'Yes,' Monckton gave a solemn sigh. 'You're quite right. That would have been wrong of me. Perhaps it was just as well the car wasn't there.'

'How did you get home?'

'I walked.'

'From Graydon Heath?'

Monckton shrugged. 'It was a nice night and it's not all that far.'

'What time did you get home?'

'Oh, I couldn't say, inspector.'

'Could anyone else tell us? Your wife?'

Monckton licked his dry lips. 'My wife is away at the moment.'

'Where were you drinking in Graydon Heath?'

'The Green Man pub.'

'Were you there alone?'

'Yes. Quite alone.'

Matthew took the photograph from the back of his note-book and held it out to Monckton. 'Do you know this man, Mr Monckton?'

Monckton peered at the photograph. He shook his head and handed it back to Matthew. 'No. I can't say I do. Who is he?'

'He's a man who was run down and killed last night by someone driving your car.'

'My God, that's terrible,' Monckton said. 'He's dead, you say?'

The surprise in Monckton's manner was unconvincing. It came too quickly, the words too pat.

'Are you sure you don't know him?' Matthew asked.

'I assure you, I don't know him, inspector. How do you know it was my car?'

'We have a witness.'

'I see.' Monckton swallowed. 'But this witness didn't see who was driving?'

Matthew tucked the photograph back into his notebook and got to his feet. 'We may need to talk to you again, Mr Monckton, so please don't leave Craynebrook.'

Monckton rose unsteadily and followed Matthew to the front door. 'Of course. Anything I can do to help.'

Matthew halted on the front step. 'Just one other thing. You were living here when Hannah Moore and her family lived next door?'

The blood drained from Monckton's face. 'Yes. I was.'

'Were you friendly?'

'As friendly as neighbours usually are.'

'Her murder must have come as quite a shock.'

'Quite a shock. It was a terrible thing to happen.'

'You told the investigating officer you weren't here that night?'

'No, that's right. I was out for the evening,' Monckton said. 'Party work.'

'Party?'

'I'm a member of the Liberal Party, inspector.'

'You're an MP?'

'Candidate,' Monckton corrected a little stiffly. 'Yet to be elected. But one of these days, one hopes.'

'I see,' Matthew smiled. 'Well, thank you for your time, Mr Monckton.'

'What do you think, sir?' Barnes asked as he and Matthew walked to the car.

'I think he's told us a pack of lies,' Matthew said, climbing into the back.

Barnes got into the front passenger seat and turned to face him. 'You think his car wasn't stolen?'

Matthew shook his head. 'No, I don't. I'm sure he was driving. I think he knows who our dead man is, and I think he wanted him dead. We need to find that car, Barnes.'

Barnes nodded. 'I'll get Uniform out looking for it as soon as we get back to the station.'

'You're going back to the station,' Matthew corrected. 'You can drop me off at the Liberal Party office, wherever that is. I want to find out more about Mr Andrew Monckton.'

Monckton watched them go, hiding behind the net curtains so they wouldn't see him. They'd believed him, he was sure of it. If they hadn't believed him, they would have taken him with them, wouldn't they?

It had been a good story. Someone had stolen his car while he was in The Green Man and run the man down. Simple as that.

Grinning, Monckton poured himself a whisky. He was going to be all right. His blackmailer was dead; he wouldn't have to pay up any more. He could even put the money back in Felicity's bank account, half of it anyway, and make up the rest somehow so she need never know. She might even come back to him.

But did he want her back? Felicity was a cow. All women were cows. He should be grateful he was finished with them. None of this would have happened at all if it hadn't been for a woman. If it hadn't been for Hannah.

Another splash of whisky went into his glass and down his throat. Why had that detective asked about Hannah? he wondered. What did he know?

Chapter Thirty-Eight

The Liberal Party headquarters in Craynebrook was a far cry from the grandeur of the Conservative Club that Matthew had visited during his Empire Club enquiries and amounted to no more than two rooms above a pub. The party agent, sitting at his desk, watched Matthew approach with apprehension.

'You're from the police?' Charlie Ezard asked.

'I am,' Matthew said. 'Detective Inspector Stannard. I'd like to ask you about Mr Andrew Monckton?'

Ezard groaned. 'What's he done now?'

'What makes you think he's done anything?'

Ezard reached for the cigarette burning in the ashtray. 'Why else would you be here?'

Matthew pointed at a chair, and Ezard nodded for him to take a seat. 'What can you tell me about Mr Monckton?'

'He's a flaming liability,' Ezard snapped, blowing smoke in Matthew's direction.

'Is he a drinker?' Matthew asked, remembering how Monckton stank of booze.

'Is he a drinker?' Ezard gave a hollow laugh. 'Inspector, that man does not know when to stop. I asked him to stand in for a fellow member at a luncheon the other week. Two bottles of wine gone before we'd even got to the dessert course. I can't tell you how many complaints I received about him afterwards. But what can I do? I'm not exactly spoilt for choice when it comes to candidates.'

'He's never been elected, I understand?'

'No, and not likely to be, either. Not now it's known he's got a drink problem. And not now he's got marriage problems, too.'

'He said his wife was away.'

Ezard made a face. 'She's left him, inspector. I don't know all the details, but rumour has it, he hit her and she walked out. Filing for divorce, and the party's not going to want a divorcee representing them.' He stubbed out his cigarette and lit another. 'Anyway, what are you here for?'

'Mr Monckton's car was involved in an accident last night,' Matthew said. 'I'm looking into the case.'

'Is he hurt?'

'No, but the man who was hit died.'

'Christ,' Ezard breathed.

Matthew took out the mortuary photograph. 'Do you recognise this man?'

Ezard peered at the picture and shook his head. 'No. He's dead, isn't he? He looks dead. Is that the man Andrew killed?'

'It's the man who was run over by Mr Monckton's car,' Matthew said as he put the photograph away. 'Mr Monckton claims his car was stolen and it wasn't him who was driving.'

Ezard raised both his eyebrows in disbelief. 'That's what he says, is it?'

Matthew nodded. 'When I spoke to him, he was quite clearly hungover. Have you known him to drive when he's been drinking?'

'He drove after the luncheon and he was two sheets to the wind then. I suppose I should have stopped him, but to be

237

honest, inspector, I was glad to see him go.' Ezard poured himself a glass of water. 'Have you arrested him?'

'Not yet.'

'But you're going to?'

Matthew didn't answer.

'Well, that's it,' Ezard said, throwing up his hands. 'He's going to have to go. The party's struggling enough as it is. We can't afford to have a murderous drunk for a candidate.'

'You think he's lying about his car being stolen? That he was the one driving it?'

'Well, that's for you to find out, but I wouldn't be surprised. And mud sticks, inspector. Monckton's reputation will be in the gutter once this gets out. And believe me, things like this always get out.'

'So, it's true,' Dickie said as Matthew stepped out onto the pavement. 'Monckton's involved in this hit-and-run.'

Matthew sighed. 'Is nothing secret in this place?'

'There's a very healthy grapevine in Craynebrook,' Dickie nodded. 'So, what can you tell me? Come on, Matthew. You'll know I'll find out sooner or later.'

'So, find out later.' Matthew moved around him and headed for the road.

'You look knackered,' Dickie said, catching him up and crossing with him.

'Thanks.'

'Going back to the station?'

'Yes.'

'I need something for the 'paper, Matthew.'

Matthew halted and Dickie did the same. 'What do you know already?'

'That an unidentified man was knocked down and killed on Cadogan Road late last night. That you've got a witness who got the registration number of the car. That you've made enquiries at the council and been given the owner as Mr Andrew Monckton. That you've interviewed but not arrested him and now you're asking questions at the Liberal Party office.'

'Then you know as much as I do.'

'Really?' Dickie looked doubtful.

'Really,' Matthew insisted. 'Print what you know, Dickie, because I don't have anything more to tell you.'

'Any luck finding Monckton's car yet?' Matthew asked as he strode into CID.

Barnes shook his head. 'Not yet. Uniform's been told to keep an eye out for it.'

'Let's hope they find it soon. The Press have got hold of our interest in Andrew Monckton. I'd like to have his car before they fill their column inches with speculation. Any new attacks reported?'

'No, sir,' Denham said. 'All quiet on that front.'

'Some good news at last,' Matthew muttered. 'Denham, I've got a job for you. I want you to find Monckton's wife. Apparently, she's planning to divorce him. Find out why. She's left him, so I don't know where she is, but try her parents first. If she's not there, try close friends, other relatives, hotels in the area... you know what to do.'

'I do, sir.' Denham sat down at his desk and grabbed the local telephone directory, flipping through its pages.

'Barnes.' Matthew took out his notebook and flipped to the back. 'I want you to take this photograph and show it to the indecent exposure victims, including the ones in Graydon Heath. See if they can identify our dead man.'

'Graydon Heath nick, sir?' Barnes asked worriedly as he took the mortuary photograph.

'Don't worry about treading on their toes, Barnes. I'll deal with them if there's any complaint.'

'Yes, sir.' Barnes frowned. 'Why would Mr Monckton want to deliberately run over a flasher?'

'That's a bloody good question, Barnes,' Matthew said.

Pinder had just started his shift when PC Rudd came up to CID and handed him a large brown envelope. 'Delivery from the Yard,' Rudd said, watching with interest as Pinder ripped open the seal.

'All right, constable,' Pinder said, pausing as he noticed Rudd hovering. 'On yer bike.' He jerked his head at the door and Rudd left, his cheeks reddening with embarrassment. Grinning, Pinder delved inside the envelope and pulled out the papers it contained. 'Sir!' he cried and hurried into Matthew's office.

'What is it?' Matthew asked as he flicked through the Liberal Party pamphlet Charlie Ezard had given him. It was dated 1923 and the group photograph on the front page was the only image the party agent had of Andrew Monckton.

'The report on the dead man's fingerprints from the Yard. They found a match.'

He held the report out and Matthew snatched it from his hand. 'Frank Arthur Crowther,' he read. 'He's got a charge sheet as long as my arm. Robbery. Pick-pocketing. Fencing.' He smacked the edge of the paper. 'Eight counts of indecent exposure and two counts of Grievous Bodily Harm. He came out of Pentonville on the fifteenth of April. The first attack in Graydon Heath was that night. First indecent exposure in Craynebrook was on the very next Sunday. The burglaries start at almost the same time.'

'They were all this Crowther.'

'Don't make that assumption. Not until we've made

240

certain. Right.' Matthew grabbed his hat. 'I'm going to see if we have anything on Crowther in our records. I want you to find out where Crowther was living. Start in Graydon Heath. Go round the pubs. Find out if anyone knew him and knew where he was staying.'

'Yes, sir,' Pinder grinned.

'Just ask questions, Pinder,' Matthew said warningly. 'I'm not sending you on a pub crawl.'

Barnes came into the office. 'All the women identified our dead man as the man who exposed himself to them, sir.'

'Excellent.' Matthew nodded, then glared at Pinder. 'Get going,' he ordered, and the young detective constable went sulkily out as Denham joined Barnes at the door.

'I found Felicity Monckton, sir,' Denham declared. 'She's staying at her parents and has confirmed she's filing for divorce on the grounds of cruelty. And listen to this. According to her father, Monckton tried to strangle her.'

Chapter Thirty-Nine

PC Rudd kicked a pebble along the pavement and watched it tumble over and over until it came to rest in the crack between two paving stones. He stamped on it, forcing it down to get stuck, imagining it was Pinder's face. Pinder hadn't had to talk to him like that yesterday, making him feel like an idiot. He'd only wanted to see what the Yard was sending CID. He'd been showing an interest, that was all.

And the goings-on in CID were so interesting. Not like downstairs, where nothing happened except for tramps pissing all over the place, drunks throwing up and prostitutes shouting obscenities. Rudd wanted to be a detective, but every application he made to become one got knocked back by Mullinger. Not detective material; that was Old Mouldy's excuse. How did Mullinger know that? Rudd knew he would make a far better detective than know-it-all Gary Pinder if only he was given the chance.

Rudd turned off the high street and headed towards the railway station to continue his patrol. He nodded greetings to passers-by as he went, but no one stopped him today and he was pleased about that, not being in the mood for chatting. He ran his eyes over the few cars parked at the station, admiring the lines of the more expensive motors. That was something to be said about Craynebrook. Its affluent residents could afford the best. Feeling a twinge of envy, Rudd moved around the cars, stroking the bodywork of some in appreciation at their sleekness.

He halted and stared at a blue Morris Cowley parked on the far side from where he stood. He knew CID were looking for a blue Morris Cowley; Uniform had been told to be on the lookout for one. Rudd hurried over to the vehicle. His breath caught in his throat as he saw the right headlight hanging from its casing. There was a wide dent in the bonnet. He pulled out his notebook and checked the registration number he had written down at that morning's parade. The plate bore the same number.

Rudd ran into the railway station and demanded to use the telephone. When the connection was made, Sergeant Turkel answered with, 'Craynebrook Police Station.'

'Sarge,' Rudd shouted into the mouthpiece. 'It's me. Sam. I need you to tell Inspector Stannard I've found the Morris Cowley.'

Edna wiped away the yolk that dribbled down her chin with the tea towel she'd draped over her chest and turned over the page of her newspaper.

Her eyes scanned the page, looking for the most interesting headlines first. She read the article about the case of mistaken identity, skipped over the one about a woman whose roof had fallen in while she taking a bath, and caught the one at the bottom of the page with the headline that read: MAN KILLED IN HIT-AND-RUN ACCIDENT. She dipped her triangle of toast in her boiled egg and read on.

"A man was killed in a hit-and-run accident on Thursday night in Craynebrook, northeast London. The victim was

taken to hospital but declared dead on arrival. He has been identified as Frank Arthur Crowther. A Craynebrook man, rumoured to be a member of the local Liberal Party, is helping the police with their enquiries."

'WILF!' Edna screeched.

There was a running in the hall and her bedroom door burst open. Wilf, still in his pyjamas and panting, cried, 'What is it?'

She thrust the newspaper at him. 'Bottom of the page,' she gasped, and moved her tray to the side.

'A woman was having a bath when—'

'Not that one,' she snapped. 'Underneath.'

Wilf sat down on the edge of the bed. 'A man was killed in a hit-and-run accident...' His voice trailed off as he read. 'Bugger me!'

'Frank Crowther,' Edna nodded. 'He's blooming dead. And did you read the next bit?'

Wilf returned his startled gaze to the newspaper. 'Crayne-brook man... Liberal Party... police.'

'That's Monckton. The police have got on to him.'

Wilf threw the newspaper aside and put his head in his hands.

'They'll be here again,' Edna said. 'They'll be coming for you.'

'Why would Monckton kill Frank?'

'Does it matter? It's all over, Wilf. We ain't going to get no more money from him, not once the police have him. And then they'll find you and you'll go inside. Oh, I knew this would happen.'

'No, Ma,' Wilf said, slamming his hand down on the blan-kets. 'I ain't going back to prison. I've got to get out of here.' He hurried out of her bedroom.

Edna threw back the bedclothes and padded after him. 'Where are we going to go?'

Wilf was pulling on his trousers over his pyjamas. 'We ain't going anywhere.'

'You what?' Edna said, gaping at him.

Wilf dragged on a shirt. 'I'm getting out of here. Sorry, Ma, but you'll slow me down. And besides, the coppers ain't going to bother you. You ain't done nothing and they can't prove you have.'

'You're going without me?'

Wilf's face hardened. 'Now, don't start. You'll be all right. You managed fine when I was inside. And as soon as things quiet down, I'll be back. Or I'll send for you. One or the other.'

He was fully dressed now, and he grabbed his suitcase and threw all his belongings into it. Wilf pushed her out of his way and thundered down the stairs. Before Edna could utter another word, he was out of the front door and making his way down the road as fast as his legs could carry him.

Matthew put one finger to the broken right headlight of the Morris Cowley and watched as it swung on its wire. He turned his gaze to the round emblem that was bent backwards and to the dented bonnet. He took out his handkerchief and used it to try the handle of the driver's door. It was locked. He did the same with the rear door, while Barnes copied his movements on the other side.

'All locked, sir,' Barnes said.

'What kind of thief bothers to lock the doors after him?' Matthew wondered. 'I want this photographed in situ, then have it driven to the station.' He headed into the ticket hall and nodded at the stationmaster, who had been peering out of the window at the police activity. 'Mr Scott?'

'I'm Scott,' the stationmaster said. 'What's going on?'

'Am I right in thinking you live here?'

'Yeah, up there.' Scott jerked his thumb at the ceiling. 'Me and the wife. What's going on with that car?'

'What can you tell me about the car?'

'It's in a right state, ain't it?'

'Do you know who it belongs to?'

'I know whose it is. He's parked it here before. But I don't know his name.'

Matthew took the Liberal pamphlet out of his pocket and showed Scott the group photograph on the front page. 'See the face that's ringed? Do you recognise him?'

Scott peered at the photograph. 'That's him. Who is he?'

'Do you know when the car was parked there?'

'It was after midnight, so that would have been early yesterday morning. I got out of bed and looked out the window and saw it pull in through the gates. I didn't see that it was all bashed up, though. It was too dark for that.'

'Did you see who got out of the car?'

'It was him.' Mr Scott pointed at the pamphlet. 'That fella you showed me.'

Matthew held up the pamphlet again and pointed to Monckton in the photograph. 'You're sure it was this man? You said it was dark.'

'It was too dark to see the front of the car but he sort of looked up as he got out of the car, and I saw his face. It was definitely him.'

With a smile, Matthew tucked the pamphlet back into his pocket. 'Thank you very much, Mr Scott.'

Chapter Forty

Matthew pulled out the chair in the interview room and sat down opposite Monckton.

Monckton looked in rather better shape than he had when they'd first met; he'd had a wash and a shave, put on clean clothes and was perhaps rather more sober, though Matthew couldn't be sure. He noticed Monckton's trembling hands and wondered just how much of a drinker the would-be politician was. The solicitor he had engaged was neat, rather compact, and even gave Matthew the thinnest of smiles.

'Do you know why you're here, Mr Monckton?' Matthew began when he saw Denham sitting next to him was ready with his notebook and pen.

'Something to do with my car,' Monckton sighed, as if he wasn't interested and the matter was entirely trivial.

'It is something to do with your car,' Matthew nodded, 'which we have now found.'

That got Monckton's attention. 'You've found it?' He looked frightened, but quickly regained his composure. He gave an awkward, humourless laugh. 'What kind of state is in? Wrecked, I imagine. Someone wanted to take it for a wild ride.' He laughed again, glancing at his solicitor. The solicitor didn't look up from his notepad.

'It is in a state,' Matthew said. 'There is rather a lot of damage from where it hit the man who now lies on a slab in the mortuary.' *Now try laughing*, he thought as Monckton's Adam's apple bobbed up and down.

'Yes, I remember you telling me the man died. It's terrible,' Monckton said, his fingers tapping frantically on the tabletop, 'to know my car was used to do that.' He shook his head. 'I don't want it back. I couldn't drive it again, not after it was used to do that.'

There it was again, the fake horror. Matthew didn't believe a word. 'When we spoke earlier,' he said, 'you claimed your car was stolen while you were in The Green Man pub in Graydon Heath.'

'Yes, that's right.'

'But you didn't report it stolen?'

The solicitor coughed. 'My client explained the reason for his failure to do so when he discovered the theft, inspector. It was his intention to report it stolen this morning when he was in a fit state.'

'Yes, he did explain that.' Matthew met Monckton's eye. 'Your car was found parked at the railway station, Mr Monckton. We have a witness who claims he saw you getting out of the car and running away.'

Monckton's eyes widened. He licked his dry lips. 'Well, that's ridiculous. No, I, er... no, that wasn't me.'

'It wasn't you?'

'No. It couldn't have been. Why would I park it at the railway station?' He appealed with a laugh to both Matthew and Denham. He was disconcerted when neither of them smiled.

Matthew slid the mortuary photograph of Crowther from the file and set it in front of Monckton. 'I showed you this photograph before and asked if you recognised the man.'

Monckton barely looked at the picture. 'I remember. I told you I didn't know him.'

'We've identified him. His name was Frank Crowther. He was recently released from prison and was the man who had been indecently exposing himself to women in Graydon Heath and here in Craynebrook.' Matthew let this information sink into Monckton's brain before continuing. 'He's also the man who collected the envelope you left behind the Dickens' novels in Craynebrook Library this past Thursday. I have another witness who states you've been leaving an envelope behind those novels in the library on the fourth Wednesday of every month for at least a year, ever since she's been working there.' The veins on Monckton's neck were standing out. He kept swallowing as if there was a lump in his throat he couldn't push down. 'What was in the envelopes, Mr Monckton?'

'I don't know.'

'Was it money?'

'No.'

'Then what was it?'

'I just said I didn't leave any envelopes—'

'No, you just said it wasn't money in the envelopes.'

'That's not what I meant.'

'To clarify, inspector, if I may,' the solicitor said. 'My client denies leaving envelopes in the library.'

'We have a witness who has identified your client. She has seen him leaving an envelope.'

'How did this witness identify my client, inspector?'

'She was shown a photograph of him,' Matthew said uneasily. He knew where the solicitor was going with this.

'I'd like to see the photograph.' The solicitor held out his hand and Matthew handed him the pamphlet showing the ringed headshot of Monckton on the front cover. 'Ah, yes, I see. This is a rather blurry image from 1923. Seven years ago, inspector. I think you'd agree a man may change a great deal in seven years. So, your identification using this photograph is something of a reach. Did you use the same photograph to gain an identification from your railway station witness?'

'Yes,' Matthew said, tight-lipped.

'Then, I'm afraid those identifications are worthless.'

'The photograph is perfectly clear,' Matthew insisted. 'It is your client.'

'According to you,' the solicitor smiled. 'I'm afraid your opinion on the matter is not quite good enough.'

Matthew put the pamphlet back into the file. 'Then your client will have to take part in an identity parade. So he can be formally identified.'

'No, no, I can't,' Monckton said to his solicitor. 'They can't make me, can they?'

The solicitor patted Monckton on the arm. 'Inspector, as my client is not under arrest, he cannot be forced to take part in an identity parade.'

'I'm confused as to why your client would refuse,' Matthew said. 'If he's as innocent as he claims, he should have no objection to having the matter cleared up.'

The solicitor chuckled. 'I'm afraid you're not going to get very far with that kind of bullying, inspector. My client is perfectly within his rights not to take part if he does not wish to do so and he does not have to offer an explanation.'

Matthew met the solicitor's eye, holding it for a long moment. *Call his bluff*, Matthew's brain was urging. He knew the solicitor would advise Monckton that he didn't need to answer any more questions and the only way Matthew could keep him here was by arresting him. But was he ready to do that? The solicitor was quite right. Identification by means of an old, blurry photograph would cut no ice in a courtroom, so he had to get Monckton identified properly.

He quickly weighed up the pros and cons of arresting Monckton now. On the pro side, Matthew was convinced Monckton had mown down Frank Crowther and he was certain Miss McKenna and Mr Scott would identify him. But on the con side, Matthew hadn't got his head straight about Monckton's involvement in Hannah Moore's murder, if he was involved, and that was a problem, for he still couldn't be sure whether the Moore murder was related to the killing of Marjorie Kirby. Was Monckton guilty only of running down Frank Crowther? Or was he guilty of murdering two women as well?

Matthew reached a decision and got to his feet. 'Stand up, please, Mr Monckton.'

Monckton stared in confusion at his solicitor, who sighed and nodded for him to agree. Monckton got to his feet and swallowed nervously as he met Matthew's eye.

'Mr Monckton,' Matthew said, 'I'm arresting you on suspicion of causing death by dangerous driving.'

'I've booked Mr Monckton and put him in a cell,' Denham said as Matthew poured himself a mug of tea. 'Here are his prints.'

Matthew looked at the page of black ink prints Denham was holding out to him. 'Check them against the biscuit tin prints,' he said, and sipped at his tea as Denham did so.

After a few minutes, Denham shook his head. 'No match, sir.'

Matthew cursed. 'And I thought we were getting somewhere.'

'We are,' Denham said encouragingly. 'The flasher's

dead, so he won't be pestering any other women, and we've got the man who killed him in custody.'

'So, just a burglar and murderer to find,' Matthew mocked. 'I'm sorry, Denham,' he said as the sergeant's face coloured. 'You're right. We should be grateful for small mercies.'

Denham nodded. 'Also, Sergeant Turkel told me to tell you Mr Kirby's down in the lobby, asking to see you. Shall I tell him you're busy?'

Matthew considered for a moment, then shook his head. 'No, I better see him. Meanwhile, get Monckton's house searched. Anything that doesn't look right, I don't care how small, I want noted.'

'Yes, sir,' Denham said.

'Right.' Matthew put down his mug with a sigh. 'If anyone wants me, I'll be in the lobby.'

Sergeant Turkel turned as Matthew entered and silently inclined his head towards the wooden bench beneath the noticeboard. Mr Kirby was sitting on the bench, eyes fixed on the floor. He was neat and well-groomed; only his haggard, grey face bore any sign of grief.

Matthew smoothed down his tie, straightened his jacket and headed over to him. 'Mr Kirby?'

Mr Kirby looked up, a little startled as if he had been miles away, then got to his feet. 'Is there any news? Have you found the man who killed my wife?'

'I'm afraid not, Mr Kirby. Not just yet.'

The haggard expression changed a little. There was confusion there, and something else. Disbelief? 'Nothing at all?' he asked.

'These things take time—'

'Are you even trying to find him?'

'Of course we are, Mr Kirby,' Matthew said, feeling sweat prickling his upper lip. 'I understand why it may seem as if—'

'Look at this.' Mr Kirby held up a newspaper and pointed to a headline. 'See what it says there? A hit-and-run accident. That's what you're investigating, isn't it? Not my wife's murder at all.'

'Your wife's murder is our top priority—'

'They why isn't there an article in the newspaper saying 'Police Hot on the Heels of Mrs Kirby's Murderer'?' He was speaking very loudly and others in the lobby were turning to stare. 'My wife's been dead less than a week and she's already old news.'

'That's not true—' Matthew began.

'I suppose she's not interesting enough, is she? There's no scandal about her. Just a working-class woman stupid enough to let a murderer into her home. Not like toffs getting bumped off by a wronged woman. You won't get your name in the 'paper for my Marjorie, will you?'

'Mr Kirby, please,' Matthew begged. Why the hell did everyone think he wanted to see his name in print?

'Please, what?' Mr Kirby spat. 'Please be quiet because I'm making a scene? I'll make a bloody scene, I promise you, if you don't find the bastard who killed my wife.' He pushed Matthew aside and stormed out of the lobby.

Matthew watched him go, conscious of the eyes turned upon him. Doing his best to avoid them, he made his way back up to CID.

'How was Mr Kirby, sir?' Denham asked as he entered, then saw Matthew's face. 'Oh. Not good, I take it?'

'Not good at all, Denham,' Matthew said. 'He thinks we're not trying hard enough to find his wife's killer.'

Denham made a noise of annoyance. 'Typical,' he muttered.

Matthew didn't reply. The encounter with Mr Kirby had upset him a good deal, not because he resented the accusation that they weren't doing their job, but because he felt Mr Kirby had had a point. He turned as he heard running in the corridor outside. Barnes burst through the door, trying to catch his breath.

'Sorry, sir,' he panted as he nearly ran into Matthew. 'But I've got an address for Frank Crowther.'

Chapter Forty-One

Stanley Tompkins was barring the door.

'You can either allow us to search the house, Mr Tompkins,' Matthew said wearily, 'or I'll arrest you for obstructing a police officer in the execution of his duty. Your choice.'

Tompkins cursed and let his arm fall to his side. 'Some bleeding choice. All right, then. Come in if you must, but I don't know what you expect to find.'

Matthew pushed past him into the hall, stepping back as Barnes and Rudd followed. They spread out, Barnes going into the front room and Rudd up the stairs. 'You've had a Mr Frank Crowther staying here?'

'That's right. Is it him you're after? Well, you're out of luck. I ain't seen him for days.'

'I know you haven't,' Matthew said. 'He's been lying on a slab in Craynebrook's mortuary since Thursday night.'

'You what?' Tompkins's mouth fell open. 'Frank's dead?'

'He was hit by a car. The driver was particularly keen on making sure he was dead.'

'Bloody hell. I've got to sit down,' Tompkins declared and shuffled into the front room, falling into an armchair that creaked beneath his weight. 'I can't believe it,' he said as Matthew followed. 'Why would anyone want Frank dead?'

'You tell me,' Matthew said, looking around the room and deciding it wouldn't be wise to take a seat. The front room was filthy and there was a very unpleasant odour he couldn't place lingering in the air. 'Did he ever mention an Andrew Monckton to you?'

'No, I've never heard of him.'

'What about Edna Gadd?'

Tompkins shook his head.

'Do you know what your friend did when he went out?'

Tompkins made a face. 'You've got his record, ain't you? You know what Frank was.'

'A flasher.'

Tompkins nodded. 'He said he couldn't help it. Said it was a compulsion with him.'

'Did he tell you what he did about his compulsion?' When Tompkins didn't speak, Matthew's tone grew harsher. 'You might as well tell me, Mr Tompkins, if you don't want to spend the night in a police cell.'

'All right, all right. Christ, you lot never get off people's backs, do you? Frank came back a couple of times and told me he'd flashed a tart. Said he'd frightened the whatsit out of 'em.'

'Is that all he said?'

'What more do you want?'

'Did he ever attack the women he flashed?'

'Attack 'em?' Tompkins frowned. 'Nah, he never said nothing about doing that. And anyway, I don't think that was Frank's style. He just liked having a bit of fun with 'em. Seeing them shocked and watching him do it. That's what he liked. And if you ask me, the women like it too. All that fuss they make is just for show.'

Matthew remembered the terror he'd seen on Miss

256

McKenna's face after Crowther had flashed her and that was still there days later, and wanted to punch Tompkins on the jaw. 'How did Crowther get his money? I'm assuming he didn't have a job?'

'Who would take Frank on with his record?'

'But you charged him to stay here?'

'Course I charged him. I ain't a bleeding charity.'

'So, how did Crowther get his money, Mr Tompkins?'

'I dunno,' Tompkins shrugged. 'He was doing favours for someone. Getting rid of stuff. You know, moving it on.'

'Fencing? What kind of stuff?'

'Silverware. Candlesticks. Jewellery. Frank knew people who'd pay for that.'

'He didn't steal the silverware himself?'

'Nah. Picking pockets was Frank's limit.'

'So, who was he getting the stuff from?'

'SIR!' Rudd thundered down the stairs, carrying what looked like a leather briefcase. 'I found this in the small bedroom at the front.'

Tompkins nodded at Matthew's unspoken enquiry. 'That's Frank's room.'

Rudd turned the case around to face Matthew. Beneath the handle was a brass plate with an inscription. Matthew peered at the writing. It read, *To Katherine and William Hayden. Wishing you a happy future together. 8th August 1919*. He opened the case. Inside was a full canteen of silver cutlery. He glanced at Tompkins. 'This was Crowther's?'

'Well, it ain't mine,' Tompkins sniffed. 'The other fella gave it to him to pass on, but Frank said he was going to keep it. I said to him, what you going to do with all those knives and forks when you can't even eat proper? But he laughed and said it made him feel like a toff just having them.'

'Who's the other fella, Mr Tompkins?' Matthew asked.

'I only saw him the once. Ugly bugger, he was. Long

yellow teeth and blond hair, almost white. Frank called him Wilf.'

'I've brought Mrs Gadd in, sir,' Denham said as Matthew hung up the telephone receiver and rubbed his ear to persuade some feeling back into it. 'She's in Interview Room Three.'

'How is she?' Matthew asked.

'Spitting feathers,' Denham said with a smile. 'Gave me an earful about how we've got it in for her.'

'Any sign of the son when you picked her up?'

'No, she was alone in the house. But I had a word with a neighbour and he said there'd been a man living there for the past three weeks.'

'Description?'

'Short. White-blond hair. Ugly.'

'That sounds like Wilfred Gadd,' Matthew nodded. 'Get the place searched.'

'Yes, sir. Oh, that reminds me. Nothing's turned up at Monckton's that's out of the ordinary.'

Matthew sighed and rose. 'Has Mrs Gadd asked for a solicitor?'

'No, sir.'

'Then we can get started. Barnes,' he said as he passed the detective constable's desk, 'you're with me.'

They made their way to Interview Room Three. Matthew told the constable who had been standing guard inside the door he could go and sat down at the table across from Edna. He was shocked by how ill she looked. Her skin had turned an ashen hue and seemed to hang from her jaws.

'I'm sorry I've had to drag you here, Mrs Gadd,' Matthew said, 'but you weren't entirely truthful at our last meeting.'

Edna folded her arms over her chest. 'I don't know what

you're talking about. And as for dragging me here, well..., I've been in worse places than this.'

Matthew didn't doubt it. He'd grown up with women like Edna Gadd, women who would belt their children for getting under their feet and who could punch harder than their husbands, but underneath that toughness was a fierce devotion to their family. They might argue like cats and dogs, but as soon as an outsider threatened them, they would close ranks and form an impenetrable wall. Matthew suspected Edna Gadd wouldn't be easy to break.

'Then, let's make a start,' he said. 'Where's Wilf?'

'I told you. My son's dead.'

Matthew shook his head. 'Wilf's not dead. He wasn't killed in France. Until the fifteenth of last month, he was in Pentonville prison serving a fourteen-month sentence for battery and burglary. And when he came out, he was living with you. So, where is he?'

'I don't know,' Edna declared. 'And even if I did, I wouldn't tell you.'

'It didn't take him long to get back to his old habits, did it? He's burgled at least two houses in Craynebrook since he got out of prison. What else has he been doing?'

'He ain't been doing nothing. I ain't telling you nothing about him.'

'All right, you can tell me what you've been doing.'

'I ain't been doing nothing.'

'You've been doing something at the library.'

'Oh, not that again.' Edna rolled her eyes. 'I get books out. I take books back when I've read 'em. That's it.'

'Does the name Andrew Monckton mean anything to you?'

A flicker of alarm crossed her face and Matthew knew the name was known to her. Edna leaned back in her chair and turned her face away.

'What's in the envelope he leaves for you to pick up? Is it money?'

Edna took a deep breath and put a fist to her heart.

'Is Wilf involved? Or is it just you and Frank Crowther?'

She glared at Matthew. 'I ain't got nothing to do with that dirty bugger.'

'Well, I know Wilf worked with Crowther. He got Crowther to fence the goods he stole, didn't he? So, did he bring Crowther in on the business with Monckton? Is that it?' Matthew waited for her to answer. When she didn't, he carried on. 'Is it blackmail, the business with Monckton? Was it money in the envelopes you picked up? Was Wilf and Crowther blackmailing him? Or was it something else your son and Crowther were up to? Like attacking women together? Trying to strangle them?'

Edna turned on him. 'Now, you shut your mouth. My Wilf would never do something like that.'

'But he did do something like that, didn't he? Wilf beat up a woman so badly she was in hospital for eight weeks.'

'He didn't mean to do that. She hit him. If she'd just left him alone, he wouldn't have touched her.'

'He was in the lady's home, robbing her, and she was sixty-six, Mrs Gadd. That's about your age, isn't it? Did Wilf really need to hurt her so badly?'

'It was a mistake.'

'Obviously, as it put him in prison for fourteen months. And coincidentally, he comes out and women are being attacked in Craynebrook, where he's busy breaking and entering.'

'No,' she said, and Matthew heard her breathing growing louder, more strained. He was getting to her. He just had to keep on pushing. 'You ain't pinning those attacks on Wilf. He's got nothing to do with them. If it was anyone, it was that Crowther.'

'It's easy to blame a dead man.'

'I don't know he did them,' Edna said, wincing in pain. 'I'm just saying if you're looking for someone to blame for 'em, you should be looking at him. Not my Wilf. You leave my son alone. He ain't... he...'

Edna's eyes suddenly widened. She stopped breathing. Her right hand went to her left arm. She clutched at it as her face contorted in a rictus of pain. Matthew watched in horror as Edna tumbled from her chair onto the floor.

'Jesus Christ,' he breathed and dragged the table out of the way. 'Call for an ambulance,' he shouted at Barnes, who rushed out, yelling for Sergeant Copley. Matthew lifted Edna's head onto his lap. 'Don't die,' he begged. 'Please, please, don't die.'

Matthew lit a cigarette, waving the match until the flame went out and tossing it aside. He took one puff, two, then jumped up from the bench, unable to sit still.

'You bloody fool,' he snarled at himself. Hadn't he thought Edna Gadd hadn't looked well the moment he walked into the interview room? He should have got her a doctor then, made sure she was fit to be questioned. Instead, he'd just ploughed on, determined to get answers to his questions, and this is where that approach had got him. Waiting in a hospital corridor to find out if she was going to live.

A nurse came out of the room where Edna had been taken. 'What's happening?' he demanded.

'There's nothing to tell you yet. The doctor will talk to you when he's ready,' she assured him and walked away down the corridor.

As she turned at the end, Mullinger brushed past her and headed for Matthew. Mullinger was in a dinner jacket and bowtie, and Matthew wondered what social-climbing function he'd been pulled out of.

'Well?' Mullinger asked.

'There's no news yet, sir,' Matthew said.

'What the hell happened, Stannard?'

'A heart attack, I think. She just collapsed at the table.'

'Were you being rough with her?'

'I was asking her questions, sir,' he said indignantly. 'That's all.'

Mullinger put a handkerchief to his forehead. 'God, this is all I need. Another death in custody.'

'She isn't dead,' Matthew pointed out.

Mullinger didn't seem to hear. 'After the Norman Kelly incident—'

'This is entirely different. Kelly hanged himself in his cell. Mrs Gadd was ill.'

'Then you shouldn't have been questioning her,' Mullinger barked.

'I know I shouldn't,' Matthew shouted back. He took another drag of his cigarette and said in a quieter tone, 'I know, sir.'

Mullinger glared at him but didn't say another word. He sat down on the bench, putting his hat next to him, taking up the rest of the space. Matthew paced, finishing his cigarette quickly and delving into his pocket to get another one from the packet when the door opened once more and the doctor came out.

'Is she alive?' Matthew demanded.

'She is,' the doctor said, 'but she's in a very bad way.'

'Was it a heart attack?' Mullinger asked.

'Yes, and rather a bad one. But we've made her comfortable for the moment. Does she have any family? They should be informed.'

'Stannard?' Mullinger asked.

'She has a son,' Matthew said, 'but we don't know where he is.'

'You should find him,' the doctor said meaningfully.

'Why can't we find the son?' Mullinger asked as the doctor left.

'He knows we're looking for him,' Matthew said, 'so he's done a runner.'

'Why are we looking for him? I haven't had any reports on a Gadd.'

'He's only come to my notice today. It's likely Gadd's responsible for the recent burglaries and he's connected with Crowther, the hit-and-run victim and Monckton, the driver of the car. It's possible he was blackmailing Monckton.'

'Over what?'

'I don't know,' Matthew sighed irritably and looked at the closed door. 'That was a question I needed Mrs Gadd to answer.'

Chapter Forty-Two

Matthew watched as Denham led the ten men out of the back door and made them form a straight line.

'All ready, sir,' Denham said.

Matthew threw the stub of his cigarette away and went over to Miss McKenna, who had been standing out of sight with Sergeant Copley behind the cages kept for lost dogs. 'We're ready for you now, Miss McKenna. All you have to do is tell me if you recognise the man who comes into the library every fourth Wednesday of the month. You're perfectly safe,' he added as she bit her lip. She nodded and took Matthew's arm.

He led her over to the line-up. Miss McKenna walked along the line, looking sideways at each man. When she'd done this twice, she hurried back to Matthew.

'Fourth from the left,' she whispered.

Monckton was fourth from the left. 'You're sure?' Matthew asked.

Miss McKenna nodded. 'It's him. Definitely.'

'Thank you, Miss McKenna. You've been very brave. Now, Sergeant Denham will see you out.'

One down, Matthew thought, *one to go*. He ordered the

line of men to move, mixing them up so that this time, Monckton was sixth from the left. Denham poked his head out of the doorway. Matthew nodded and Denham brought Mr Scott into the yard.

'Mr Scott,' Matthew said, 'I just need you to identify, if you can, the man you saw getting out of the Morris Cowley parked in the railway station car park and running away.'

'That's him,' Mr Scott said without hesitation, pointing at Monckton. 'That's the one.'

'I need you to look carefully at every man, Mr Scott. Take your time.'

'I don't need to. It's him all right.'

'There's a procedure we have to go through,' Matthew explained patiently. 'So, please. Take a good look at each man.'

Grumbling under his breath, Mr Scott did as Matthew instructed. He peered into each man's face, then moved to stand beside Matthew.

'It's him, I tell you,' he said, pointing again at Monckton.

'Thank you, Mr Scott.' Matthew nodded at Denham to see him out and watched in satisfaction as Copley led the other men away. The solicitor couldn't argue with these positive identifications.

With no one yet telling him what to do, Monckton had remained where he was. His hands were shaking; he was, Matthew thought, probably in desperate need of a drink.

'Take Mr Monckton back to the cell,' Matthew said when Denham returned. 'And have the doctor give him the once-over. I want to make sure he's fit to be questioned.'

The doctor pronounced Monckton well enough to be interviewed and Matthew headed for the interview room.

'Well, Mr Monckton,' Matthew said, taking a seat at the

table. 'You've been formally identified by two witnesses. Do you have anything to say?'

'My client has no comment to—' The solicitor broke off as Monckton put a hand on his arm. He stared at Monckton in surprise.

'It will be good to tell it,' Monckton said. He groaned, tilting his face to the ceiling, and sank back in his chair. 'I'm so bloody tired of it all.'

'Tell what, Mr Monckton?' Matthew asked.

Monckton met Matthew's eye. 'It was me. I killed him.'

'You killed Frank Crowther?'

Monckton nodded. 'My car wasn't stolen. I was at The Green Man pub that night. I'd been there all evening, drinking. I drank a lot. I always drink a lot. Anyway, I was driving home and I saw him, Frank Crowther, rolling a cigarette as he crossed the road, and I thought, you bastard. I'm going to get you. So, I drove the car straight at him. He went down and he didn't move. I drove over him again and made sure he wasn't moving. It sobered me up, hitting him, enough so that I was able to work out my car would be a mess and questions would be asked, so I decided I would park it somewhere and claim it had been stolen. I parked it at the railway station and walked home. It was late and I didn't think anyone had seen me.'

'Mr Monckton,' the solicitor said, 'I really don't think you ought to say another word.'

'What does it matter now?' Monckton said wearily. He looked at Matthew. 'What more do you want to know?'

'Why did you kill Crowther?'

'Because he was blackmailing me. Had been for six years. Ever since Hannah.' Monckton fell quiet.

Matthew's heart beat faster as a piece of his puzzle seemed to fall into place. 'You were her lover?'

'If you can call it that. I was more of a plaything, as it turned out.'

'Did you kill her?'

'No, I didn't.'

Matthew frowned. 'But if you didn't kill her, why did you submit to blackmail?'

'Because I was there that night and somehow, that Crowther fellow knew it.'

'You were at the party?'

'At the party? No. I wasn't invited to the party. Not that I would have gone if I had been. I didn't like her friends. They weren't my sort of people. Some of them called themselves artists – writers and painters – but they were layabouts, mostly. I had hoped to see her that night after I came home, but when I heard them laughing and the music, I went to bed instead. But I wasn't sleeping well, and I woke up in the early hours and I couldn't hear anything from her house. The party was over. I was surprised because Hannah's parties usually went on till dawn. I had this idea she'd ended the party early because she'd taken one of her men friends to bed. She'd been cool with me for a few weeks and I was convinced she had someone else. She denied it, but I didn't believe her. I thought I'd catch her at it, so I climbed over the fence between our gardens and went into the house by the kitchen door. I knew it would be open. Hannah never locked her doors. I went up to her bedroom and saw she was alone in the bed. At first, I thought she was asleep, but then I looked a little closer and saw...' He closed his eyes at the memory. 'I saw she was dead. I hurried back to my house. I should have called the police, I suppose, but I knew how it would look.'

'You mean the police would suspect you?' Matthew asked.

'That, but also how guilty I'd look in the public's eye. I was just getting started in politics and I didn't want to do anything that would scupper my chances of becoming an MP. It would get out that I'd been seeing a married woman, and a married woman who did drugs...' He shook his head. 'The 'papers would have had a field day. So, I kept quiet. I didn't say a word. And then the letter arrived.'

'What did it say?'

'It said 'I saw you. I know you killed Hannah Moore.' And an instruction to put twenty pounds in the library on the fourth Wednesday of every month or else the police would come knocking.' Monckton shrugged. 'So, I paid the money. I've been paying it ever since.'

'Did you know who was blackmailing you?'

'May I?' Monckton pointed at Matthew's packet of cigarettes.

Matthew shook a stick out for him and lit it.

Monckton blew out a plume of smoke. 'Not then. Not until a week ago when I received another letter saying the price of silence had gone up. I now had to pay fifty pounds a month.' He shook his head. 'I didn't have the money. I put the twenty in the usual place and included a note saying I couldn't pay what he was asking and begging him to under-stand. It didn't work. I was sitting in the park when that Crowther sat down beside me and told me I had to pay up.' He took another drag. 'So, I forged my wife's signature on a cheque and drew out a hundred pounds from the bank so I could pay the extra thirty. I knew it was only putting the problem off for a little while, but I didn't know what else to do. And then I saw Crowther crossing the street. After every-thing I've told you, is it any wonder I killed him?'

'So, where does Edna Gadd fit in?' Matthew asked.

Monckton frowned. 'Who's Edna Gadd?'

'Wilfred Gadd?'

'I don't know them. Who are they?'

'I believe Edna Gadd has been collecting your hush

money for the past six years, possibly in collaboration with her son.'

Monckton leant forward. 'Are you telling me it wasn't that Crowther fellow who's been blackmailing me?'

'It isn't clear yet,' Matthew said, gathering up his papers. 'You'll be charged with the murder of Frank Crowther and your confession typed. You'll need to read and sign that it's correct. For now, though, Mr Monckton, you'll be returned to your cell.'

'Excellent result, sir,' Denham said as he and Matthew returned to CID.

'Yes, it is,' Matthew agreed, allowing himself a smile, which dropped off his face as soon as he saw Mullinger standing by his desk. 'See if anything has come in on Wilfred Gadd,' he said to Denham before heading for the superintendent. 'Did you want to see me, sir?'

'I want an update, Stannard.' Mullinger's tone implied irritation that he'd had to seek Matthew out.

'Monckton's just confessed to killing Frank Crowther, sir. He believed Crowther had been blackmailing him for the past six years.'

'He was being blackmailed for what?'

'For killing Hannah Moore. Monckton was at the house that night, after the guests had left, but he claims he found Mrs Moore already dead. Then he got a blackmail note, saying the writer knew he'd killed her and to pay up to keep it quiet. He paid because he was worried his innocence wouldn't be believed and his political career would be over before it started.'

'Do you believe him?'

'I'm not ready to believe him just yet,' Matthew said. 'He's a drunk, and according to his father-in-law, he tried to strangle his wife the other day when they were having a row. Now, that could be something or it could be nothing. I want to hold onto him while I conduct further enquiries.'

'But your feeling is?'

Matthew was surprised by the question. Mullinger had never struck him as a man who appreciated gut instincts. 'That's he's telling the truth about Hannah Moore.'

Mullinger tutted. 'What about the Kirby killing? I trust you haven't forgotten about that?'

'No, I haven't forgotten,' Matthew said. 'I'm working on it.'

'Good. At least I can tell the Press we've caught one murderer.' Mullinger reached into his pocket and drew out a folded paper. He handed it to Matthew. 'The court order to interview Oliver Moore.'

'Thank you, sir. Is there any news on Mrs Gadd, sir?' Matthew asked as the superintendent headed for the door.

'I spoke to the doctor this morning,' Mullinger said. 'There's no change in her condition and he's not hopeful of an improvement. Have we located her son yet?'

Matthew shook his head. 'We're still looking for him.'

Denham came in as Mullinger left. 'Was that the Super asking about Wilfred Gadd, sir?'

'Yes. Do you have something?'

'I've got his record.' Denham waved a file. 'A few convictions for pick-pocketing when he was young. Nothing during the war. Presumably, he was serving. A few charges for robbery in the early twenties. Then it all goes quiet. Either he stopped or he just got better at his work and didn't get caught. Then December 1928 comes the conviction we know about when he got locked up. Released a few weeks ago. Used to live in Whitechapel before moving to Leytonstone. But this is the interesting thing, sir. I've got hold of his prison record. Apparently, he wasn't allowed to go into the washrooms without supervision because he would break the mirrors. The prison doctor reckoned it was a trauma caused by the war. He's definitely our burglar, sir.'

'But is he our killer?' Matthew wondered.

'The mirror was smashed at the Kirbys,' Denham pointed out.

'And at the Moores.'

'It's obvious, then, isn't it, sir?'

Matthew shook his head. 'I wish it was.' He got to his feet. 'I've got the court order to interview Oliver Moore. Let's get over to Driscoll's Care Home and see what he's been up to.'

Chapter Forty-Three

Dr Avery rose from behind his desk when Matthew and Denham were shown into his office. 'This is harassment, inspector. I had hoped I'd made my position clear at our last meeting.'

Matthew held up the paper Mullinger had given him. 'A court order, Dr Avery. So you see, I am going to question Mr Moore.'

Dr Avery snatched the paper from Matthew's hand and quickly scanned the text. 'I do see,' he said stiffly. 'Then I wish it to be on record that I strongly advise against subjecting Mr Moore to questioning and strenuously object to your actions, inspector. If Mr Moore's mental health suffers from your questioning, I'll be holding the police entirely responsible.'

'It's noted, Dr Avery,' Matthew said.

'And I insist on being present during your questioning.'

'That's fine by me.'

'Very well.' Dr Avery handed back the court order. 'I believe Mr Moore is in the day room.'

Matthew put out a hand. 'Before we see Mr Moore,

doctor, can you tell me if you keep a record of your residents' comings and goings?'

'Yes, we keep a log.'

'I'd like to see it, please.'

Dr Avery's mouth contorted in irritation, but he put his head outside his office door and spoke to his secretary. She came in with a green ledger and held it out to Dr Avery, but he flicked his hand at Matthew and the secretary gave it to him.

Matthew set it down on Avery's desk. He took out his notebook and flipped to the page where he had made a note of all the dates on which the attacks had occurred. Oliver Moore, Matthew saw, had been out of the care home for all of them. He closed the book and handed it to the secretary with a thank you.

'Satisfied, inspector?' Dr Avery asked.

'Yes, thank you. I'll see Mr Moore now.'

Dr Avery strode out into the hall, Matthew and Denham following at his heels. Oliver Moore was sitting by the window when the three men entered the day room. Dr Avery went up to him and put a hand on his shoulder.

'Oliver, there's a policeman here who would like to talk with you.'

Matthew kept his eyes on Oliver and saw the older man's jaw tighten and veins stand out on his neck. He neither looked up nor turned around but watched Matthew draw near out of the corner of his eyes.

'Mr Moore, I'm Detective Inspector Stannard,' Matthew said, pulling up a chair and setting it down in front of Oliver. 'I need to ask you some questions. Will you talk to me?'

'Yes, if you want.'

'Thank you. I see from the home's logbook that you go out every day.'

'Yes. I go for a walk.'

'And sometimes of an evening, too?'

'Sometimes.'

'Where do you go when you go out?'

Oliver shrugged. 'I just walk. No particular place.'

'Do you walk into Graydon Heath? Into the town?'

Oliver frowned. 'I think I may have done, now and then.'

'What about Craynebrook? Do you go walking there?'

'I don't know. I just wander around when I go out. I don't plan to walk anywhere in particular.'

'Do you meet anyone when you're out for a walk?'

Oliver shifted in his seat. 'Why are you asking me these questions? What have I done?'

'You haven't done anything, Oliver,' Dr Avery interjected.

Matthew held up a hand to silence him. Dr Avery's mouth tightened at the impudence. 'Do you meet women on your walks?'

Oliver stiffened. 'I don't go out to meet women, inspector. What kind of a man do you think I am?'

'What kind of a man do you think I'm implying you are?'

'Inspector!' Dr Avery cried as Oliver's hands curled into fists.

Matthew ignored him. 'Do you know an Andrew Monckton?'

'Yes,' Oliver said, obviously surprised by the question. 'He was a neighbour of ours. Many years ago.'

'Mr Monckton has recently admitted he was having an affair with your wife in the period before her death. Were you aware of this affair?'

Oliver rose and turned away. 'I won't have you talking about Hannah like that.'

'Were you aware of the affair, Mr Moore?' Matthew pressed.

'My wife did not have an affair. She was not that kind of woman.'

'What kind of a woman?'

'You're painting her as some sort of whore.'

'You don't care for those kind of women?'

'Of course I don't. No decent man does.'

'They offend you? When you see them on the street?'

'I try not to notice them, inspector.'

Dr Avery leaned over Matthew's shoulder. 'You're upsetting him, inspector,' he whispered in his ear.

'I can see that,' Matthew returned quietly. He waited until the doctor had retreated before continuing. 'Where did you go on the night of your wife's murder, Mr Moore?'

'Inspector!' the doctor cried again as Oliver spun around and gripped the back of an armchair, his mouth open in horror.

'Dr Avery, I'd appreciate it if you kept quiet,' Matthew said angrily. 'Mr Moore?'

'I don't want to talk about that,' Oliver said.

'Where did you go that night?'

'I didn't go anywhere. I was with my friend, Major Kirwin, at his flat in town.'

'Major Kirwin has admitted to me you and he parted shortly after dinner and that he doesn't know what time you returned to his flat.'

Oliver frowned. 'No, that's not true. He told the other policeman—'

'Did you return to Craynebrook that night? Did you go home?'

Oliver stared at him, his breath coming fast. 'I didn't...'

'You're confusing him, inspector,' Dr Avery said. 'I cannot allow you to continue.'

'You can't stop me, Dr Avery,' Matthew reminded him.

'I can stop you if you're endangering the health of my patient. I'm aware of the rough tricks policemen use to get their man, as I understand it's put, and I—'

Matthew had had enough. He jumped up and rounded on the doctor. 'I'm trying to find out whether your patient, doctor, has killed two women and attempted to murder four more. Now, I'm not using any tricks, rough or otherwise, to find that out, and if you try to obstruct me again, I shall instruct my sergeant there to place you under arrest. Is that clear?'

'This is outrageous,' Dr Avery blustered, stepping away from Matthew. 'That I should be so abused in my own—'

'No, no, no, no, NO!' Oliver cried. He put his fists to his temples and screwed up his eyes. He swayed, then straightened and glared at Matthew, a fierce stare that shocked him. Oliver raised his fists and lunged at Matthew, grabbing him by the lapels.

But Matthew was ready for him and held his ground, gripping his wrists and tugging while Denham grabbed Oliver around the waist and pulled him away. Oliver struggled, but Matthew and Denham were too much for him, and he was forced to release Matthew. Denham bundled Oliver to the floor.

'What are you doing?' someone cried.

Matthew, trying to catch his breath, turned to the young man standing in the doorway. 'Who the hell are you?' he demanded, too angry for courtesy.

'I'm Dominic Moore,' Dominic cried, staring in horror as Denham cuffed Oliver. 'Leave my father alone!'

Matthew checked his appearance in the mirror in Oliver's bedroom, making sure none of his suit's stitching had come apart in the struggle. He brushed himself down, straightened his tie and ran a hand over his hair to smooth it. What a bloody fiasco that had been.

Denham rapped on the open door. 'Mr Moore's been taken to the station, sir.'

Matthew nodded. 'What's Dr Avery doing?'

'He's shut himself in his office. Said something about police brutality and that he's washing his hands of the whole affair.' Denham sounded remarkably unconcerned.

'Then he's just made our job easier.' Matthew attempted a smile but couldn't quite manage it.

'It all got a bit rough in there, didn't it, sir?' Denham said, looking around the room. 'I wasn't expecting him to react like that. Still, he's in here for a reason, I suppose. Probably should be in a nuthouse, not a care home.'

Matthew opened the wardrobe door. 'What's the son doing?' he asked as he looked through the few clothes hanging up.

'Sitting in the day room. I think he's waiting for you.'

'Good. I need to question him.' Matthew sighed. He had been hoping to find a pair of brown overalls or an overcoat, flat cap and scarf among Oliver's possessions, evidence that would mark him out as the murderer of Marjorie Kirby and the attacker of Joanne Cooper and the other women, but the wardrobe contained only shirts and trousers. He moved to the chest of drawers.

'I reckon we've found our killer.' Denham said as he searched the drawers in the bedside cabinet. When Matthew didn't answer, he looked over at him. 'Don't you, sir?'

'He's certainly got a temper,' Matthew said, pulling open the bottom drawer and finding folded pullovers. He rummaged beneath them. His fingers touched something hard and smooth and he drew it out. It was a scrapbook rather like the one his mother kept. Pasted to the pages were newspaper clippings. 'Look at this,' he said to Denham. 'He's cut out and saved the newspaper articles about his wife's murder.'

Denham looked over Matthew's shoulder at the scrapbook. 'I reckon that proves it. Why would you keep articles about your wife's murder if you didn't do it?'

Matthew flipped over more pages. Not pasted in, but just slipped between the pages, were other documents – letters from Major Kirwin, birthday and Christmas cards from Georgina, and a few letters from Dominic, the last written on a letterhead from a P&O ship called the *SS Rahasy*. He closed the scrapbook, tucked it beneath his arm and turned to Denham.

'Let's go and talk to Dominic Moore.'

When Matthew entered the day room, he found Dominic sitting in an armchair, knees together, with a box of cigars upon his lap. The young man watched Matthew and Denham approach and waited until Matthew had sat down in the opposite armchair before speaking.

'Why have you taken my father away?'

'He's helping with our enquiries, Dominic,' Matthew said, thinking he looked so young and distraught, to address him as 'Mr Moore' seemed inappropriate. He reminded him so much of Georgie, not in looks, but in manner. Georgie, too, often seemed younger than his years and just as delicate, as if a puff of wind would blow him over.

'What enquiries?'

'Do you read the newspapers, Dominic? Do you know what's been happening in Craynebrook?'

'The murder, you mean?'

Matthew nodded. 'That, and the other attacks on women.'

'You think my father has something to do with those? You're mad.'

'I don't think so.'

'He's not involved,' Dominic insisted. 'He can't be. My

father would never do anything like that. He's never hurt anyone in his life.'

'He tried to hurt me,' Matthew pointed out. 'You saw that for yourself.'

'He was defending himself.'

'He attacked me because he didn't like what I was saying.'

Dominic looked down at the box of cigars. 'I was going to give him these as a present,' he muttered.

Matthew gestured to Denham to get his notebook out and make notes. 'I'm glad you're here, Dominic. I've been wanting to talk to you.'

'To me? Why?'

'I want to ask you about your mother.'

Dominic's face paled. 'I don't want to talk about her.'

'I understand it's difficult,' Matthew nodded, 'but it's also necessary. You weren't at home the night your mother died?'

'No, I was staying with my grandmother. Mother was having one of her parties and she didn't want me there.'

'Did she usually make you leave if she was having a party?'

'Yes. Sometimes I refused, but when I knew Father wasn't going to stay, I agreed to go to Grandma's.'

'Did you know who was going to be at her party?'

'Her usual friends.'

'Do you know if she had a particular friend she was planning on seeing that night?'

'What do you mean by particular friend?'

Matthew hesitated, not sure how to phrase it. He didn't find it easy asking a son about his mother's sex life. 'Someone she didn't want her other friends to know about. Someone she kept a secret.'

'Well,' Dominic said with a laugh, 'if she had a secret friend, I wouldn't have known about them, would I?'

'You didn't hear her say anything? Speak to anyone about them?'

'No.' There was irritation in Dominic's monosyllable.

'You were with your grandmother when she found your mother the next morning?'

'Yes. Grandma went into Mother's bedroom. She shouted at me to stay out when I tried to go in. I didn't know why.'

'Did you notice anything odd about the house when you returned?'

He shook his head. 'It looked like it always did after Mother's parties. A mess.'

'You didn't notice then that the house had been burgled?'

'No. Grandma made me go over the road to Mother's friend while she called the police. I never went back to the house after that.'

'You went to India soon after your mother's death?'

Dominic made a face. 'Grandma made me. She said she'd arranged a job for me there. I said I didn't want to go, that I didn't want to leave Father, but she insisted. It was only supposed to be for a few months, but it was six years.'

'That's a long time to be away from your family.'

'I got used to it. And Father wrote to me and said it was best I stayed there for a while.' He looked sorrowfully around the room. 'If I'd known it was as bad as this here, I would have come back earlier. How long are you going to keep hold of him?'

'As long as necessary,' Matthew said. 'It is a very serious matter I need to question him about. Unfortunately, your father doesn't seem inclined to cooperate, so it may take some time.'

'He doesn't want to cooperate because he had nothing to do with those women,' Dominic insisted. 'You're picking on him. It's not fair. Father hasn't hurt anyone. You'll see, and then you'll have to let him go.'

Chapter Forty-Four

Wilf bent low over his pint of beer, scowling at the sounds of people talking and laughing around him. He hated them for being happy and carefree when he had had to run away from his home and leave his mother behind, and all because that stupid git Frank and that idiot Monckton had ruined everything. He should have listened to his mother; she had been right about everything. She'd told him he shouldn't have involved Frank, and she'd told him not to demand more money from Monckton, and he'd ignored her and gone his own way. And this was the result.

Wilf looked up as someone approached his table. He'd chosen one in the corner where no one had reason to pass by, hoping he'd go unnoticed. As much as he felt at home to be back in Whitechapel, being on familiar turf had its drawbacks. He had friends here, but he also had enemies. Enemies who wouldn't hesitate to turn him in to the law.

The stool on the other side of the table was kicked round, and Alfie Crane plumped himself down on it. Wilf relaxed at the sight of his old friend.

'I thought it was your ugly mug,' Crane said with a grin, putting his pint jug on a spare cardboard coaster.

'Hello, Alfie,' Wilf said. 'Good to see you.'

'And you. What are you doing back here?'

'I had a bit of bother where I was.'

'What sort of bother?'

'We had the police sniffing round. A bloke I was working with got himself run over and my name came up. Thought it best if I made myself scarce for a while.'

Crane nodded understandingly. 'Well, that explains why you're here and not with your mum. I reckoned it would have to be something serious to keep you away from her.'

'I don't like it, Alfie,' Wilf said. 'But Ma understands why I had to leave her. As soon as things quieten down, I'll send for her. I don't like it in Leytonstone, anyway. I want us to come back here.' His eyes narrowed at Crane. 'What you looking at me like that for?'

'Don't you know?' Crane asked.

'Know what?'

Crane pulled a rolled-up newspaper out of his pocket, laid it on the table and put a finger to a column of text. 'This is under Police News. "Craynebrook Police were questioning a Mrs Edna Gadd in connection with a spate of recent burglaries and a hit-and-run accident when she was suddenly taken ill and rushed to hospital. She is described as being in a stable but serious condition".' Crane took a swig of his pint. 'Your mum's in a bad way, Wilf.'

Wilf snatched up the newspaper and frantically read the article. 'Bloody hell, Alfie. I didn't know about this.'

'Makes you wonder what they did to her, don't it?'

'What do you mean?'

'You know what the police are like when they want people to talk. Maybe they got a bit handy with your mum.'

Wilf stared at him for a long moment, then shook his head. 'Nah, they wouldn't have done anything to her. Not an old lady like my ma. Would they?'

'I wouldn't put anything past them. Where you going?' Crane asked as Wilf scrambled to his feet.

'What d'you mean, where am I going?' Wilf snapped. 'I'm going to see Ma.'

Crane pushed Wilf back onto his stool and shook his head. 'You don't want to do that, Wilf. They'll be waiting for you, expecting you to turn up. That's why they've put that bit in the 'paper. And then they'll nab you and you'll be back inside before you can blink.'

'But I can't just leave her,' Wilf protested. 'Ma'll be wondering where I am. She'll think I don't care about her.'

'Your mum will understand,' Crane assured him. 'She won't want you to risk being caught going to see her. You've got to sit tight, Wilf. It'll be all right. She's in the best place, ain't she?'

'You reckon she'll know why I ain't been to see her?' Wilf asked despairingly.

'Course she will,' Crane nodded. 'Come on, drink up. I'll get the next round in and we'll drink to your mum.' He rose and looked back down at Wilf. 'I'd like to know which copper it was put her in the hospital, though. Your mum was always good to me and I'd make that copper pay, I can tell you.'

Wilf followed Crane with his eyes as he went to the bar and ordered their drinks, laughing with the barman. Wilf's lips curled. Crane was all talk. He didn't give a toss about Edna.

Wilf got up, pushing people out of his way, and stormed out of the pub.

'Has the doctor looked him over?' Matthew asked Barnes as he met the detective constable outside the interview room.

Barnes nodded. 'The doctor said he's a little rattled, but Mr Moore's lucid and up to being interviewed.'

'What about a solicitor?'

'Sergeant Copley telephoned Palmer & Knight and Mr Palmer was free. He's in there with him now, sir.'

'Fine,' Matthew said. 'He's been booked in? Fingerprints taken?'

'Yes, sir. They're on my desk.'

'Good. While I'm in there, I want you checking Mr Moore's fingerprints against the prints taken from the Kirby biscuit tin. Check carefully. And if there's a match, you come in and tell me. Understood?'

'Understood, sir.'

Matthew nodded and turned to Denham. 'You're with me,' he said, and they both entered the interview room.

Oliver Moore was sitting at the table. Beside him was Joseph Palmer, whom Matthew had met during the Hailes and Spencer trial.

'Nice to see you again, Mr Palmer,' Matthew said.

'And you, inspector,' Palmer said as seats were taken.

'Your client is aware of what's going on?'

'Yes. I've explained why he's been arrested.' Palmer cast a worried glance at Oliver, who was biting his nails.

'Your client has been seen by a doctor, Mr Palmer,' Matthew said to reassure him. 'And I will bear in mind Mr Moore's mental state. Though you must appreciate, the matter I need to question Mr Moore about is very serious.'

Palmer nodded. 'I do understand, inspector.'

Matthew opened his file. 'Mr Moore, are you aware that several women have been attacked over the past few weeks in Graydon Heath and Craynebrook, and that one woman has been killed?'

Oliver took his hand away from his mouth. 'Mr Palmer told me.'

'Are you also aware that the woman who was killed was strangled?'

Oliver nodded.

'The attacks and the murder all took place on nights and days that the care home logbook shows you were out.'

'I go out every day.'

'Are you alone when you go?'

'Mostly.'

'On your walks, Mr Moore, do you remember attacking any women?'

Oliver's face screwed up. 'I don't... I didn't...'

'Inspector,' Palmer warned.

Matthew nodded. 'We searched your bedroom at the care home, Mr Moore, and found this.'

Denham put the scrapbook open on the table between Matthew and Oliver.

Oliver stared at it. 'That's mine.'

'You've pasted in newspaper clippings. Why did you do that?'

'They're about Hannah.'

'To be specific, they're about your wife's murder. Aren't they rather strange things to keep as mementos of your wife?'

'Are they?' Oliver shook his head. 'I don't know. It was just something I did.'

'On the night of your wife's murder, you claimed you were with Major Kirwin all night.'

'I was with him.'

'But not all night, Mr Moore. Major Kirwin has made another statement to me that he lied to my predecessor and that you, in fact, left him after dinner at about 9 p.m. Did you return to Craynebrook? Did you go back home?'

'No, I didn't.'

'So, where did you go?'

'I don't remember.'

'I'm sorry, Mr Moore, but I find that rather hard to believe.' Matthew tapped the scrapbook. 'You have all these clippings to remind you of that night. And it was a memorable night, wasn't it? If my wife had been murdered, I'm pretty sure I'd know where I was at the time. I'd also feel guilty that I wasn't with her. That I hadn't been there to protect her.'

'Hannah didn't want me with her. She didn't need me.' Oliver closed the scrapbook and pushed it away. 'I'm not talking about Hannah any more.'

'Then let's talk about the recent attacks,' Matthew said. 'How well do you know Craynebrook?'

'Quite well, I suppose.'

'Do you know Wellington Road?'

Oliver shrugged.

'A woman called Marjorie Kirby was killed on that street between the hours of ten and three on Tuesday. She was killed in a very similar way to your wife, Mr Moore, at a time when, according to the care home's logbooks, you were out.'

'I don't know any Marjorie Kirby.'

'What do you think of women, Mr Moore?' Matthew asked. 'Do you like them?'

'I don't have any reason to think about women these days.'

'Because you don't want to?'

'Because women are no longer a part of my life.'

'Your mother's a woman. Isn't she a part of your life?'

'Mothers are different. They care about you. It doesn't matter what you do, they'll always love you.' Oliver looked down at his hands. 'At least, most mothers do.' He turned to Palmer. 'I'm so tired. I don't want to answer any more questions. I want to go home.'

'I'm afraid that's not a choice you have, Mr Moore,' Matthew said, growing impatient. 'You're under arrest. If you don't answer my questions, I'm going to have to assume there's a reason and that you've got something to hide.'

'Inspector,' Palmer cut in, 'I don't think your assumptions have any—'

There was a loud, urgent rap and the interview room door burst open. Panting, Barnes stopped a moment to catch his breath and Matthew waited, expecting him to say Oliver's fingerprints matched the prints on the Kirby's biscuit tin.

'I'm sorry to interrupt, sir,' Barnes said, 'but there's been another attack.'

Chapter Forty-Five

Matthew sat down on the sofa, his hat in his hands, and addressed the woman crying opposite him in the armchair. 'I'm very sorry, Mrs Burstow.'

'Sorry?' Mr Burstow cried. 'My wife was nearly killed on our very own doorstep—'

'Yes, Mr Burstow, I know,' Matthew said.

'Bloody useless.' Burstow shook his head. 'All these attacks and this lunatic still hasn't been caught.'

Matthew let Mr Burstow rant on. Barnes was bristling by the door, the implication that the police had been twiddling their thumbs irking the young detective.

'I need you to tell me what happened, Mrs Burstow,' Matthew said when her husband paused for breath.

Mrs Burstow sniffed into her sopping handkerchief and took a deep breath. 'I was outside, going through the bin. One of the children's toys had been thrown away by accident and I was sorting through the rubbish to find it. I was bent over, looking through the bin, when I felt someone come up behind me. I turned, and this man put his hands around my throat.' Her hands went to her throat to show Matthew how. 'He was squeezing and I couldn't breathe. But I struggled with him and we fell. He fell on top of me, still squeezing my throat. I grabbed hold of the bin lid and hit him with it. His hands loosened and I screamed. I screamed for Michael.' She held out her hand to her husband, who gripped it with both of his. 'And then he ran off.'

'Karen had left the front door open,' Mr Burstow said. 'I was in the kitchen and heard her scream. I ran out to the front and found her on the ground.' He shook his head at the memory. 'Just look at her throat.' He pointed at his wife's neck. There were dark bruises on the skin.

'Can you describe the man who attacked you?' Matthew asked.

'He had on a flat cap and a scarf over his face,' she said. 'That's all I can remember.'

'It's the same man as killed that Kirby woman, isn't it?' Mr Burstow said.

'It certainly sounds like it, Mr Burstow,' Matthew agreed. He waited for another verbal onslaught, but Burstow seemed to have blown himself out and he just shook his head again. Relieved, Matthew turned back to Mrs Burstow. 'I'd like a doctor to have a look at you.'

'Oh, I'm all right,' she protested.

'I'd be happier to have a doctor confirm that.' Matthew gave her his most charming smile. It worked, as it usually did. She smiled back and nodded. 'And besides, I need an official report of your injuries.'

'Will I have to go to court?' she asked in alarm.

'Huh,' Mr Burstow said, glaring at Matthew. 'They've got to catch him first.'

Matthew fell down into his chair and lit a cigarette, blowing the smoke up towards the ceiling as he laid his head on the back and closed his eyes.

He'd made a complete balls-up of the entire investigation. He'd gone from having too many suspects — the husband, the lover, the burglar — to having just the one, and now that suspect looked like he was out of the running. Oliver Moore couldn't have attacked Mrs Bristow, and by that reckoning, almost certainly hadn't killed Mrs Kirby, even if he had killed his wife. And now Matthew was having his doubts about him killing his wife. Monckton could have lied about killing Hannah, he supposed, but he just couldn't see it. If Monckton had killed her, he would have confessed it, surely, along with the murder of Frank Crowther? So, who did that leave? As far as Matthew could make out, only the burglar, who had almost certainly been Wilfred Gadd. And yet, Gadd killing Hannah didn't make much sense, especially not when he was black-mailing Monckton for her murder.

Matthew heard footsteps in the outer office and glanced through the partition window, scrambling to his feet as Mullinger entered the room. He was going to get a carpeting, Matthew knew. Knew, too, that he deserved one.

'Mrs Burstow?' Mullinger asked without preamble.

'Shaken and bruised, but she's all right,' Matthew replied. 'She struggled with him and he ran off.'

With a sigh, Mullinger sat down in the chair by Matthew's desk. He gestured for Matthew to resume his seat. Surprised, Matthew obeyed.

'At least we don't have another murder on our hands,' Mullinger said. 'So, Stannard, you're the brains at this station. Who the devil is it? Who's attacking these women?'

'I don't know, sir,' Matthew admitted. 'Before, I was certain it was Oliver Moore, but—'

'But he's downstairs in the cells and so has the best alibi he could have.'

'And the MO is the same as all the other attacks, so it

would be absurd to say he did all the others and someone else this one.'

'Agreed,' Mullinger said. 'What about this burglar? Perhaps DI Carding was right after all and the burglar killed Hannah Moore?'

That was something Matthew didn't want to admit. He'd been so sure Carding had been lazy and that the notion a burglar would strangle upon being disturbed rather than banging a woman over the head was nonsense. But had he been wrong about that? He'd been wrong about Oliver Moore, after all.

He glanced at the Hannah Moore case file on his blotter. 'I'm certain the man who killed Mrs Kirby is the same man who killed Hannah Moore,' he said, knowing this was stretching the truth; he wasn't certain at all, he just felt it. 'I'm going to go through everything again. The attacks, the Kirby murder, the Moore murder. The answer's in the files. It has to be.'

Mullinger considered for a moment. 'I think you should know, Stannard, that I'm under pressure to call in a detective from the Yard. There's a growing consensus at Headquarters that we are unable to find this killer. I'm reluctant to agree to passing this over, but ultimately, it won't be my decision.'

Matthew's mouth had gone dry. 'I understand, sir. When will you know if that's what they're doing?'

'By the end of tomorrow. You have until then to make some headway, but after that...' He shrugged and got to his feet. 'Do your best, Stannard, with the time you have left. I'd rather like to prove Headquarters wrong about us.'

Chapter Forty-Six

'Oh, not too much,' Georgina said with something like a giggle as Robert Stubbs topped up her sherry glass. 'I'll get tipsy.'

'It'll do you good,' his wife, Deirdre, insisted as she offered a tray of hors d'oeuvres. 'You're looking very peaky, Georgina. You're not getting out enough.'

'It is lovely to have an evening out of the house,' Georgina admitted, thinking how eagerly she had dressed not an hour before, relieved she didn't have to spend another dinner trying to draw Dominic into conversation.

'What's on the menu tonight?' Richard Lacey asked.

'Rib beef,' Deirdre replied with a smile.

'Oh, my favourite,' Lacey declared, licking his lips. His twinkling gaze landed on Georgina. 'And how are you, Mrs Moore?'

'Oh, well enough,' Georgina said, smiling up at the widower, and invariably her dinner companion on the rare occasions she was invited out to dine. It irked her a little the two of them were always invited together, just so there wouldn't be an uneven number of men and women around the dining table. It was quite petty of her, she knew, but it would be nice if, just once, she was invited for herself rather than to make up the numbers.

'And Oliver?' Lacey went on. 'How is he these days?'

'Fine,' she said, the somewhat untruthful statement issuing immediately from her lips.

'I understand young Dominic has come home? That's nice for you, isn't it?'

'It's lovely,' she nodded, and took a rather large sip of her sherry.

The lie brought with it a sense of guilt. Georgina knew she really shouldn't feel so resentful towards her grandson, but there was no denying how much of a strain she found his presence in her house. It wasn't that he did anything in particular to upset everything; it was just Georgina felt as if she was constantly walking on eggshells, desperate not to upset him or say something she shouldn't. Having reconciled herself to the fact that Dominic would not be returning to India, she was now hoping it wouldn't take him too long to find a flat for himself, even if it meant she would have to talk him out of taking his father with him. That was something that must never happen.

She only half-listened while Richard Lacey chattered on about this and that, nodding and smiling whenever he paused, which wasn't often. Lacey was an enthusiastic talker about himself, and usually Georgina resented his lack of interest in her, but tonight she welcomed it, as it meant she wasn't expected to contribute much to the conversation. Her attention wandered and she cast wistful glances at Joan and Benjamin Travers over by the china display cabinet. Georgina sometimes chatted with Joan in the hairdressers when their appointments coincided and had always enjoyed their conversations, but she enjoyed talking with Benjamin even more. In an unusual act of boldness, Georgina excused herself from Lacey, cutting him off in mid-sentence, and headed for the Travers. Benjamin was examining the latest addition to Deirdre's porcelain collection, pointing out details to his wife, when his eye caught Georgina coming towards him and she saw him stiffen. Why was that? Georgina wondered.

'Georgina,' Joan cried, leaning in to brush a kiss across her cheek. 'It's been ages.'

'Yes, hasn't it?' Georgina nodded. 'Almost six months.'

'No!' Joan looked aghast. 'It can't be as long as all that. Can it, Ben?'

'I think it might be,' Benjamin said, replacing the figurine on the glass shelf. He closed the cabinet door carefully and, with a tight smile, said, 'Good evening, Georgina.'

There it was again. Something in his manner that suggested he found her presence uncomfortable.

Joan put a hand on Georgina's wrist, her expression pitying. 'How's Oliver?'

'Fine,' Georgina lied again, wishing people would stop asking so she didn't have to think of him for at least a few hours. 'He's doing very well.'

'Oh, that's good, isn't it?'

'Yes. Isn't it?'

They sipped at their sherry.

Joan cleared her throat, glancing up at her husband. 'And Dominic? How is he?'

'He's fine, too. Glad to be back, I think.'

'Is he?' Joan asked earnestly.

'Yes,' Georgina said, a little perplexed by her tone.

'And does he have any plans now he's home for good?'

'Oh,' Georgina said, wondering how Joan knew Dominic wasn't returning to India. 'Well, he says he's going to look around for a job that suits him. And he wants to get a place of his own, of course. He won't want to be living with me for too long.'

'But it must be nice for you to have him in the house. I imagine you must be quite lonely with Oliver in the—'

Benjamin cleared his throat noisily.

'—with Oliver where he is,' Joan amended.

'I'm used to it,' Georgina declared defiantly. 'And I quite like being on my own. I find Dominic has so much energy – you know what the young are like.'

'Oh yes, we all know about Dominic's energy,' Joan murmured into her glass.

'What was that?' Georgina asked.

'Nothing,' Benjamin said, giving his wife a warning stare.

But Georgina shook her head. 'No. You said something. What did you mean?'

Joan's shoulders slumped. 'I shouldn't have said anything. Georgina, forgive me.'

'For what?' Georgina demanded.

Joan shrugged. 'We all know why Dominic's come home.'

Georgina frowned. 'Yes. He was tired of India.'

'Oh, my dear,' Joan said, putting her head on one side. 'India was tired of *him*.'

'I don't understand.'

Joan opened her mouth to reply, but Benjamin put his hand on her shoulder. 'That's quite enough. No, Joan. Enough has been said. We don't want to gossip.'

'What gossip?' Georgina begged.

'You'll have to ask Dominic,' Benjamin insisted.

'Maybe that would be for the best,' Joan agreed. 'Speak to Dominic, my dear. Let him tell you.'

A gong was banged in the hall, and Deirdre stood in the doorway, arms raised to make her announcement. 'Dinner is ready!' she sing-songed. 'Come along, everyone.'

Lacey promptly appeared by Georgina's side and crooked his arm at her. 'Shall we, dear lady?' he grinned.

Chapter Forty-Seven

Matthew set down his cup of coffee and rubbed his tired eyes. He glanced at the clock on the wall. Half-past two. He should have gone home hours ago.

He'd been through all the pages in the Hannah Moore case files, all through the statements made by the attempted strangling victims, and had found nothing that told him who he should be looking for that he hadn't already known.

Matthew dug out the details on each of the victims. He began with those who had been killed, Hannah Moore and Marjorie Kirby. Then he fished out the details of the women who had been luckier, who had got away with their lives. He made a new list, jotting down their particulars. After fifteen minutes, he had finished his list, and he sat back in his chair and studied it.

All the victims were in their mid-thirties and had dark-brown hair, were of medium build and around five foot six. But there, the similarities ended. Some were married with children, others were unmarried and childless. Some were middle class, others working class. Matthew shook his head; there was nothing for him there.

With a sigh, he grabbed Oliver Moore's scrapbook and

flipped it open. He read the newspaper clippings. There was nothing new there, so he turned to the letters, Major Kirwin's first. Kirwin wrote of cricket matches and the horses he had bet upon, of what fellow army officers had been up to and the odd news story that had caught his interest. There was nothing personal, nothing enlightening, and Matthew set them aside to turn to the letters from Dominic.

Dominic's early letters reminded Matthew of Georgie. The handwriting was neat, the product of many school hours spent copying letters into exercise books, but there were spelling mistakes and badly phrased sentences that suggested Dominic had not been the most academically minded of students. Despite these flaws, the letters' meaning had been clear enough – Dominic loved his father. Not once, Matthew noticed with surprise, did Dominic mention his mother.

Matthew came to the last letter Dominic had written, the one with the *SS Rahasy* letterhead. It was very short and read, *Dear Dad, I hope this letter finds you well. I'm writing this from the ship. It's been rather lonely on board. There's no one I know to talk to, so I'm so looking forward to seeing you and Grandma again. We dock at Tilbury tomorrow, so hopefully, I'll see you very soon. Your loving son, Dominic.'*

Yawning, Matthew's tired eyes fell upon the date Dominic had written just below the letterhead – 22nd March. He frowned. There was something odd about the date, and he didn't know why. Matthew reached for his notebook and flicked through the pages until he came to the notes he had made for his meeting with Georgina Moore. She had said she met Dominic at the train station on Wednesday 16th April. So, if the ship had docked on the twenty-third of March, where had Dominic been during those three weeks?

Matthew jumped up from his desk and grabbed his hat from the stand. 'Barnes,' he yelled. 'I need the car right away.'

It was just before 6 a.m. when Matthew arrived at the office of The Old Peninsular and Oriental Steam Navigation Company and asked to speak to someone who could provide him with information. The steward on the door, unused to such early callers, hemmed and hawed, but then held up a finger as a thought struck him. 'Mr Reynolds will be able to help you.'

He took Matthew to an office lined with bookshelves stuffed with oversized ledges and round tables laden with papers. The steward called, 'Mr Reynolds?' and a small, neat man with a large moustache popped up from behind a stack of books.

'Yes?'

'Here's a policeman to see you,' the steward said, pointing at Matthew.

'I'm after information about a recent voyage, Mr Reynolds,' Matthew said and introduced himself.

'I'll leave you to it,' the steward said and disappeared.

Mr Reynolds came towards Matthew. 'What information is it you require, inspector?'

'The *SS Rahasy*'s voyage in March,' Matthew said.

'Ah, the *Rahasy*,' Mr Reynolds said knowingly, but then frowned. 'I thought the investigation had been concluded.'

Matthew started. 'What investigation?'

'The investigation into the man overboard. Well, woman overboard, I should say.'

'I'm not aware of any investigation, Mr Reynolds,' Matthew said.

'Oh, I see.' Mr Reynolds hurried over to a bookshelf and pulled out a ledger. 'Everything was, of course, recorded. We're very particular about that here at the P&O.' He flicked through the ledger's pages. 'Yes, here we are. The *SS Rahasy* left Bombay on the twenty-eighth of February. It's a three-week journey, give or take a day or two for bad weather, which had her docking in Tilbury on the twenty-third of March.' He watched as Matthew took out his notebook and noted his words down. 'The unfortunate incident occurred on the last evening. A Mrs Pauline Bowen was lost overboard.'

'Was the sea rough?' Matthew asked.

'Not at all. It was a very calm night, I understand.' Mr Reynolds coughed delicately. 'I'm afraid the poor lady jumped. At least, that was what the police believed. We have a copy of the coroner's report.' He moved to a bank of wooden filing cabinets at the far side of the room and opened a drawer. He pulled out another folder and handed it to Matthew. 'As you see, the coroner determined Death by Misadventure.'

'That's not the same as suicide.'

'No, but I believe the lady left no note and that no one actually saw her jump, so it was thought to put her down as a suicide would have been...' he waved his hand, 'too much of an assumption?'

'As you say,' Matthew agreed, 'but without a note or witnesses, to say it was suicide, whether officially confirmed or not, is rather a leap. Might she not have simply fallen overboard?'

'Oh,' Reynolds shook his head, 'highly unlikely, inspector. The railings on the ship are waist high. She would have had to climb over them to fall. And as you will see from the witness statements made at the inquest, several people reported she was in low spirits.'

Matthew flicked to the witness statements. Mr Reynolds was correct. The few passengers who had engaged with Mrs Bowen during the voyage reported her as seeming down in the dumps and rather lonely.

'Her marriage had broken up and Mrs Bowen had decided to leave her husband and return to England. The Tilbury police were satisfied the lady ended her own life. No blame, I can assure you, was apportioned to the company.'

Matthew flicked through the file. 'Where's the passenger list?'

'That's a different file, inspector.' Mr Reynolds took another file from the cabinet and flicked through the pages, handing Matthew another sheet of paper.

Matthew ran his eyes down the list of names until he found Dominic Moore listed. 'What's this red mark next to this name?' he asked.

'That means we've had correspondence from the passenger.' Mr Reynolds flicked through the file. 'Yes, here we are. Mr Moore contacted us on the twenty-fifth of March to enquire after an item of jewellery he believed he had left in his cabin. He asked us to forward it to him should it be found.'

'And was it found?'

Another rifling through the file. Another piece of paper pulled out. 'Here's our reply,' Mr Reynolds said. 'Dated the twenty-seventh of March. A brooch had been found in his cabin and was duly sent on to him.'

Matthew smiled with satisfaction as he read the letter. The brooch had been sent on to Mr Dominic Moore, care of The Bentley Hotel, Graydon Heath!

Chapter Forty-Eight

Steam was coming through the hole in the tureen sitting on the breakfast table. According to Lucy, Dominic had asked for kedgeree the night before, so Georgina supposed that meant he would be down for breakfast.

'Thank you, Lucy,' she said, unrolling her napkin. 'You can go to the kitchen now. Don't come back in until I call you.'

Georgina had seen the look of perplexity upon her maid's face at the unusual instruction, but offered no explanation. Lucy closed the door and Georgina waited. It was another fifteen minutes before the door opened and Dominic entered.

'Morning, Grandma,' he said cheerily.

Georgina's stomach churned at the thought of turning his good humour sour, as she knew she must. 'Good morning, Dominic.'

He pulled out the chair and sat down. Lifting the lid off the tureen, he breathed deeply. 'Lovely,' he said, and spooned the kedgeree onto his plate. 'Lucy's got the knack of making this just right, hasn't she?'

'I'm glad you like it, Dom,' Georgina said. 'Did you enjoy yourself with Daniel last night?'

'It was all right,' he shrugged.

She helped herself to a smaller portion. 'Aren't you going to ask me if I had a pleasant evening?'

Dominic looked up at her. 'Yes, of course. Did you?'

'Not particularly.'

'Oh. Why not?'

'I heard something that rather confused me. About you.'

Dominic stared at her, his jaw working as he chewed. 'What about me?'

'I don't really know. My friends wouldn't go into any detail. But they gave me the impression something happened in India to make you come home.' He threw his fork down on the plate, making Georgina jump at the clatter it made. Dominic sat back in his chair and looked at her, his expression unreadable. 'But you told me you wanted to come home. So, which is true?'

Dominic continued to stare at her.

'I'm not angry with you, Dom,' Georgina went on, 'but I do want to know the truth. Why have you come home?'

'I don't like you talking about me to other people,' he said after a long moment, picking up his fork again. 'That's not nice.'

'I wasn't saying anything unpleasant.'

'Talking about me behind my back.'

'That's not how it was, Dom. But please answer my question. Why exactly have you come home?'

'Because I wanted to,' he said through gritted teeth.

Georgina took a deep breath. 'I don't believe you.'

'Maybe I don't care whether you believe me or not,' Dominic said, his fist tightening around the fork. 'Maybe I don't care what you or your friends think.'

'You're under my roof, Dominic,' Georgina said, her blood pounding in her ears. She'd never seen her grandson

302

like this before, so angry. It frightened her a little, but she had to know. 'I insist on you telling me the truth.'

A shiver ran through her as Dominic turned his eyes upon her. They were the eyes of a stranger, not her grandson at all.

Matthew drove like the devil back to Craynebrook.

Dominic Moore! Matthew tried to tie all the facts in his memory together. Dominic Moore had been in Craynebrook when his mother was murdered. He had been on board a ship where a woman appeared to have committed suicide, but whose body was never found. Dominic had arrived in England the very next day, the twenty-third of March, and stayed in a Graydon Heath hotel rather than going home to his grandmother, which put him in the area for the attacks on Agnes Trent and Margaret Longford. On the fifteenth of April, he had come to Crayne-brook and the attack on Joanne Cooper had taken place less than a week later. They couldn't all be coincidences.

The car pulled up outside the station. Matthew threw open the door and rushed up the steps to the lobby. He hurried past Turkel, who stared at him in astonishment, and bolted up the stairs to CID. 'It's Dominic Moore,' he declared, bursting through the door.

Denham and Barnes, both seated at their desks, stared at him in astonishment. Lund came to stand in the doorway of his office.

'What's this?' he asked.

'We got the wrong Moore,' Matthew panted. 'It's not the father. It's the son. He was staying at a hotel in Graydon Heath during the first attacks, then he moved to Craynebrook. And there was a woman on board the ship he came to England in who supposedly threw herself overboard. But her body was never recovered and her description is similar to the other women. Mid-thirties, dark-haired.' He took a deep breath as his brain made another connection. 'Just like his mother.'

'Wait a minute,' Lund held out his hand. 'You're saying this Dominic killed these women and his mother?'

'That's exactly what I'm saying. Listen. The Moore's neighbour, Miss Jernigan, told me Hannah had no time for her son, that she neglected him. In Dominic's letters to his father, there's not one mention of his mother, not one sentence about her. Straight after the murder, his grandmother ships him off to India to get him out of the way. Or out of our way? Nothing like the Moore murder happens in Craynebrook for six years. Then Dominic comes back, first to Graydon Heath and then to Craynebrook. In both places, women are being attacked and one woman is strangled. Now,' Matthew appealed to all three men, 'tell me that's a coincidence.'

Barnes got to his feet. 'You're right, sir. We should bring him in.'

Denham nodded. 'The same.'

'Lund?' Matthew asked.

Lund stared at Matthew for a long moment. Then he pushed out his bottom lip, took a deep breath and said, 'Let's go get the bastard.'

People were standing at their garden gates, staring up at Georgina Moore's house when the police car pulled up at the kerb. Some of them hurried forward as Matthew climbed out, but he didn't need them to tell him something was wrong inside the house. He could hear the screaming for himself.

Matthew rushed up the path and banged on the front door. 'Open up. Police,' he yelled. The screaming broke off, and Matthew pressed his ear to the door. Hearing nothing, he looked in at the window, but the net curtains prevented him from seeing inside. He banged again. 'Open up. Police.'

There was running and someone or something thumped against the door. A yelp and scrabbling – Matthew briefly saw fingers snatching at the stained-glass window – then more screaming. He pushed against the door. The latch must have been turned during the struggle and it gave way under his pressure. As he burst into the hall, Matthew was just in time to see Dominic dragging Lucy into the kitchen before slamming the door shut.

Matthew charged at the kitchen door and it flew open. Dominic was backing away, one arm around Lucy's waist, the other gripping the tie he had wound around the maid's neck. He yanked at it and the girl gurgled. Her face was bright red and her hands scrabbled at the fabric digging into her skin. Georgina was slumped in a corner of the kitchen. She looked terrified.

'Let her go, Dominic,' Matthew said.

Dominic gave the tie a yank. Lucy's head jerked backwards and her eyes bulged.

'It's all over. You're not getting out of this.'

'All this?' Dominic laughed, but there was no humour in it. 'You've got no idea what all this is.'

'No?' Matthew countered. 'Marjorie Kirby? Pauline Bowen? Your own mother?' Dominic's smug expression faltered. 'You killed them, didn't you? And all those other women you attacked. You would have killed them too if you could.'

Dominic's gaze darted from Matthew to just over his shoulder where Denham had appeared, then to his grandmother in the corner and finally to the girl in his arms. Matthew had seen that look before. It was the look of a man searching for an escape route, and he hoped Dominic wouldn't work out that the best means he had was in his arms. All he had to do was hold the maid hostage and Matthew would have no choice but to let him leave the house. Once he was outside, he could shove Lucy away and run. There would be a chase. Dominic might get away, he might not. But Matthew didn't want to take that chance.

Barnes appeared at the open back door and caught Matthew's eye. Dominic hadn't heard him and Matthew signalled with his eyes for Barnes to keep quiet. If he could keep Dominic's attention on him and away from the back door, Barnes might just be able to take Dominic down.

'Why did you do it, Dominic?' he asked. 'Why attack and kill those women?'

'They were whores. All of them.'

'Not all of them,' Matthew said. 'Marjorie Kirby wasn't. Nor was Pauline Bowen. Your mother wasn't.'

'My mother was the biggest whore of all. I know what she did with her men friends. I heard them at it. And heard them laughing at my father, calling him a fool. And as for the other women. They were just as bad. Women with children who shouldn't even be thinking of things like that. Cheating on their husbands. Giving themselves to any man who came along and took their fancy.'

'Is that what happened with Pauline?'

Dominic's lip curled. 'She wanted me to take her to bed. I taught her a lesson.'

'And Marjorie Kirby?'

'She invited me in. Offered me tea and cake.'

'Is that all she did? Offered you tea and cake?'

'I knew where that would lead. It would have been have some tea and cake and then come upstairs with me. I wasn't going to fall for that.'

'Why did you break the mirror?'

'I knew it had happened before with Mother,' Dominic said. 'It made that other policeman think a burglar had killed her. So I broke the mirror to confuse you. And it worked, didn't it? You didn't know it was me all along?'

'No, I didn't.' Matthew glanced at Lucy. Her eyes weren't bulging anymore, so the tie around her neck must have slackened a little. *Just a little more*, Matthew begged. 'So you taught those women a lesson? And what about your mother? Did you teach her a lesson too?'

Dominic smiled. 'That's right. I climbed out of the bedroom window here and went home. It was easy. Grandma always went to bed early. She didn't know I'd left.'

Matthew heard Georgina whimper. 'So, you planned to kill your mother?'

Dominic shrugged. 'I thought it was time she was gone. I knew Dad would be out of the house, so he couldn't be blamed. And I knew there'd be plenty of people coming and going, drinking, out of their heads on drugs, so I knew I wouldn't be noticed. But it was even easier than I expected. They'd all gone and Mother was in bed. It was so easy. I just put my hands around her throat and squeezed. And then I came back here and went to bed.'

Lucy gurgled, and Dominic tightened his grip on her waist.

'So, what about her?' Matthew asked, nodding at Lucy. 'What has she done to deserve this? She's not a whore.'

Dominic glanced down at the girl. 'She will be given half a chance. All women turn into whores.'

'But not now she isn't. Let her go, Dominic. Why add another murder to your list?'

'Why not?' Dominic scoffed. 'What difference does one more make?' He gave the tie a vicious yank. Lucy spluttered and made a choking noise.

It was now or never. Matthew nodded at Barnes, and the detective constable burst into the kitchen and kicked Dominic's legs away from under him. Dominic fell back onto the tiled floor, pulling Lucy down on top of him. His hold on the tie loosened and she scrambled away, screaming. Matthew held his arms out to her and she threw herself at him, clamping her arms around his waist and sobbing against his chest. Barnes was on Dominic in an instant, pinning his arms to the floor. Denham went to Barnes's aid, pressing the shouting, struggling Dominic's face into the floor as Barnes clamped on the handcuffs.

'All right, sir?' Denham asked, looking at Matthew.

Matthew nodded. 'Well done, you two. Get him out of here.'

Matthew pressed a glass of brandy into Georgina's hand. 'Drink that,' he ordered and waited until Georgina took a sip. 'Better?'

She nodded and took another. 'I can't believe it,' she said, and her voice was cracked and broken. 'That Dom did all those terrible things.'

Matthew pulled the other armchair nearer and sat down. 'You had no idea?'

She shook her head as tears fell. 'I thought Oliver killed Hannah. That's why I didn't want you to talk to him. It's why I put him in the care home. I know it was wrong of me, but you didn't know Hannah. She was a terrible woman. Dominic was right about her. She treated my son abysmally and Oliver didn't deserve that. The way he was when he came back from the war... It wasn't his fault, but Hannah never saw it that way and she was always on at him. Even in front of Dominic. I never realised how that made Dominic feel about her.'

There came a mewing from beneath Georgina's chair and a small furry head poked out between her feet. Matthew bent down and picked the kitten up, putting it on his lap and stroking its head.

'Dominic brought that home,' she said, looking at the creature with disdain. 'He wanted to look after it. To see him with it, you would never imagine he could hurt anything. He was so gentle.' Georgina sighed. 'He called it Mussmer. I had to look it up. It means revenge. I suppose he thought it was a very clever joke, calling it that and me never knowing.'

'He does seem proud of what he's done,' Matthew nodded, tickling the cat's chin. He looked across to Georgina, his brow furrowing as his eyes caught the serpent brooch pinned to her left breast. It didn't seem right for her, some-how, and it made Matthew wonder.

Georgina saw him looking and she unpinned the brooch from her blouse and handed it to Matthew. 'Dominic gave me that when he arrived.'

Matthew examined the brooch. It didn't look new. 'Do you know where he got it?'

'India, I suppose,' Georgina said with a sniff. 'I didn't like it, but I wore it because he gave it to me. I'll throw it away now.'

'I think I'll take it, Mrs Moore,' Matthew said, pocketing the brooch. 'Evidence,' he explained when she frowned at him. He left it at that. He didn't want to tell her he suspected it was a brooch Dominic had taken from Pauline Bowen.

She seemed too weary to wonder any further. With a sigh, Georgina said, 'I think Dominic must have done something similar in India to what he's done here, inspector. You should talk to Benjamin Travers. He and his wife are friends of mine. I saw them the other night and they let slip that Dominic was made to leave India. Ben wouldn't tell me why, but I can guess.' She reached over to the side table and taking up the newspaper and a pencil, scribbled an address on the blank edge. She tore off the strip of paper and handed it to Matthew. 'Talk to Ben. He'll tell you, I'm sure.'

'I will,' Matthew assured her, seeing the old lady close

309

her eyes. She was worn out, he could tell. He would have liked to talk to her longer, find out more about Dominic, perhaps get some answers to the many questions going around in his head, but he felt the kindest thing he could do at that moment would be to leave her alone. 'I'll be off now, Mrs Moore,' he said. 'But I don't like to leave you on your own. Is there anyone who can sit with you?'

'There's Lucy—' Georgina began, then her face crumpled. 'Is she all right? Is she being looked after?'

'A constable's with her and I'll get a doctor to make sure she's all right. Don't worry. But can I get a neighbour to come in and keep you company?' he pressed.

'No, I don't want anyone,' Georgina said, resting her head on the back of the chair.

Matthew rose, cradling the cat in his two hands and bending to set it on her lap.

'No, don't,' she said, jerking away.

'I'm sorry,' Matthew said, holding the wriggling animal to his chest. 'I thought you'd like—'

Georgina shook her head. 'I don't ever want to see it again. I didn't want it in the first place. Drown it, if you want, but get it out of my house.'

Chapter Forty-Nine

Oliver was in the interview room with Joseph Palmer. Matthew sat down at the table and offered him a cigarette. Oliver took one and Matthew lit it for him.

'Do you have more questions for me, inspector?' Oliver asked.

'No, Mr Moore,' Matthew said. 'I'm afraid I have some bad news for you. We've arrested your son.'

Oliver's expression was strangely blank. 'Because he killed Hannah?'

Matthew stared at him in astonishment. 'You knew?'

Oliver's hand trembled as he held the cigarette to his lips. 'I didn't know. I suspected. Hannah treated Dominic so very badly. I understood her treating me that way – I was a nuisance, a pain – but Dom didn't deserve what she meted out to him.'

'Why did she treat him so badly?' Matthew asked.

'I don't know. She wanted a child, or so she told me when we married, but when Dom came along, she seemed to change her mind. Hannah complained he took over every-thing, that she didn't have any life of her own left. She even blamed him for ruining her figure and her health. She'd suffered quite a bit carrying him. And she wasn't a woman to bear her dislike silently. Hannah told him she wished he hadn't been born every chance she got. From his youngest days, Dom knew his mother didn't like him, didn't want him. And I wasn't any help. Thank God for Mother. She cared for him far more than either I or Hannah did.' He started. 'Does Mother know about Dom?'

'She was there when we arrested him. He was threatening the life of her maid and there was a very unpleasant scene. But Mrs Moore is all right, I assure you.'

'Good God,' Oliver breathed and ran his hands over his face. 'Poor Mother.'

'Inspector?' Palmer cut in. 'The recent attacks?'

Matthew nodded. 'Dominic committed those too.'

'So, I presume,' he went on, 'you'll be releasing Mr Moore without charge?'

'We will,' Matthew said. 'There's no reason to hold him any longer.'

Miss Halliwell set down the tea tray, gave Matthew one of her best smiles and left the office, closing the door behind her. Mullinger reached for the coffeepot and poured the hot black liquid into two fine china coffee cups.

'An excellent result, Stannard,' he said, handing Matthew one of the cups.

Matthew helped himself to a biscuit. 'Thank you, sir.'

'Yes. Two murders and several violent attacks cleared up with one arrest.'

'Three murders, sir,' Matthew corrected. 'Dominic Moore killed Mrs Pauline Bowen on the *SS Rahasy* as well.'

'Oh yes,' Mullinger's lips curled up in a smile. 'Three murders, one of which was passed off as a suicide by the Tilbury police. I expect they'll have to answer for failing to investigate that one properly.' His pleasure in that thought was evident and Matthew hid a smile behind his coffee cup. 'Dominic Moore has confessed, I take it?'

Matthew nodded. 'Yes, he has, and to all the attacks, including the Graydon Heath ones. I've informed their CID.'

Mullinger frowned. 'You should have left that to me, Stannard. It would have been a pleasure to tell their superintendent we were right after all.'

Matthew registered the use of Mullinger's 'we'. 'Sorry, sir, I didn't think.'

'And of course, I've told Headquarters the good news,' Mullinger went on, taking a third biscuit from the plate. 'They were very complimentary. Invited me up for a meeting at the end of the week to give them a complete account.'

'Have they, sir? That's good of them.'

If Mullinger noticed the sarcasm in Matthew's words, he didn't show it. He leaned forward and tapped the report Matthew had given him to read. 'What's this about India?'

'Information received from a Mr Benjamin Travers. He got Dominic Moore a job in the Indian Civil Service as a favour to Mrs Moore, but ever since Dominic arrived, there had been a series of attacks on local Indian women, similar to those he committed over here. It was thought a purely native affair at first, but then it became clear an Englishman was involved. The police narrowed it down to Dominic, but not being keen to implicate him in the attacks and risk rousing anti-British feeling, they suggested Dominic be quietly removed from India.'

Mullinger nodded approvingly. 'Quite understandable, of course. Best course of action to get him out of the country, keep it all hush hush.'

Matthew didn't agree, but he kept his opinion to himself.

'So, Monckton and the father? Neither of them were involved?'

'No. Oliver Moore, though his whereabouts are unknown for that night, really did just go for a walk, it seems. He's been released back to the care home. As for Monckton, his story about finding Hannah Moore dead appears to be true.'

'So, was the Moore house burgled that night or not?'

'Hard to say without questioning Wilfred Gadd, but it would make sense. I reckon Gadd burgled the house after Hannah had been killed, broke the mirror because of the trauma he suffered during the war, and somehow saw Monckton either enter or leave the house, put two and two together and reached the wrong conclusion that Monckton killed Hannah Moore. Then decided to make capital out of what he'd seen.'

'But the mirror was broken at the Kirbys.'

'Dominic Moore did that to put us on the wrong track, to make us look for a burglar again. But he left his fingerprints on the biscuit tin.'

'So, we would have found him eventually,' Mullinger said.

'Not necessarily,' Matthew said with a sorry shake of his head. 'Not unless we had a reason to take Dominic's finger-prints. But for that, we would have nothing to match the biscuit tin prints against.'

'Yes, well,' Mullinger said, 'let's keep that to ourselves, shall we? And I don't know if you've heard? The vandal with the red paint?'

Matthew had forgotten all about the vandalism. 'What about them?'

'They've been apprehended.' Mullinger consulted a paper on his desk. 'A Mrs Virginia Cryer. Quite extraordinary, a woman doing that. But PC Rudd came across this Mrs Cryer about to throw red paint over a gravestone in the churchyard. Apparently, she believed it marked the body of a war profi-teer. The woman seems to have an anti-war fixation. She's admitted the other incidents and been charged. So, that's all been nicely cleared up.' The telephone on his desk rang and he picked up the receiver. 'Yes, Miss Halliwell?... No, that's all right... Yes?.... I see. Thank you.' He hung up and stared stonily at Matthew. 'The hospital called. Edna Gadd died an hour ago.'

A lead weight landed in the pit of Matthew's stomach. He stared into the bottom of his coffee cup. 'I'm sorry to hear that.'

'It's very unfortunate, of course,' Mullinger went on, 'but under no circumstances can we be considered to be at fault. The woman had a heart problem. Her heart attack could have happened at any time. That's what I will be telling the Press, Stannard, and you're to do the same. Is that clear?'

Matthew nodded. 'Perfectly clear, sir.'

'Well, it's been a busy few weeks.' Mullinger slurped the last of his coffee. 'I expect you're exhausted.'

'I am rather tired, sir.'

'Then get yourself off home. I've told Lund he's on call for the night, so you won't be disturbed. Get some rest. That's an order, Stannard.'

Matthew got to his feet and buttoned up his jacket, surprised at the superintendent's solicitude. 'Thank you, sir. I'll do that.'

Chapter Fifty

Dickie was waiting for Matthew on his front step when he arrived home. He grinned and held up two bottles of stout. 'Congratulations. I hear you got a result.'

'I did,' Matthew nodded, smiling. 'But it doesn't mean I'm giving you an interview.'

'I'm not after one, old boy.' Dickie waggled the bottles. 'Thought you might like to celebrate.' He noted Matthew's expression. 'No?'

Matthew shook his head. 'Thanks, but Pat's coming over and, to be honest, I'm knackered. When she's gone, I'm just going to go to bed.' He saw Dickie's disappointment and offered, 'Maybe tomorrow night?'

'If you like,' Dickie said, putting the bottles into his coat pockets. He nodded at the box Matthew was carrying. 'What have you got in there?'

'Oh, nothing,' Matthew said, pushing past Dickie to his front door. 'Just something for the flat.' He fumbled in his pocket for his keys.

'Did you hear about Nancy Price?' Dickie asked.

Matthew turned back to him. 'What about her?'

'The appeal we signed. The Home Secretary accepted it.

She's not going to hang. Life imprisonment instead.'

'I'm glad,' Matthew said. 'She didn't deserve to hang.'

'Pity about Edna Gadd, though.'

'You've heard?'

Dickie nodded. 'Mullinger made a statement, and for once, he was right in what he said. It wasn't anybody's fault. I had a word with the doctor and he said he's surprised she lasted as long as she did. You were just unlucky it happened when you were questioning her. So, don't beat yourself up about it.'

'Thanks, but I can't help feeling guilty.' Matthew fitted his key into the lock.

'Well, I'll be off, then,' Dickie said. 'Give me a call tomorrow if you fancy that drink.'

'I will. Goodnight, Dickie.'

Matthew pushed the front door open and wearily climbed the stairs to his first-floor flat. Balancing the box against his chest, he opened his door and made his way to the sitting room. Putting the box down on the table, he folded back the flaps and delved inside. A rough tongue licked his hand and Matthew smiled as he lifted the kitten out.

He set it down on the floor and watched as it explored its new domain on clumsy legs. Going into the kitchen, he opened a tin of tuna and forked it out onto a saucer, placing it on the floor. The kitten purred as it ate. Matthew poured milk into another saucer and set this down by the tuna.

'You're going to need a new name,' he said, and returned to his sitting room to pour himself a whisky. Taking it into his bedroom, he set the glass down on the bedside table next to his *Wisden Cricketers' Almanack*, still waiting to be read. As he pulled at the knot in his tie and kicked off his shoes, he felt movement behind him and turned.

Standing behind the bedroom door was a man with white-blond hair and a cosh in his hand.

Also by C. K. Harewood

Under Cover of Darkness (exclusive to subscribers)

The Empire Club Murders

<u>Coming Soon</u>

Death of a Blackbird

Scan the QR code to visit www.ckharewood.com

Printed in Great Britain
by Amazon